4 RIVERSIDE CLOSE

DIANA WILKINSON

BLOODHOUND
— BOOKS —

Print ISBN 978-1-913419-43-1

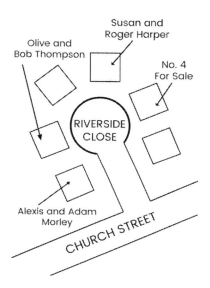

Olive and
Bob Thompson

Susan and
Roger Harper

No. 4
For Sale

RIVERSIDE
CLOSE

Alexis and Adam
Morley

CHURCH STREET

HOUSE FOR SALE

I open the front door and let him in, smiling all the while to put my guest at ease but making sure to tuck myself tightly behind the door. The neighbours might be watching.

'Join me.' I laugh light-heartedly. He flinches at the words but he is too slick, too cool to look unsettled. Such demeanour wouldn't sit easy on his arrogant shoulders. Bastard. But I remind myself he's far from perfect. It's all been an act. I let out a short contemptuous laugh, enjoying my private thoughts. Paying to meet women smacks of desperation.

'A drink?' I offer, smiling as I lead the way to the kitchen. Perhaps he thinks I am like the sales agent, a slick purveyor of words and underhand tactics linked to obscene commissions. He stands and stares at me, as if I am mad. Beads of perspiration have settled on my brow and I have to wipe the drips away with my gloved hand. He glances round at the front door but will be remembering that I locked it securely behind us.

I knock back a whiskey from a half-drunk bottle and hand my guest a glass before wandering towards the patio doors. 'Cheers,' I say while I stand and look out across the bijou virgin square of grass. It's *empty and soulless, like my prey. I turn round to face him, the wait finally over.*

'Sit down. We need to talk.' I indicate a chair into which he relaxes while watching me lift a bottle of wine from a display rack under the cupboards. Of course he likes fine wines. Maybe he thinks we're going to share some intimate secrets. Instead of popping the cork, I walk slowly round behind him, raise the bottle high in the air and before he has time to flinch, I smash it down hard on the back of his head. His body jerks weirdly. His right foot twitches and then tries to push up away from the chair and I think of a headless chicken trying to escape. I lift my own foot in response and stamp down violently on top of his and hear the satisfying crunch of decimated bones.

Then I move round to the front of his chair, amazed by how easy it's been. His head is slumped awkwardly to one side and for a brief second I fear he might already be dead. I delicately run a jagged shard of green glass, taken from the smashed bottle, across his perfect cheeks and poke the end through the skin. As I circle his eyes, jabbing ever more persistently with the tip, he finally opens them. I let out a deep breath, relieved he is still conscious. I deftly tie his legs and arms to the chair, securing them with strong cord to prevent him from slithering to the ground.

'I'm glad you could come,' I say, staring into his eyes. My voice is high-pitched, edged with hysteria. His lips are moving as he tries to speak but I can't hear anything. I mimic his efforts, excited by his fear and by my control. I give mock encouragement. 'Speak up. What's that?' I push my ear close to his mouth.

I wait until he once again slips out of consciousness and I extract the small paring knife from my pocket. I need to complete my task. I put my left hand over his lower face which I pull firmly to the left, the tension exposing the right side of the neck. With the edge of the knife facing forward, I stab the neck slightly behind the ear, before jamming it in to the hilt. Then as I sharply pull the knife back out, I project it

4

forward ripping through the arteries and opening a hole in the neck. As the blood gushes forth, I know my task is done.

A phone buzzes in my pocket, making me jump, disturbing the silence and bringing me back to reality. I need to leave, back out the way I came in through the patio doors. I assess the scene. There is not much to tidy up. There is no hint of my blood; I am certain of my efficiency. Once I've showered and changed, I'll head off and burn my clothes. Epping Forest will inter the evidence. The police won't come looking as I'll be last on their suspect list. Once I have washed the whiskey glass, scrubbing away rogue traces of DNA, I move towards my exit.

I close the door gently behind me and smile over my shoulder one last time at the sight of the blood-spattered kitchen. The wet red floor is like the River Styx, flowing seamlessly through the gates of hell. My savagery will lie in wait as a warning against immoral filth and as a lesson to the unfaithful.

I am hit by a chilling ghoulish silence outside and cautiously hover for a moment to make sure there is no one about. I hold my breath, waiting, listening. Finally, when I am certain I am alone, I begin to move forward.

There is a small river running along behind the close. It trickles merrily and eventually disappears under a bridge before it enters a shady copse on the edge of the motorway. I tread gently across the grass and squeeze through the unlocked gate at the bottom of the garden, grateful that the river made such back garden portals desirable. No one in the close bothers to keep them locked. The arseholes think it is such a safe neighbourhood.

An owl hoots from somewhere nearby and the noise makes me falter. The full moon is brightly accusing as it stubbornly lights my path which is being muddied by more continual pellets of rain. I pull my collar up and glance heavenwards thanking the gods for the downpour which is already wiping away any hint of my presence.

A rustle behind urges me on with greater speed. It will be a fox, sneaking through the damp grass, scavenging for scraps. Perhaps I should look back. I don't.

This is my biggest mistake.

1

CAROLINE

My laptop is open at the *Join Me* homepage. I brace myself, preparing to scroll through the profiles. It's the first thing I do every morning when I get out of bed. I sit at the small desk in our bedroom and start to browse. Soon I'm staring at the head and shoulders snapshot of a new member.

'She doesn't look too bad.' I jump backwards as Jason's hands suddenly alight on my shoulders. The words 'too bad' make me wince. I don't want his opinions.

'Too pale, and I thought you didn't like redheads.'

'Expensive-looking jewellery though.' He's good at spotting the luxuries, the wealth. I'll give him that. The gold chain seems to be pulling her down and the heavy earrings are elongating her freckled lobes.

'What's she into?'

'Usual. Gourmet dining, fine wines and...' I hesitate. My casual tone tries to stifle the nausea. I don't really want to say it. 'London Zoo.' This is the marker, the red flag. Bored housewives like Susan Harper aren't into zoos. Jason's profile sucks them in with his showcased photographs and fanciful desire to visit the lions at Regent's Park. This is our dangled carrot.

'Looks like a good choice. What do you think?'

I don't want to say what I really think. The words 'tart' and 'whore' perch precariously on the tip of my tongue. I have to remind myself that *Join Me* is my creation, my master plan. It's meant to keep Jason close and keep me in control. I can only share him because he belongs to me but it's tough. Every day it's getting tougher.

He walks away, perhaps sensing the tightening in my shoulders and clenching of my jaw, and pauses as he reaches the bathroom door. 'Join Me?'

It's our interminable joke but I can no longer share the amusement. It's only recently that I've sensed wry sarcasm every time he asks the question. The levity in his tone contrasts starkly with my own misgivings. I don't reply, furrowing my brow in feigned concentration. He takes my silence as a negative and I soon hear the shower crank up as he slips away from view.

I close my eyes, trying to calm my fears. The anxiety has made my palms sweat. I wipe them on my jeans and remind myself that Jason's not perfect.

He has a small dark shape, etched deeply above his coccyx, slightly off-centre. The raised ugly red outline, with its ragged serrated edge had at first startled me but soon threw my obsessive insecurities a lifeline; a smattering of crumbs.

'Ouch!' I screamed when it had appeared that first time out of nowhere, affronting me with its blackness. I had recoiled, loosening my wet relentless grip from his body. I remember falling back hard against the pillows. 'Cramp,' I lied. I winced, rubbing my left calf furiously while keeping my eyes averted.

'Oh that's my map of Brazil,' he announced proudly; a cartographer at home with his work. 'Look, it's broad across the top, thinning all the way down to Sao Paulo. It's a tattoo,' he lied. I remember how he had run his finger along the coastline. But it isn't a tattoo. It's a simmering festering dormant birthmark; grotesque and branding.

My gaze is automatically drawn towards the frosted pane and I torture myself watching the soap suds lather his perfectly tanned silhouette. I try to visualise the South American land-mass, willing it to give me some respite from my obsession. Jason. He is my god and I am in his thrall.

I determinedly click the screen back to life and scroll down to payments. There are three more enrolments. Harry 888 says he's twenty-five but with his black horn-rimmed glasses and balding pate he would be lucky to pass for fifty. The Tower of London and Buckingham Palace are on his wish list. Roly 676 is an accountant, an avid reader with a steady job and a penchant for heady cocktails. He wants to tour the wine bars of London. I guess he's married. I'm skilled at reading between the lines. Katie 145 is single, plain and mousy. She won't have any money, school teachers don't, but she fancies a trip down the Thames. Wild abandoned sex will be her fantasy but Jason has ignored her repeated invitations.

'Christ. Will you stop sneaking up on me?' I stiffen. Jason has crept across the carpet, stealthy as a panther. Dangerous. He's hovering behind me.

'Sorry, couldn't resist it.' He will be grinning, all perfect dazzling teeth. His aftershave makes me cough. He's been preparing for his date. 'Don't forget I'm meeting Jocelyn tonight.'

I swallow an acid retort.

'How could I forget?' I grit my teeth, knowing I can't forget. Until he's safely back home again, I'll picture the scene, rewinding and replaying the masochistic images. I'll see them in my mind's eye, laughing, drinking and more; so much more. Jos 040 is drowning in lust for my husband. Her desperation is lining our pockets.

'She's promised to bring me two grand. Remember?' It slips

off his tongue, effortless, unemotional, with a hint of pride ringing through; pride at his unrivalled success. It's for us, after all.

Jocelyn has fallen for Jason's lies of lucrative investment opportunities. Her *Join Me* profile highlights that she's into champagne haunts and Italian cuisine. She has joked privately with Jason that she has no interest in sightseeing. She's a trophy wife from Essex; easy pickings.

'Why are you in jogging clothes? You've just showered.'

'I need some fresh air and I'll pick up the paper while I'm out. Do you need anything?' He is standing in front of the long mirror running fingers through his lustrous wavy hair, checking his appearance. Photo-shoot perfection is how he likes it.

'No, you're okay. Don't be long.'

After he closes the door, I listen to him jog lightly down the stairs. A thunderstorm has built up outside and I move to the window and greedily stare down at my husband. He's pulling the hood of his sweatshirt up before slowly bending down to retie his laces.

The skies open and for a moment I hold my breath, hoping he will turn round and come back indoors. He doesn't but instead sets off, slowly at first, then building up pace as he heads ever more rapidly down the street. It might be a trick of my imagination but he seems to be running crazily, with intent, away from where he's come.

He's trying to put as much distance as he can between us.

2

SUSAN

The rain splashes against the window, large opaque globules slither down the pane; wet and woeful, like February. Everything is so dull. Outside in the close there isn't a soul about. Random cars dot the driveways, teasing with hope of post-apocalyptic life. The circular bulb of the cul-de-sac seems like the end of the world, preventing the dullness from escaping.

I stifle a yawn, reaching at last for the teasing glass of Sauvignon. I double-check the time, having promised myself I wouldn't succumb until five o'clock. One minute past. I close my eyes and let the cold nectar glide down my throat, relishing the almost-instant relief from the boredom. Tucking my legs under the swivel chair, I sit up straighter and pull myself closer in towards the computer. I finger the flyer sitting beside me on the desk and enter the web address. *Join Me*. The ladies at the gym have been chatting casually about the appeal of the website's intriguing invitation to have fun around London with strangers but no one has enrolled yet. Or so they say.

The screen finally springs to life.

JOIN ME

Enrol and Enjoy London's Sights Together

Heritage, Cultural, Dining/Fine Wines, London Fun
Tate Modern, British Museum, Royal Opera House, National Portrait Gallery...

The homepage is bright and sunny, blue and yellow, with an orange rainbow effect running through the text. A sudden clap of thunder outside makes me jump, a violent accompaniment to the images of joy and happiness. The wine is helping to veil the tackiness and is teasing me to browse further.

The profile synopses, however, are what taunt my imagination more than the bright and breezy sightseeing blurb. It's shared fun that appeals rather than the bricks and mortar of the Tower of London. Unless I sign up I can only romanticise about the characters whose faces peer out from the screen. I jiggle Roger's Newton's Cradle in front of me, jangling the balls from side to side, jabbing a forefinger at each end to coax the heavy metal shapes backwards and forwards. Click, click, click.

WHERE WOULD YOU LIKE TO GO?

Enrol, create a profile and list your interests
Join a Members' tour or organise your own
Invite Members along to share culture and fun

A sudden ring at the front door startles me. Carefully secreting the wine glass behind the curtain, I sit tight. Perhaps they'll go away.

'Do you want me to get it, Mrs Harper?' Natalie, our childminder, yells down from upstairs. She's in the make-believe world of Lego building and Disney movies, under strict instructions not to disturb me until six o'clock.

'It's okay, Natalie. I've got it.' This seems preferable to having Tilly and Noah back under my feet too early.

At the front door, I peer through the spyhole and manage to make out the distorted images of two strangers. Praying it's not Jehovah's Witnesses, I open the door.

'Hi. Oh, you must be... em?' I hesitate. 'Sorry. I can't

remember your names. Roger did tell me...' For the life of me, I don't remember anyone telling me. I feign ecstatic interest in the new arrivals to the close. The woman is petite and pretty but slightly on the mousy side, although her Nike trainers suggest she might be a potential jogging companion.

'Alexis and Adam. Morley. We've moved in across the road and wanted to say *hi*. Also wanted to apologise for the removal van this morning. The men took ages and I think your husband had a bit of trouble reversing.'

'Oh don't worry. I'm Susan, by the way, and that'll have been Roger in the car. Would you like to come in for a cup of tea or perhaps something stronger?'

We shake hands, very formally and I brace myself against having them in, unenthusiastic about impending small talk. I politely tempt them by opening the front door slightly wider, letting the cold damp air invade the hallway.

'No thanks. That would be lovely but we really need to get on with the unpacking so we'll have somewhere to sleep tonight. We wanted to introduce ourselves.' She turns towards her husband. I wait for Adam to add something. He stands slightly back from his wife, a cold unfriendly set to his lips.

'It's been a long day but thanks for the offer,' he says, withdrawing a limp hand. He's rather nondescript and aloof. Not like Roger who is tall, striking and very imposing. Adam complements his rather plain companion.

As I close the door behind them, I feel a dreary mood settle over me again. The realisation that they will be unexciting reliable neighbours has accentuated my boredom. We'll be able to share sugar cubes and teabags.

I wander back into the study, only half an hour of peaceful solitude left before Natalie has to go home. While I kick-start *Join Me* back to life, I peek out through the window and see the Morleys standing by their front door. She has put a key in the lock and seems to be struggling. He brushes her to one side and takes the key from her, proceeds to open the door before extracting it and holding it up, pointedly in front of her nose with a triumphant smirk, as if to say, 'See. That wasn't so difficult now, was it?'

I down the last of the wine, before topping it up from the bottle by my feet, and decide to sign up. Hell, why not? *Join Me* is just a more sociable version of Facebook. It seems to be about making friends and sharing fun rather than 'in-your-face' bragging of what exotic destination you and your family have visited. Unfriending contacts has taken up more of my time recently than requesting them.

I use my personal credit card, the one Roger doesn't control, and register with my private Yahoo email address. I'll pick my moment to tell Roger about the site, once it's a fait accompli. He won't mind, I'm certain, because he knows I toy with Facebook even though he still manages to tut every time it's mentioned.

It's not that I don't love Roger. It's rather that high-powered solicitors have little spare time for fun, and fine dining has been replaced with trips to McDonalds or Burger King. Romantic dinners have become a dim and distant memory.

I click the continue button, methodically working through the terms and conditions until I finally come to payment. Then it's done.

I browse; online shopping springs to mind as I begin clicking on the teasing photographs which are the visible tips of hidden icebergs. The members are all duller than I could have imagined, especially the men. Bob 123, Leonard 785 and Jerry 100 have all lied about their ages. They must have. As I squint at their profile pictures I find it hard to imagine that all forty-something's are balding, bespectacled and bearded. I smile at Bob 123's ambition to visit the London Dungeon. Some members haven't added their ages. Perhaps they think this doesn't matter when it's the sights that are on offer. However, I must admit that Percy 901, who looks about ninety, wouldn't be my first choice of companion. I can see why he's left his age out.

I then scroll through looking for those who claim to be in their thirties and those who might be into less serious pursuits. The *London Fun* section draws my eye.

LONDON FUN:

London Zoo, Thames River Boat, City Bus Tour, A Trip to Harrods...

The excitement is starting to pall when I see him. Vince 666. His smile lights up the screen. It's wide and winning. His white teeth are perfect. His eyes are a chocolate brown, his skin a pure olive tone. Six foot two apparently. He works in finance in the City, in futures trading and lives in London. I decide to add gourmet food to my interests and, for fun, London Zoo. I hate zoos but as this is first on Vince 666's bucket list, it's too tempting. Perhaps it's the wine working but what fun!

I have ten minutes left to perfect my draft profile and decide to change the first picture I chose. I looked quite stunning in my twenties and glancing at the gilt-framed mirror beside me, I fool myself into thinking that I might still pass for twenty-five. I stare for a couple of minutes at Vince's picture and my stomach does a little flip. Imagine. I could invite him to share an experience.

'Mrs Harper?' There's a gentle rap on the door before it's tentatively opened and Natalie pushes her head round. 'I need to get going.'

'Sorry, Natalie. I lost all track of time. Give me a minute.'

I quickly log off, clear the browser's history, clicking the X on the top right-hand corner of all recent screens and shut down the computer. Roger would be expecting to find sites advertising city mini-breaks, ski chalets or even dog rescue shelters. He's toying with Tilly's incessant request for a puppy, pretending that it's never going to happen. Roger tries to keep us all happy. I would rather explain face to face how *Join Me* works than he comes upon it by chance.

As I switch off the light and head out into the hall, Noah runs up and jumps into my arms, screaming 'Mummy! Mummy!'

I pull him close, kissing his perfect round little crown and realise I'm looking forward to Roger getting home.

3

CAROLINE

I slouch low in my seat, feigning interest in the gym brochure, head bent in manufactured concentration. I glance up intermittently to get a better look.

Susan Harper stands out from the crowd. It's her shock of thick unkempt auburn hair; long and loose, straggling round her shoulders. She's tall and skinny, dressed entirely in black with skin-tight leggings clinging savagely to her bones. The myriad of stubborn freckles that cover her face and arms make me smile. They'll not appeal to Jason. Airbrushed from her profile picture, they have presented me with an unexpected gift. A thick band of sweat rings her brow, a saintly halo of exertion.

'Coffees? My turn.' Her voice is imperious but gratingly high-pitched. 'Everyone for cappuccinos?' Susan has pushed her way to the forefront of the gaggle of ladies. A determined army talking fast and furiously, battling to be heard, they nod in unison. Two tables are pushed together, towels and kit bags tucked haphazardly underneath.

I amble towards the bar, timing my arrival. Susan is trying to jiggle three drinks in her skeletal fingers, pushing the receptacles tightly together, trying to steady the swirling contents. Dark sinewy veins snake up the back of her hands.

'Here. Let me help.' I lift a couple of coffees, offering to carry them over to the waiting group. A witches' coven.

'Thanks,' Susan says, smiling back at me.

'A pleasure.' I set the mugs down and turn to go back to the bar.

'You're welcome to join us.' Her smile is pleasant but cloying. She needs to be liked.

One of the ladies clears a seat beside her and pats it with a firm rap of her hand. 'Plenty of room,' she says.

I hesitate, unsure. My plan had been to bump into Susan alone, hanging around the changing rooms or lockers. I look round the café, unwilling to be derailed too easily. I could pretend to be waiting for someone, play for time. Instead, with a slight nod, I agree to join the circle.

'Thanks. I'll get my drink.'

I was right to guess that she might belong to the Fitness Forum. Her *Join Me* profile makes claims of Pilates and Zumba, and the gym's exorbitant joining fees made it a likely choice. Also it's the nearest private club to Riverside Close where she lives.

A heavy music beat is pulsating round the room, loud and energetic, confusing my thoughts. I'm reluctant to be noticed. Jason can't find out I'm following members who catch his eye. He would wonder why and it would be difficult to explain. A date is in the diary for him to meet up with Susan later in the week, so I need to be careful, not do anything rash. The thumping noise pulses round in my head as I reach for my coffee.

'A bit noisy.' A man at the table next to the ladies grimaces. He has been watching and tries to engage me in conversation, perhaps surmising that I might prefer his company. I ignore his efforts, smile weakly, and instead move towards the empty chair Susan has slotted in next to hers.

Conversation is in full swing but it's light and meaningless, staccato words bouncing back and forth. School runs, mid-week tennis lessons and vacuous asides about the weather.

'I'm Susan, by the way.'

'Caroline. Carrie to my friends.'

'Are you a new member?' she asks.

'I'm thinking of joining but not sure I can justify the fees.' I finger the brochure, leafing lightly through the pages. It gives me something to do.

'It's worth it if you do the classes. They're all included.' Each of the ladies in turn endeavours to sell the package, willing me to join them.

Susan looks at me when conversation turns gossipy, apologising for the non-inclusive nature of the topics. She extracts a scrunchie from her handbag and pulls her tangled red mane back from her face, knotting it loosely at the nape of her neck revealing an ugly mole under her left ear. I can't help staring. It reminds me of Jason's branding landmass.

'Sorry. We can't help ourselves. Typical bored housewives,' Susan says with mock self-chastisement. She sips her coffee, small delicate little mouthfuls, gripping the mug firmly in both hands and appears to be letting the mellow chatter waft over her, in one ear and out the other. Her mind is elsewhere.

She's meeting Jason on Friday and is holding the guilty secret close to her chest, tightly minding it like the hot steaming liquid. It will be the first time for them to meet. Fine wines and champagne is her thing apparently. Of course, I don't believe her claim that she's also keen to visit London Zoo.

Something makes me blurt it out. Perhaps it's my inherent impatient streak but a sudden lull in the conversation gives me the opening.

'I've had an interesting flyer through my letterbox. *Join Me.* Anyone heard of it?' It appears like I'm trying to join in, bring a subject of worth to the table. The ladies stop drinking for a second as conversation dries to a trickle. Their attention is caught by the newcomer.

'Shit.' I watch Susan as coffee misses her mouth and the milky liquid hits her black vest. It's a knee-jerk moment.

I hand her a serviette, watching the manic attempts to scrub away the first traces of guilt.

'Yes. We were talking about it last week,' says one member of the group; a small pale-faced *mumsy* type. 'I wouldn't have the time. Have you joined?'

'No, but it looks fun. Maybe if I'd a bit more spare time.' I stand up, gently pushing my chair back. 'It was nice to meet you all but I need to get going.' I smile from one lady to the next.

Susan suddenly stands up. 'I think I'll make a move too. Waitrose beckons. See you all next week?' She does a phoney little exaggerated wave of her right hand, flapping it theatrically from side to side in front of the ladies, before extricating her kit bag from under the table.

We walk out together towards the car park, shivering in unison as we pull our coats tight. Susan has regained her composure, the spilled coffee incident forgotten.

'Do you live nearby?' she asks as we reach our cars, parked near to each other.

'Off the Archway Road. Not far from Highgate tube station. You?'

'Riverside Close. It's nearer Hampstead than Highgate.' She clicks her car key and a gleaming black BMW saloon beeps open. 'Not too far from you.' She hesitates, as if unsure whether to kiss me on the cheek or shake my hand. I wonder if the mention of *Join Me* has left her feeling uneasy.

'Yes. Perhaps we could meet up for coffee sometime,' I

suggest. I click my own car fob and notice one of the back lights isn't working. As I throw my handbag across the passenger seat, I sense her hovering, although she's standing by her car door.

'Hey, why not come round for coffee one morning?'

I start up my car, pull the door closed and zip down the window.

'Yes. That would be nice, thanks.'

Susan takes a scrap of paper from her bag, leans it on top of her car bonnet and scribbles down a number.

'Here. Give me a call.'

'Will do. Sounds like fun.' I pocket the number safely before driving off, waving my hand out the open window. I watch her in the mirror as she slides into her expensive car. She has no idea she's being played. That's the way I want it.

As soon as I got together with Jason, I gave up on girlfriends. I'd always been the mousy dreamer, the dowdy hanger-on who harboured Cinderella dreams. As I drive away from Susan, I shiver at the thought of ever needing a girlfriend again. Jason is all I need. I never want to go back.

I had always felt a masochistic draw to be in the company of beautiful people. It seemed to give me worth. Jade had been my so-called best friend since university but we used each other, feigning a mutual empathy. It was a two-way arrangement. She needed me to keep her company on nights out and I in turn got invited to the best parties and coolest events, simply because I was her best friend.

Jade was beautiful. Well, beautiful on the outside but pitted and ugly on the inside. She was selfish and arrogant, driven by her looks rather than brains. However, she underestimated me once too often and the night Jason arrived on the scene would be the last time I saw her. I eventually changed my phone number when she persistently tried to get in touch. She was finally forced to get the message. I might be plain on the outside but determined as death on the inside. People never look deeply enough; that's their problem.

'Don't look round. You'll not believe the guy who's walked in,' she'd said.

I didn't look. There was no need. If Jade's eye landed on someone then no one else got a look in. We were at a nightclub, celebrating a reunion of sorts as we hadn't seen each other for several months. Also getting drunk always seemed like a good idea. The music was deafening, thundering through the psychedelic strobes, blocking out coherent thought and conversation.

'Is it safe to look yet?' I played along, dry mouthed and disinterested. Jade was like an exotic fish in an aquarium, all eyes drawn to her smooth bright colours as she slithered and weaved among the lesser, more insignificant, life forms.

'Not yet. Oh my god! He's coming this way.' She flicked her long hair coquettishly from one side to the other and back again, and then coiled it on top of her head before letting it cascade once more over bare tanned shoulders. Posing in skyscraper heels, her hips shimmied while she straightened her sheer silk dress.

I got used to people staring, asking me if she had a boyfriend, where she came from and if I could get them her phone number. I fell into the role of leftover sidekick only the desperate or realistic would turn to.

'Jeez this music's loud. Hi.' I heard the voice before I turned and saw the person. He was holding his hands theatrically over his ears. Jade answered for both of us.

'I know. I can't hear myself think!' she yelled, miming his

action of putting hands over her ears, gritting her teeth in mock horror.

'Can I get you ladies a drink?'

Jade nodded and wiggled her near-empty champagne flute in the air while he stood there, lips closed but upturned in wry amusement. His eyes did the talking. Even through the dark hazy atmosphere, my attention was drawn to the deep brown magnets. When he turned in my direction, my gaze dropped and my cheeks burned.

We stood in silence as he ordered the drinks, scared if we looked away he might be gone.

'Here. Champagne for the ladies.'

Jade's outstretched hungry hand hovered empty in the air. 'Careful not to spill any,' he said. His fingers brushed my hand and with barely a glance, he passed the second glass towards my friend's greedy out-splayed fingers.

'Thanks.' The voice came from somewhere but not from me.

We settled in a corner, the three of us. Jason had come alone. He didn't need sidekicks. I sat among the beautiful people and for the first time since I'd met Jade, I was aware of someone more dynamic, more physically perfect than she was.

'Isn't he bloody gorgeous? Have you ever seen anyone so cool?'

Jade was beside herself, a bitch on heat. Jason had popped out to make a phone call and she was already planning on how to get rid of me.

'Listen, he's coming back. You wouldn't mind popping to the loo and giving me five minutes alone with him?' Jade guzzled her champagne, downing friendship and decency in one gulp.

'He's the man for me. Christ, Carrie. I think I've found Mr Right.'

On cue, I excused myself. Old habits die hard and I headed for the exit. I'd catch a taxi back to King's Cross and take the train from there back up to Highgate. I wouldn't be missed. It was in that moment I decided never to see Jade again.

Destiny had different plans though. It intervened in the guise of a drunken teenager, balancing glasses cheek by jowl, who staggered across the room. A band of uneven carpet and unsteady footing sent a Bloody Mary straight in my direction.

'Shit. I'm sorry.' A bright red stain, thick like fresh blood, coursed down my top and rapidly seeped through the flimsy material. 'Shit, shit, shit,' he repeated. 'Let me get you a cloth.' The smell of tomato juice made me gag. 'I'm really sorry.'

'Don't worry. It doesn't matter. I'll clean myself up.'

I pushed past, desperate to escape, and soon found myself sitting in a toilet cubicle willing the night to end, nauseous from the congealed gunge stuck to my chest. I heaved racking silent sobs as the floodgates burst their dam.

'Carrie, are you in there?' Jade was soon working her way along the cubicles, banging heavily on each door, her voice screaming over the background noise. But she was in a hurry. I sensed her irritation. My stony silence was no match for her determination.

I slowly pulled back the lock and faced her.

'What the fuck's happened to you? You look like death. Christ, Carrie.'

'Thanks.'

I walked over to the basins and turned the cold tap up full. I cupped the icy liquid in both hands and threw it over my face, staring in the wide cracked mirror at the huge black tears of misery deposited by dissolving mascara. But I no longer cared.

'Don't make it worse. Please,' Jade said as she peeled her consoling arm from my shoulders. Embarrassment and frustration had already taken the place of pity. I scrubbed my red blotchy cheeks with a tissue and scraped at the black gritty sediment until I couldn't see.

'Don't worry, Jade. Go and enjoy yourself. I'll be fine. I've got a taxi waiting,' I lied. I dripped soapy water from my hands into the sink and put them under the dryer. A monsoon of hot air drowned out my friend's voice until it evaporated into thin air. I watched her tousle her hair in the mirror and reapply lip gloss and eye liner with a practised steady hand.

I gave her a wan smile, slung my bag over my shoulder and said goodnight.

'Night, hun. I'll call tomorrow. Wish me luck,' she shrieked. Excitement was written large across her face as she turned towards the toilets. She waved me off, a flippant little gesture, like swatting away an irritating fly.

Jason was standing outside the ladies.

'You okay?'

'Not really,' I said as I wiped wet residue from my neck with a sleeve.

'Come. I'll see you out.'

Like a disgraced child, I followed as he took my arm. I felt his fingers burn warmth through my shivering body. We squeezed through the sweaty gyrating mass until we reached the back door where the cold night air hit us with its wall of ice.

'Where to?'

'Highgate. Archway Road. Thanks but I'm okay now.'

He walked towards the row of taxis, spoke through a window and then came back as a cab pulled alongside.

'Here. Let me.' He stretched across and opened the door. I wasn't sure at this point whether to kiss him on the cheek or to slink silently into the back seat. Mortification at my appearance and acrid smell pushed me towards the latter.

'Thanks again.' I kept my head down, scared to look and see pity in his eyes.

But instead of turning and heading back into the nightclub, he slipped in beside me and pulled the door gently to.

'Highgate please. The Archway Road up near the tube station.'

As the cab pulled away, we both spotted Jade out of the window. She was standing by the back door of the club scouring her surroundings for Jason. I was sure she wasn't looking for me. Her eyes scanned left to right and back again with an occasional glance over her shoulder. Her long tanned arms encircled her chest as she gripped them tight across her body against the chill.

'Duck,' he said and we laughed in unison, hunching down from view below the glass. His arms wrapped tight around me and pulled me ever lower. 'That's what I call a close shave.'

That was the moment I fell in love with Jason.

4

ALEXIS

We start to unpack the boxes together. Adam is on call but has promised faithfully that unless there's a dire emergency, I will have his full co-operation this evening. Bonnie, a friend's dog and our temporary house guest, is watching avidly; but from a distance. She's waiting for me to summon her, brandishing a treat, but Adam's admonishing finger has rendered her immobile; but watchful. Her ears are up.

'Stay.' He stares her down. Then suddenly his mobile goes off.

'Adam Morley,' he announces in his very important voice. The doctor on call needs to have gravitas. He's talking to someone sycophantic from work. I carry on tearing newspaper from mugs and glasses, stacking them on the coffee table. I bang the receptacles down on to the wooden surface, making deliberate noise until Adam moves towards the door into the hall. His voice echoes off the empty walls.

Bonnie treads warily towards me, tail down, unsure.

'Come here.'

She snuggles in beside me, hiding behind my bent knees, trying to make herself invisible.

'Yes, I see. Yes. Hmm, hmm,' Adam mumbles. He makes fed-up gestures in my direction, miming frustration with raised eyebrows and theatrical sighs. The person on the other end doesn't know he has commitments. He doesn't tell them he's unpacking cases of belongings pertaining to starting a new life in a new home.

'Yes, I understand. I'm on my way.' I knew he was a doctor when I married him. I liked the respect that went with his profession. 'I'm sorry,' he says, clicking his phone off. 'Leave it. I promise I'll do my share tomorrow. It's a burst appendix.' It sounds impersonal, like a burst pipe. He turns quickly, no interest in my reply, having already decided he needs to get going, and starts to head upstairs. His bare feet move firmly across the wooden boards in the hall.

'Can't someone else cover this once?'

He stops, turns back. 'Alexis.' The one curt word implies there'll be no discussion. Bonnie slinks down further behind me. 'You know the score. It goes with the job. Emergencies happen.' There's no room for manoeuvre. He's the breadwinner.

'Yes but you promised.'

He moves closer and looks down at me but, without further comment, shoos Bonnie back into the corner.

'Can't you put that bloody thing in the garage?'

I don't answer. Instead I carry on ripping paper with barely tempered aggression and then move towards the television and switch it on. At least he managed to plug it in before he got the call. With that, he walks away and disappears upstairs to change.

Five minutes later, dressed in a work suit accessorised with a weird jazzy psychedelic tie, Adam reappears and bends down and kisses me on top of my head. The clock leaning against the wall shows it's 7.30pm.

'I shouldn't be too late. But don't wait up,' he says. 'I'll see you in the morning.'

'Whatever.' I offer a weak conciliatory smile. 'Hope it goes okay.' But he's already heading towards the front door.

I move to the window, still void of curtains, and watch Adam's car disappear out the close towards Church Street. I look round the circular confine, imagining happy families behind the closed doors. Bonnie's jumping up and down, barking with little relieved yelps, willing me to lift her up. Her body, soft and downy, relaxes into my chest. She's happy now we're alone. I've decided that one day I will buy myself a dog. One day if Adam is not around. Bonnie has already become attached even though I'm only looking after her for a few days; a favour for a friend.

I watch a large black 4 x 4 pull up outside the Harpers' house. It will have passed Adam's saloon on its way into the close. I wonder if the men did a pleasant but emotionally distant acknowledgement gesture through their blackened windows. I pull back from my vantage point, hiding behind the wall, and peek out across the road. I see Susan Harper's husband step out of his car and proceed to put his key in the front door. He is tall and dark skinned with slickly gelled hair sticking to his scalp. Perhaps I'll pop over again at the weekend, making some excuse about locating the stopcock or perhaps give them our spare keys. It looks as if I'm going to need company.

Should be back by midnight. A few complications. Ax

It's ten o'clock when Adam's text pings through. Perhaps I'm being paranoid but a burst appendix surely doesn't take four hours. Bonnie has fallen into a deep trusting slumber by the time I turn off the lamps. I settle her in the utility room before creeping upstairs in the dark. The wind has picked up outside and seems to be howling through a gap somewhere in the house. Perhaps it's the bare walls and floors that are turning up the volume on every tiny noise and making me anxiously alert. Lack of through traffic makes the close feel cut off from the real world.

I keep my onesie on as I climb into bed, glad that I remembered to throw the duvet and pillows loosely into the car so we would at least have some bedding for our first night. The tightly sealed champagne bottle with the two crystal glasses sits accusingly on the bedside table next to where Adam will sleep. I want him to feel guilty.

The small bedside light throws its beam onto the folder. I keep it hidden in my bedside drawer away from Adam's belittling eye and slowly spread out the contents in front of me before I start reading the downloaded articles on the latest tracking devices, home surveillance and PC forensics.

I've decided to stick to my original plan. The burst appendix incident has spurred me on to use Adam as my guinea pig. However, I won't let on, giving him the benefit of the doubt; innocent until proven guilty. An alarming increase in his overtime and late-night emergencies has helped me decide.

'A private detective? For Christ's sake, Alexis. I think you need to get real. Get a proper job.' His derision has slowly turned from irritation to anger. 'Why not get a better teaching post?' He mocks when I tell him that I've wanted to follow in my father's footsteps since I was about six.

'It's not some pipe dream. It's what I want to do. The way you wanted to be a doctor.'

'I wanted to be an astronaut first.'

As I settle down under the duvet, bunching up the pillows

behind me, my mind races ahead, working out how best to tail Adam and monitor his movements. If I'm wrong, I won't own up, and maybe in years to come, I will own up to Adam about how I honed my skills. Perhaps in middle age we'll rekindle a shared sense of humour and enjoy the joke.

Dad taught me to follow my instincts. His career in the Met, forty years, was cut short by one too many high-speed car chases but not before he'd shared thousands of clues and cases with me, teaching me how to interpret data to catch the villain. I swallow hard, blinking back the memories.

It was at the hospital Christmas party that niggling doubts first surfaced. Debbie was a junior nurse but we never got introduced. I remember her being loud and raucous, big and buxom, and Adam pointedly avoiding her. When she headed in our direction, Adam took my arm and steered me away in the opposite direction. This happened twice; one time too many.

'That was a bit rude.' There was something in the way the nurse stared after us that alerted me. I watched her down a plastic beaker of punch. Her wild eyes made looks to kill.

'Oh ignore her. The nurses can't hold their drink. Always the same at these bloody dos.' Adam rapidly propelled me off into a far corner where a huddle of smartly dressed consultants was holding a more cerebral conversation. He thought I didn't notice his backward glance though, the admonishing stare directed towards Debbie. That was the second clue.

My eyes become heavy, the lids straining to stay open, when I decide to put the file away and turn off the light. It's shortly before midnight and there's still no sign of Adam.

Suddenly I hear a determined barking from downstairs. Bonnie is awake. She usually sleeps through the night. I sit up, straining my ears for other noises, a door opening or closing, rogue footsteps on the stairs. There's nothing; barking and then silence. I get out of bed and, using the torch on my mobile, make my way along the landing, following the white streak of light down the stairs through to the back of the house.

'What's up? Come here, you.' The barking has subsided, replaced by faint whining noises and Bonnie's stubby little tail is swishing furiously back and forth. 'You know I can't take you upstairs.' I carry the little body through into the kitchen and reach up for the biscuit treats. Her consternation is quickly forgotten, as she gobbles down the reward. She licks my face, her wet sticky tongue probing my neck and cheeks.

We hear a car pull up in the driveway. Resignation grips Bonnie as I hurriedly put her back in the basket. She won't lie down, not yet, but watches me intently.

'Shh. Be a good girl. I'll see you in the morning.' Her small bright eyes cut through the darkness and as I close the door, she knows now to be quiet. She'll not bark again tonight. Not now that Adam is home. We share an instinctive unease.

5

ALEXIS

I drive cautiously through debris and fallen branches strewn across the leafy suburban avenues. Storm 'Nathan' has deposited a trail of destruction in its wake but at least the persistent rain has abated and I soon reach the High Road which is clear except for the clogged arteries of London traffic. A bright frost-free day is essential for my plan. I've had to be patient.

Adam left later than usual this morning, spending what seemed like an eternity toying with his full-bran muesli. His bowels are an obsession.

'There's too much cholesterol in that,' he had said, pointing towards my warm croissant, 'and you'll put on weight.'

'I'll take the risk. Anyway I don't know how you can eat that rabbit food.'

'It's not about enjoyment, it's about discipline,' he said, spooning up the dregs of browned milk. 'Don't you want to live till you're a hundred?'

By the time I managed to leave the house it was around ten o'clock. There was no one about outside and as I got into the car, I was hopeful that rush hour might have abated. Within the cosy confines of Riverside Close it's easy to forget that London never sleeps.

It's a good hour later before I pull up outside the lock-up in Camden. The red paint is peeling off the up-and-over door whose colour no longer makes it look so revolutionary and garish. Grey steel can be seen breaking through the glossy façade. I sit for a moment in the car recalling Trent's pride in his purchase.

'What do you think, sis? Cool eh?' He had unlocked the metal shutter and rolled it up and over, leading me proudly inside.

'Very,' I'd said. You couldn't help but love Trent's enthusiasm. Every idea was the next big thing. 'This time next year we'll be millionaires.' My little brother was Del Boy in the making.

'A ramp here, stacking shelves against this wall, and I'm thinking of selling tyres. It'll work,' he'd said, willing me to get fired up by the damp grey walls and broken concrete floor.

I finger the key which is strung around my neck, hesitant for a second, before inserting it into the slot. The metal rollers creak as I push the door up. Flakes of rust attack my eyes and momentarily blur my vision.

The reek of oil hits my senses first before I manage to open my eyes and take in the sight of tools littering the floor and benches. I find a switch which turns on a single dangling electric light. Typical. Trent wouldn't have thought to disconnect the electric supply before he upped sticks and left. The lone bulb sheds an eerie glow around the room. Torn stained overalls lie strewn across spare tyres and a rusting broken down ramp fills the centre of the space.

In the far corner I spot what I'm looking for. There's a dirty green tarpaulin on top but the outline of my brother's pride and joy is distinct. I strip back the cover and look at the sleek black machine. A Kawasaki Ninja 250R. I finger the faring, remembering how little protection it offered as I clung petrified but exhilarated to Trent's body as we sped down the motorway. Fear and exhilaration were like the flip sides of the same coin.

I remember his patience teaching me how to master his new toy, spending tireless hours with me at a disused airstrip showing me how to skid, slide and build speed. We were a good team but it's painful to remember. I miss him and wish he'd come home.

The black helmet is clipped to the handlebars, waiting for my brother's return and for him to hop back on. I lift it off, pull it over my head and then throw my right leg across the seat before I try to bring the engine back to life. The key is still in the ignition and with a single turn, it kick-starts the machine into spluttering action.

After filling the bike with petrol, I practise weaving in and out of the endless traffic. I drive, gingerly at first, to Riverside Close, timing the journey and back again. By five o'clock I decide to stop off at a café near the hospital for a strong coffee to recharge my batteries and prepare for the night ahead. It could be a long one. I've at least a couple of hours to kill.

I reread the text messages from Trent while I savour the hot drink. I had gingerly asked if it was okay to use his bike, half expecting a firm negative.

> Of course you can, Sis. Enjoy but be careful. It's not a toy.
> Love you. Trent xxxx

The messages bring us closer, the miles between not so

gaping when his words light up the screen. America is suddenly comfortingly round the corner.

> Of course I'll be careful. Miss you. Wish you'd come home. A xxxx By the way you'll have a big electric bill waiting for you!!

He promises he'll be back next year. It seems a lifetime away. Trent would understand what I was doing; encourage me to follow my heart. I close my eyes and conjure up his smug reply, 'I told you so' when I explain about Adam. Trent never did like him. The thought doubles my determination, and my doubts.

I click the phone shut, pulling back from my reverie and drain the last dregs of coffee. Reattaching the helmet, I head back out into the biting night air. There's work to be done.

It's seven o'clock when I see Adam exit the hospital. He told me he'd be late as he promised to go for a few beers with colleagues. But he never drinks with co-workers after work, preferring to keep an aloof distance. I wait behind a bus shelter, tucked out of view as he strolls to his car. Tonight I'll find out where he's really going.

I've attached a small video camera to the front of the bike and as I tail Adam's car closely up towards West Hampstead I click the setting to *on* when he slows down outside a block of flats; Waverley Mansions. I park across the road, swivelling the front of the bike outwards at an angle so that the recorder has a clear view of the driver exiting. He waves to someone on the first floor. A woman is standing by the window, expectant. Adam has a bunch of flowers in his hand and as I squint through the black visor, I know the night recorder will have captured the roses. It will also have captured the blurry image of Debbie, the nurse from the hospital, waving down at him.

I feel nauseous, and fear I might throw up. Gut instinct was right. Optimistic logic has been encouraging me to ignore the pessimistic misgivings but I think I've known all along. I watch him press a key on the entry pad and can see his smile under the glow of the porch light when he whispers something into the mouthpiece; something familiar. I can also make out that the roses are red. He lets himself in and disappears from view.

It takes me about ten minutes to gather myself, decide what to do. A red-hot anger replaces the shock and a spur-of-the-moment idea springs to mind. I get off the bike and reach for the small toolbox secreted under the black leather seat. I open the tiny metal container and run my fingers along the contents. At one end, between a couple of spanners and some spare valves, is a thin pointed awl with a long metal spike. Perfect.

A black-clad motorcyclist in the night is well-nigh invisible to the naked eye. I'm insignificant and uninteresting. The dull street lights and empty pavements play into my hands and as I scour the street, I'm confident there's no one about.

I drive the pointed tip firstly into the driver's side front wheel, plunging it with all my might. It sticks and I have to heave and tug to get it back out. I put my ear close to the rubber and hear a very faint hiss. I work my way round the car and unscrew all the valves before dropping them down a drain.

The awl gets stuck in the fourth tyre and it won't budge. I bend down and am almost completely underneath the car trying to prise the tool loose, when a young couple pass by. It's lucky they're too enrapt to notice me. I lie quietly, hoping that my blackness is fusing with the night and that I won't be spotted.

I breathe more easily when they turn a corner and disappear from view. In a last-ditch attempt to wreak as much havoc as possible, I remember the penknife; a 1960s Boy Scout model with flick blade. Trent had pestered my father to have it since he was a nipper and finally got the prize on his eighteenth birthday by which time such implements had been banned.

I leave the awl in place and scramble back up and head for the toolbox. I was right. The penknife is easy to spot with its white skeleton logo. The blade flicks open, its sharp edge smooth and glistening. I take it back to the car and effortlessly slash all four tyres, watching as the air slowly leaves their fatally wounded forms.

I look up towards the upstairs window before I get back on the bike. The curtains are closed and I can just make out the silhouettes of two people, motionless, behind the flimsy veil. I swallow hard, biting back the bile, and without further delay, strap the helmet on and start up the engine. I need to get back; first to the lock-up to drop the bike off then home to Riverside Close.

Yet as I pull away, I realise that our new house will never be home.

I'm under the duvet with all the lights out when the front door opens. A long way off, I can hear Adam untie his laces and place his shoes by the front door. Of course he'll not want to wake me, despite the slashed tyres.

He creeps upstairs, undoing his tie with his right hand and taking off his work jacket which he slings over his left arm. I know he's doing this because this is what he does every Friday night when he gets back after midnight. He'll be wondering why I'm not calling out to say 'is that you?' It's later than usual so he'll assume I'm asleep. He will be exhausted, angry and exasperated.

I glance at the clock. Three o'clock. As I close my eyes in feigned slumber, I wonder if he'll tell me, in the morning, why he had to get a taxi back and where his car tyres got slashed.

6

OLIVE

I'm sitting at the window, staring out across the cul-de-sac. To the outside world I'm not sure if it is my age or appearance that renders me invisible. Hunched down by the window, the net curtains afford me a flimsy screen that keeps me hidden from neighbourly glances. Bob has slotted into old age with surprising ease. His irritating habits are driving me ever more insane. He reluctantly agreed to go and hit some golf balls with an old friend this morning, insisting that he would be back in time for lunch. He doesn't like to leave me on my own but I find myself wondering why. I shout at him incessantly, carping at his petty-mindedness and lack of ambition. This drives me madder than it does him. His ambition disintegrated in his early forties after he left the army. He was never the same after the stints in Northern Ireland; post-traumatic stress is now the label attached to his disturbing war experiences. Counselling wasn't for him though. He decided to take up painting and decorating instead. He has been under my feet ever since.

I get up and wander towards the kitchen. I feel like twenty-one inside, but as I peer into the hall mirror, I see that wrinkles line my face like a map of the world. The thickly etched furrows are like isobars of discontent. I'm not sure where they've all come from as I'm religious in avoiding the sun. Our last overseas holiday was in 1990 when Bob surprised me with cheap flights to Malaga.

I put the kettle on and listen to the silence. If Bob wasn't around or dropped down dead on the golf course, I do realise that the silence wouldn't be so welcoming. Everything forbidden has its appeal and I smile at the thought. Those were the days.

I take my tea and biscuits over to the window, relishing the warmth reflecting off the glass panes, and pull back the curtains slightly before I settle back into my seat. I like sitting by the window, watching the world go by. I can only do it when Bob's out of the way, which is rarely. The cul-de-sac has seen plenty of comings and goings over the years. The average age of the inhabitants has dropped significantly as money comes earlier to the young.

I dunk the ginger snap in the hot milky liquid and suck up the softened sugary mess. That Susan Harper has started coming and going more regularly, dressed up smartly rather than in her leisure gear. I watch her lock up, scan the driveway and get into her car. It is mid-morning and I think she must be going out for lunch; somewhere posh no doubt. She only ever offers up a cursory remark in my direction when she unwillingly has to communicate about some neighbourhood concern or the weather. She's not interested in Bob or me. We are too old with nothing to offer in the way of status or excitement. Perhaps she has to suffer her own elderly parents and has no spare charitable time.

I sip my tea, musing that I could offer her a lot in the way of advice and experience. I do wonder who her mystery lunch date might be though. She would have no interest in my affair all those years ago as she would see that as a totally different matter. What would I know about love and excitement? I'm nearly eighty years of age with knowledge limited to knitting, baking and the odd spot of gardening.

I peer round to the left, hoisting myself slightly out of my seat, and watch Alexis Morley leave the house. She waves at Susan. Alexis is a pretty little thing, tomboyish with short blonde wavy hair and reminds me of my younger self. She notices me and waves with a natural trill of her fingers. She walks down her short driveway and moseys up mine and rings the bell.

I set my cup down and lever myself up out of the chair using one of its arms for support. Alexis has her finger poised by the buzzer ready to press it again when I finally manage to reach the front door.

'Hello.'

'Hi Olive. I'm off to the supermarket and wondered if you needed anything from the shops.'

'That's very sweet of you.' I smile. Perhaps she can see past the wrinkles but I'm not sure. She has only moved in recently. 'I'd be very grateful if you would pick me up a newspaper. *The Telegraph* please. If you're sure it's no trouble.' I overturn the glass jar sitting on the hall table by the door and scrape together the money. I put the coins in one of the plastic bank bags which Bob keeps in the drawer for collating the different denominations.

'Would you like a cup of tea?' I ask, knowing that she won't stop. No one has time for anything these days and sitting by the window in a lifeless cul-de-sac with an old woman is not a young person's idea of fun. Alexis has started going out every morning, in casual dress, around the same time. I think she leaves the close about eleven but I can jot the time down later.

'That's very kind, Olive, but I need to get going. I've a lot to do.' She smiles. Her teeth are small and straight and her eyes crinkle at the corners as she takes the plastic bag. I become aware of my veined hands with their arthritic claw-like spindles next to her smooth delicate fingers. My circulation is not good; it's the Raynaud's that stops the blood circulating. Alexis walks back down the path, promising to push the paper through the door when she gets back. I suspect this will be her good deed for the day.

It's around midday when Bob phones to say that he'll be stopping off for a pint with his friend at the golf club. He hopes I don't mind. I'm delighted. I have one more hour of peace and quiet.

I get out my small diary and jot down a few notes. It's my favourite pastime, a hobby to keep me busy and my brain alert. Every day I note down small insignificant events that have taken place in Riverside Close. I log Susan Harper's departure, Alexis' visit, and am about to put my diary back in the drawer when I notice a large car cruise up and into the empty drive opposite; the drive at number four Riverside Close. It is Mr Herriott the estate agent. He'll soon be launching into his slick sales patter with an eager potential purchaser. He humours me when the client arrives and I hobble across the road, pretending that his smarmy charm is inherent. I know otherwise.

I'll potter over again this morning and annoy him with my weak neighbourly winsome smiles. I do wonder at my venom, and as I pull on my tweed coat and woollen hat, I am amused by the subterfuge so easily provided by old age. I'll smile like the little old lady I have become and try to block his sale yet again. What fun.

7

ALEXIS

I arrive late for the seminar. It was a spur-of-the-moment thing, a last-minute enrolment.

Rewinding through the grainy images of the cheap red roses fuelled the determination to pursue my new career with increased vigour.

The back streets of Luton snarl in one-way traps through the concrete jungles. The flyover takes me the wrong way as my satnav leads me in the opposite direction. My Mini speeds back round the roundabout, slithering over the damp surface, until I finally spot Dean Street on the left, neatly tucked away between a kebab shop and a Romanian food store. There's nowhere to park and by the time I manage to cram my car between two white vans half a mile down the road, I'm sweating and agitated.

The office block is the only four-storey building on Dean Street which appears to accommodate mainly eating establishments and tattoo parlours. I race up the concrete stairwell, two at a time, until I reach the fourth floor. Breathing heavily, I sidle through a set of bulky swing doors situated at the end of the landing and find myself transported back in time to school assemblies. At the front of the hall, the speaker, a smart Asian gentleman whom I assume to be Mr Kabal, the programme organiser, is in full flow, enunciating loudly from behind a wooden lectern. When he spots me, he halts mid-sentence.

'Please, take a seat. We've only just started.' He beams.

The heat in the room is suffocating as I take my place in the first vacant slot. I scrabble for my notepad and pen when a young suited teenager taps me on the shoulder from behind and hands me a printout of the day's itinerary. I nod a silent *thank you* as I take off my leather jacket and swing it over the back of my chair and prepare to become immersed in the event.

We cover everything from listening devices, live-action surveillance and vehicle tracking to twenty-four-hour monitoring. For a moment I close my eyes, visualising Adam and Debbie. I can still see her long bleached-blonde hair hanging loose and dishevelled as she drew the curtains closed. It's hard to forget. I imagine the 'live action' which took place and my resolve hardens. He'll pay, arrogant cheating bastard. I reopen my eyes and scan the room, wondering how many of the attendees want to set up round-the-clock monitoring on their own partners. I can't imagine all the attendees have ambitions to become private detectives.

'Our methods guarantee results,' rounds off Mr Kabal, smiling broadly at his rapt audience.

At the coffee break I pop outside to check my phone. Adam is staying away tonight; Milton Keynes on a neurological conference. That's what he's telling me. He's left a message saying he'll phone when he gets to the hotel. The message will make him feel better. Lies will offer a temporary balm and he'll then be able to enjoy himself, convinced I'm at home devoid of suspicion.

'Hi. I haven't seen you before.' The young man who offered me his printout when I arrived, smiles. 'I'm Gary.' He extends a sweaty palm by way of introduction. He tries to deepen his high-pitched voice while proffering a timid handshake. He's only now becoming an adult.

'Alexis. Alexis Morley. Yes, this is the first time I've been to one of these things,' I say. He hands me a watery coffee in a plastic cup, which I can't hold for the heat. He laughs when I jiggle the receptacle from one hand to the other before setting it down on the windowsill.

We chat about the latest snooping equipment and devices, and swap phone numbers. I don't take his card but tap his details into my phone, under a fictitious name. I'm learning new skills quickly. No paper trails. Adam thinks I'm catching the train up to London to meet a friend for lunch and then taking in a show. As far as he's concerned, I'll be sleepily exiting the theatre around the time he's likely to be bedding Debbie in Milton Keynes.

Gary sits beside me when the lecture resumes. I'm not sure whether he sees me as a mother figure or an attractive older woman, a Mrs Robinson fantasy. He whispers asides to me during the increasingly boring oration which has moved on to mobile phone and computer forensics. He makes me laugh with perky little quips from behind his hand. His levity is helping to lift me out of my stubborn gloom.

I soon find myself realising that with the need for at least two people on twenty-four-hour surveillance operations, Gary and I might be able to link up. He's starting to look like a possible answer to my more pressing requirements. He also assures me he's great with a camera.

~

46

I'm glad to get out from the hot sweaty atmosphere and am soon waving Gary off as he disappears into a neighbouring kebab shop. It's almost dark and the parked cars, jammed cheek by jowl on the pavement, are slowly being kick-started into life in preparation for the rush-hour journey home. As I set off to find my car, I stop and peer through the window of a darkened tattoo parlour situated next to the office block. Inside are two leather-clad men with straggly beards hovering over a young teenage girl, who's probably in her early teens. She has a myriad of metal studs protruding from her left ear and her pink hair is gelled into spikes with a purple streak running through the middle. Her appearance screams rebellion. She's angry. As I ease the door open, I decide to join her. I'm angry too. The knowledge that Adam will so totally disapprove spurs me on. I can hear him justifying his distaste by using medical terminology to describe the more severe, potentially life-threatening, side effects of my actions.

'I'll be with you in a minute.' One of the bearded artisans smiles at me. 'Perhaps you'd like to have a look through our catalogue.' He points with his whirring metal etcher towards a pile of magazines on the table, talking in a deceptively sing-song effeminate voice. Looks can be deceiving. The girl stares in my direction without emotion, maintaining a carefully controlled and threatening façade.

'Thanks.' It doesn't take me long to find what I'm looking for. It stares back at me from the page: a tiny image of a detective hiding behind a huge magnifying glass. It's perfect. A red rose or tiny heart might once have caught my eye. Now the single word 'Adam' with a blood-smeared knife superimposed through the characters entices me with a graphic savage appeal. I decide on the subtler detective image; it signifies a future. Adam is my past and I'll try to wipe all traces of him from my memory.

The small tattoo sits proudly above my coccyx. Adam no longer follows my naked body with his eyes and I wear shorts and T-shirts in bed. However, I decide that before I confront him with all the evidence I'll reveal the tattoo, do a twirl, and tell him when the sculpting took place.

8

SUSAN

I'm feeling self-conscious sitting in the stuffy tube carriage wearing an above-the-knee leather skirt with my bony knees peeking out over the top of the leather boots. I try to relax, keeping my eyes peeled straight ahead. There's a man sitting opposite, about my age, early forties, his hair with a hint of grey at the temples. He's engrossed in a tablet, his fingers sliding slickly back and forth across the screen when he suddenly looks up and catches my eye. He looks away hastily. A wry smile crosses his lips and suggests amusement, or perhaps pity, thinking mutton dressed as lamb. I close my eyes to block him out.

I pull my coat more tightly round me although I have to loosen my scarf. Sweat is starting to play havoc with my make-up. I extract a small A to Z and recheck the location of the champagne bar. Vince contacted me, delighted he had found someone other than himself who was interested in wild exotic animals. That was only five days after I'd enrolled.

I see you're a fellow lover of zoos. Fancy joining me on a trip next week? Meet at Regent's Park perhaps? Vince

I waited two days before declining, using the icy conditions and snow forecast as an excuse. Trudging round the zoo in minus degrees doesn't really appeal.

Perhaps we could share a glass of wine and set a date to see the animals in the New Year? I'm a real lover of fine wines too! Vince

The suggestion came back a day later. It was the stubbornness of the snow, I tell myself. The thick white blanket dulled the noise all around, and my world became even quieter and more claustrophobic. Roger told me not to drive until the ice had cleared and Natalie was happy walking the kids back from school. I might not have needed an excuse but this seemed as good a one as any. So I blamed the weather for my response to the messages.

Ok. I'm up in London on Friday. Perhaps a quick drink and I'll bring my diary? If not, happy to wait till the New Year. Susan

His reply bounced back within five minutes, a disconcerting ping, as I was closing down the laptop. It was as if he'd been waiting, hovering or perhaps it was timing, coincidental.

Friday's perfect. I'm also up in London that day! Le Ciel est Bleu off Regent Street. Great selection of wine and champagne. 6 o'clock any good? Vince

My stomach is in knots as I step out onto the platform. Butterflies are battering my insides and I want to turn back and re-enter the safety of the carriage but it's too late. Rush hour is in

full swing and I'm batted back and forth, like a volleyed tennis ball smacked with intent, between the dark-suited men. The doors have slid closed again. I rest for a moment on a metal bench, draw breath, and watch the train rumble away in the distance, commuters packed tightly and hanging precariously from the dangling straps.

Two men sit beside me; too close, talking in foreign tones. I feel uneasy and grip my handbag more tightly. *Two minutes* till the next train. I'll go home; it's all been a ridiculous exercise. One of the men moves in closer and I can feel his arm rubbing against mine. He smells of sweat and oil, a rancid combination. *One minute.* There's a rumble approaching from the other end of the tunnel and a warning horn blasts through the muffled silence as headlights appear. I jump up, pushing away the dirty stained fingers that have wound themselves round the leather strap. No one's watching. No one cares. This is London. I struggle to get away but finally manage to disentangle the stranger from my bag, before pushing and shoving wildly past the hordes, climbing the stairs two at a time in an effort to reach the exit gates.

By the time I'm outside on the street, there's no air left in my lungs. I keep checking over my shoulder but no one's following. Or perhaps they are; it's difficult to be sure as the faces all pass in a blur. I feel safer outside, the brown icy sludge already beginning to melt, heralding firmer, more familiar footing. I pull my collar up round my ears, slinking down, and try to make myself invisible. I can't go back into the underground, I need air. The strangers might be loitering. Vince suddenly seems like a safer option. One drink and then I'll go home.

The side road where the champagne bar is situated is off Regent Street. It is ten minutes past six when I stop outside Le Ciel est Bleu. It's dark inside. I nervously push open the door and scan the tables. I needn't have worried about not recognising him. He is sitting at the bar with his back to the entrance. He doesn't need to look round. He knows he'll be sought out; it's something in the outline, the bearing of his shoulders. The assurance of the silhouette draws me forward. I approach tentatively, unable to turn back. Perhaps I should. My leather skirt and boots give out the wrong message. A work suit would have helped me feign high-powered business sense but it's all too late.

'Susan,' he says with a raised questioning eyebrow, turning and sliding effortlessly off his stool. He extends a hand, smooth, warm and strong. It mirrors the rest of him. A musky woody scent clings to him. I blush, my cheeks inflamed to match my hair and I wonder what the hell I'm doing here.

'Vince.' I smile.

'Here, let me take your coat.' Self-assured, relaxed.

I'm tongue-tied and embarrassment mingles with a distinct frisson of fear. A bottle of champagne nestles in a silver ice bucket on the bar and Vince asks the waiter to 'bring it to my table'. I flinch at the word 'my'. Perhaps Le Ciel est Bleu is a regular haunt or perhaps he works next door.

Whatever, it's clear that Vince is on familiar terms with the young bartender.

'No problem, sir.'

I slowly relax as the minutes tick by. The champagne hits my senses, the bubbles fizzing warmly down my throat. I drink too quickly. Conversation starts to flow as we cover subjects ranging from favourite movies to holiday destinations, current affairs, and even skim over religion. It is all so easy and really very pleasant. We avoid talk about relationships, past or present.

There seems no need. I can hear laughter, sporadically crackling through the atmosphere and realise it's mine.

'So, fine wines, eh?' Vince clinks his champagne flute against mine, his eyes crinkling in amusement. 'Red or white?' He's toying with me, playing a game. It's difficult not to be flirtatious, he makes it so easy. As I sip the fizzy clutch, I think of Vince as one of the finer things in life.

'I like both. Red with the meal, white beforehand.' I hear my own voice, trying to impress.

'I'm a red man myself. Merlots, Malbecs and Riojas.' He tops me up, and then narrates tales of wine tours around France, Spain and Italy. I listen, mesmerised. I wonder if he's worked out that I'm in my early forties, married with two children. I want to tell him but it doesn't seem relevant and I don't really want him to know. It might spoil the moment. Also I don't ask about his background as there seems no need to know that either.

'Do you really want to go to the zoo?' His eyes tease me with intensity as he suddenly changes the subject. I have to look away. 'Favourite animal?' he asks. He turns the bottle upside down in the bucket. It's finished. There's an unwelcome finality in the action.

'Sometime definitely; but not in this weather. It's far too cold. Maybe in the spring.' I do a mock shiver. 'As for my favourite animal, it's got to be the lion.' I repeat Noah's favourite; King of the Jungle. Of course it is Vince's favourite animal too. It had to be. We laugh and it's as if we're playing a weird game, knowing all along that neither of us really fancied such an outing.

'Listen, I've got to get going. It's been lovely.' I don't want to go but sense danger lurking close to the surface. I stand up rather too suddenly, straighten my skirt and fidget with my gloves but my head starts to spin. I should have eaten. 'Oops.' I stumble.

'Are you okay?' Vince puts a hand across to steady me. The room is turning, round and round, too fast.

'Yes, fine thanks. I think it's the heat and alcohol.' He pulls me gently back down into my seat, leans across and pushes a stray hair back from my face, smiling into my eyes. It's hard to bring him into focus.

'Can we do this again? I've really enjoyed it.' His face is up close to mine, his breath tickling my cheeks. 'You're beautiful, Susan. Do you know that?' I can't move, my legs have collapsed under me and I have to grip the chair arm to ground myself. He leans forward and plants a soft kiss on my lips.

'Sorry, I couldn't help that,' he says and draws back again. He's teasing me.

'Your coat, madam.' The waiter's hovering, a smirk on his lips. Something tells me he's seen it all before. Vince doesn't get up but watches as I button up my coat and sling my bag over my shoulder.

'Thanks. Bye, Vince.'

'Bye, Susan.'

It's a long walk to the door, but I keep going. I don't look back.

I sit like a statue, concreted to the spot, on the train ride back to Hampstead, ignoring the screaming admonishments accusing me of deceit. I can't think straight. My leather skirt is sticking uncomfortably to my thighs and mascara has crept into the corner of my right eye. I poke a finger in, scratching relentlessly and try to blink away the irritation. It occupies my mind for a few seconds; a welcome diversion from the mental angst.

A young couple opposite is holding hands in companionable silence, their smugness grating. Suddenly I feel old, bitter. The train screeches through the dark, pulling in and out of tunnels, dragging us along in its wake. The young woman smiles at me, perhaps she knows, can read my thoughts. But when I notice her boyfriend grip her hand more tightly, I realise she meant to impress him with her warmth; her charitable pleasantries to strangers. That's what you do when you're young and in love.

As I climb the stairs again, out into the chill night air, my phone pings. I notice a text from Roger and two missed calls.

Hi. Just wondered how you're getting on. Kids in bed. See you soon. X

As I stand in the freezing cold, watching my breath vaporise, I wonder why he's texted. I never text him when he goes out with friends, certainly not as early as eight o'clock when his message was sent. Perhaps he suspects something but there's nothing to suspect. I told him I was shopping with a friend and having a bite to eat afterwards. I decide not to reply. I'll be home in fifteen minutes and need to move, help the frozen blood circulate through my veins.

Walking back down the hill towards Riverside Close, I notice a voicemail message on the screen. I take my glove off again, shoving it momentarily into my mouth, and click to listen.

Hi Susan. Lovely to meet you. Hope we can do it again soon. Vince.

I delete the message, frantically looking left and right in case Roger might have strolled up to the tube to meet me. I switch off the power. He'll be worrying that I haven't replied but I'll be home soon. My left leg starts to cramp, the cold frosty air constricting the blood flow. I inch forward, one step at a time, and need all my concentration to avoid the rogue patches of ice lining my route.

On reaching Riverside Close, a huge wave of relief floods over me. I've made it; all in one piece. I hesitate by our front door, and wonder why I've been so worried. The warm bright lights are welcoming and I've really done nothing wrong; nothing with intent, that is.

I tuck the phone back into my handbag and decide not to say anything to Roger about the evening. It's all been a big mistake, a weird turn of events that conspired to make things happen the way they did. I'll delete myself off *Join Me* or perhaps share the site's intrigue with Roger. Perhaps we can join a group outing to the London Eye. I can decide tomorrow. For now, I'm glad to be home.

As I turn the key in the lock, a rogue thought kicks in. White lies and secrecy, Roger says, make up the first rung on the ladder to adultery. It's his job; divorce cases. Affairs and infidelity are his speciality.

9

CAROLINE

Jason's at home. I know his every move. Staying in control requires that I'm always one step ahead of the game. It's eleven o'clock when I quietly insert the key in the lock. I've been out. Jason thinks I've been socialising with the bored housewives from the gym, swapping anecdotal tales of errant husbands. He never asks for names or details; he's not that interested. In reality I've been biding my time in the seedy pub up the road.

Once inside, I check my appearance in the hall mirror and tousle my hair for effect. I need to look my best. Old habits die hard but something tells me Jason won't notice. I think he takes me for granted.

From my vantage point, I can see his bare feet resting on the coffee table but I can't see his face which is out of view.

'Hi,' he yells over the noise of screen shooting. Guns and car chases. His feet don't move. He's relaxed, content. I don't answer but creep up behind him and plant a kiss on top of his head. I close my eyes for a second and inhale his scent.

'How were the kept ladies?' His tone is mocking but he doesn't let his eyes wander from the onscreen massacre. I bristle.

I want to ask how his tart was and feel an uncontrollable urge to throw nasty disparaging remarks in his direction. I don't. I know better.

'Well, thanks.'

He doesn't look up.

I unwrap my scarf, strip off my gloves and go back into the hall and hang my coat over the end of the stairs. The pub's cheap wine has turned my stomach but I automatically go to the fridge and uncork a half-drunk bottle of rosé. The top up will help bury the demons. The alcohol will soften the lurid images and a couple of sleeping pills will render me unconscious; until tomorrow. Relief from the mental torture is always fleeting.

Jason turns up the volume, a clear message that he'd rather not talk. He senses the wine will agitate me and he's right.

'What time did you get back?' It's a simple question, part of my job. 'It's Friday and you usually get home later.' I'm trying to be pleasant, businesslike, but his unemotional responses wind me up. We made a pact that we wouldn't discuss details pertaining to his trysts, only making rare exceptions when money became an issue.

'Eight o'clock. Do you mind if I watch the last ten minutes? The film's nearly over.' He smiles but his tone is dismissive.

I watch him through the alcoholic haze, still mesmerised by his perfection. The chiselled jaw and full sensual lips. I stare at him, unbelieving in such physical beauty. A desire to run my fingers through his thick brown hair threatens to overcome my resolve. Nearly three years have flown by since we got married. I still can't believe he's all mine. Or is he? The doubts are always there, more and more intense. I can manipulate his liaisons but there is always the unforeseen. The not-to-be-trusted third parties cause the problems, the unknown menacingly threatening. The nagging knot in my stomach returns. I go upstairs, carrying the wine glass with me.

Jason's linen jacket is slung over the back of the chair. I rifle the pockets as per my nightly ritual, peering closely at the collar for signs of stray hairs; straggling red strands perhaps. Masochism has become a hobby. I'm not sure who he was meeting tonight although I know the times. I've been trying with increasing difficulty to blot out names and faces. Names bestow lives and personalities and make it real. I like the number identifications that attach to the profiles. I enjoy mocking his women by calling them by a number. They're like prisoners after all. Their profile pictures mirror the numbered mug shots of convicted felons, imbuing them with a demeaning identification.

The gunfight is still blasting up from downstairs so without hesitation I check the inside pockets. There's nothing unusual, a few loose coins alongside his precious pens, a gift from his late mother apparently. That's what he says. Entertainment receipts are thrown innocently into the receptacle beside the bed. They invite my scrutiny but there should be no need because they're unhidden and will be entered as business expenses. I'll log them tomorrow.

I sometimes wonder if perhaps he's clever and not entirely at ease with our working partnership, hiding the occasional entertainment receipt from me. I open out the scrunched-up pieces of paper and notice one for a small bistro in Golders Green. This wasn't in the diary. When was he there? Monday evening. I pocket it. He'll not notice as he left it there, in the middle of the pile, oblivious to my suspicions.

'What are you doing?' His voice behind me makes me jump.

'Jesus! You startled me. I didn't hear you come up.' He wanders over and lifts his jacket from the back of the chair and hangs it neatly in the wardrobe. He does this every night, taking great care with his expensive outfits. He glances at the collection of receipts, unconcerned by my interest and ignores the fact that I've been going through his pockets.

He kisses me on the cheek, blocking my way as I head to the bathroom to brush my teeth.

Once inside, I lock the door and sit on the toilet seat for ten minutes, finishing my glass of wine which is stuck to my fingers.

Jason's in bed when I creep back out and in the darkness, I can make out his sleeping shape under the duvet. He's left the curtains open as he doesn't like sleeping in a blackened room. A full moon stares through the small square window, unblinking and all-seeing. Childhood nightmares haunt him apparently.

I'm jealous of his body and his perfection and am tempted to slide in under the silken covers alongside him. I could then imagine for tonight at least that he is completely mine. In the warmth of slumber I pretend that he'll belong to me forever.

I resist the temptation, however, as the urge to check the website is ever present. Jason had time this evening to browse and get lured into his next seedy little encounter. I have my suspicions as to whose profile pictures he'll have been viewing and feel an urgency to check up on the activity. Instead of yielding to the moment, I bend over and kiss him on the top of his head and whisper 'goodnight'. He murmurs 'I love you', before he slips silently into his own dark world of sleep. I'm jealous of the night. It has taken him away from me again.

I go back downstairs and start up the computer. *Join Me*'s screen flickers into life. I keep the main lights off and let myself get sucked into the glaringly lit underworld filling the monitor. The home page is bright and dazzling. The azure blues and sunshine yellows give no hint of dubious intent. They're happy colours, Jason says; deliberately unthreatening.

I wipe away a stray tear that's settled stubbornly in my eye as I scroll down the new recruits. I'm not sure how I've been reduced to this. My obsession with Jason has led me to the brink of madness but I can't let up. I read the numerous emails, asking why we only operate in London. Do we have any profiles to display of interesting people living further north? Yorkshire perhaps?

I persuaded Jason that *Join Me* had to start small; locally. Start small and expand cautiously is my business premise. We need to get it right before we can conquer the world. The truth is that I need all the ladies to live nearby. I won't be expanding up north, or south into Cornwall. It would be too far to travel; too far away to keep control.

I was right. Jason has been online browsing the profiles since he got home. Susan 789 has been watched a dozen times or so over the past few days. Meeting her at the gym, in the flesh, has spurred me on. I know Jason has already met her but I haven't asked to know more. I stare at her profile pictures, noticing that she's added a couple more coquettish action poses but they look nothing like her. Clever airbrushing has smothered the imperfections.

I jot down her address, checking it against the payment details. I knew it was Riverside Close, she did tell me, a small upmarket cul-de-sac about half an hour's walk away. I now have the house number. I haven't decided yet whether to call her first or turn up out of the blue on the doorstep. Whatever I decide, Monday will be the start of a wonderful friendship. Susan Harper will welcome me as her new best friend.

10

CAROLINE

I set out at 10am, waiting until Jason has gone out. Although he's been summoned by Francine to help with some new household disaster, today I don't worry. Today I've purpose of my own and don't have time to wallow in doubts about his past life.

When I first met Jason, he was living in Highgate with a woman called Francine. When I finally felt compelled to ask about her, find out more, his tone was flippant, hinting at a lack of depth in their relationship which helped sooth my concerns.

'It's never been serious with Francine. She sort of looks after me,' he said.

'What do you mean?'

'She owns a four-storey house in the village and in return for odd jobs, she lets me live there rent free. It suits us both.'

'Why would she do that? Surely she hasn't that many odd jobs.' I sounded churlish, childish and disbelieving. 'What age is she anyway?'

'Fifty. Old enough to be my mother!' He had laughed as if this was the punchline to some well-rehearsed joke. If he was trying to lighten the mood or spare me hurt by his tone, it worked. It suited me to believe the latter.

By the time we had become an item and moved in together, she no longer seemed to pose a threat. If she was distraught or heartbroken by her abandonment, I could only surmise. He never really talked about her. The future then became my main concern, not the past.

Yet she hovers in the background like a ghost not done with haunting; a pesky irritating thorn in my side, like a splinter of wood embedded under my skin, stinging when bothered. Jason still scampers back when summoned; if a door falls off its hinges or the back garden needs tending. He says it's the least he can do. I suspect it is guilt.

The arctic temperatures are persistent but the snow has cleared and I walk with steady tread past the imposing Georgian mansions that skirt Porters Wood. The dull gloom of February has been replaced by a crisp brightness which stubbornly tempts me with hope and happiness. I turn my head towards the stark silent landscape. The tightly packed barren trees, like soulless skyscrapers, draw my eye. A woman is strolling peacefully across the carpet of mulched rotting leaves, holding tightly on to a toddler. I think it's a girl but the thick clothing makes it difficult to be certain.

Sadness seeps through the sunshine and skims skittishly over my resolve. Beaver Glade is tucked away behind the trees. It's a small clearing with swings and roundabouts. Jason took me there once when we first got together and whirled me round on the circular platform until I felt so dizzy I thought I might throw up. I hesitate for a second. Memories persistently taunt me and self-torture is my nemesis. A couple of clouds shaped like sheep have appeared overhead. I will count them tonight.

I stop at the junction of Church Street where it joins Riverside Close. There's no one about. A red VW Beetle is tucked neatly into a handkerchief-sized driveway, and a blue Audi into a similarly sized gravelled driveway opposite. I take a deep breath, flatten my hair into some semblance of order and push my gloves into my pocket. A cul-de-sac seems a strange place to live; a way in but no way out.

I walk slowly towards the top of the dead end as my eyes scan the exclusive enclave. Perhaps the residents are members of a tight inner circle, like the Freemasons, which mirrors their environment. I spot Susan's black BMW in the top right-hand corner of the sac. A wooden sign etched deeply with the words *Windy Pines* is bolted to the gate; it suggests individuality. However, the house is identical in construction and design to *Sunny Elms* next door. Perhaps the names are meant to help the postman but I'm sceptical. They ooze pretension with a glaring lack of pines and elms anywhere to be seen. A *For Sale* sign marks out the plot on the other side of Susan's. *4 Riverside Close.* It's waiting for a new owner to imbue character.

Susan's front door opens before I reach the bell. She must have been watching out for me since I called; in hindsight, a wise decision. I need her to be at home today. My plan can't wait any longer.

'Caroline. Come in, the kettle's on,' she says in a welcoming sing-song descant. We kiss each other on the cheeks. Perhaps it's my imagination but her weight seems to have plummeted since I met her at the gym. Bones are sticking out through her skin-tight top, shoulder blades protruding symmetrically like knife edges from her back.

'I'm only just returned from the gym. Come in. Did you walk?'

'Yes. It's lovely out. I don't mind the cold as long as it's bright.' I close the door and follow my hostess into her kitchen. It's glossy and slick, modern accessories teasing the eye. A designer strip light hangs down over the breakfast bar which is constructed from a huge slab of dark glossy granite. It's polished to perfection like Susan, although more substantial.

'Coffee? Or what about a glass of wine?' She's overly enthusiastic, as if she hasn't seen anyone for days and I'm like some stranger she's pulled in to her castle, desperate for company.

'Wine sounds good. Never too early in the day. Thanks.' I settle myself on one of the fine leather bar stools and finger the strip light. It pops on automatically.

'Love the light,' I say.

Susan has extracted a small cleaning cloth from a cupboard under the sink and wipes the surface before she sits down. She polishes quite violently.

'Did you go to Pilates?' I ask while sipping the wine. It's delicious, cold and welcome. Susan toys with her mint tea but then decides it's rude not to join me in a glass of something stronger and she returns to the fridge and sets the newly opened bottle between us. We both know it won't last long.

'No. I managed about half an hour on the treadmill.' She pats her concave stomach. 'I need to get rid of this.' She points at imaginary middle-aged spread, trying to pinch at non-existent fat.

I smile. I'm surprised by her obsessive nature. I was expecting a more devil-may-care type of woman.

She sets the polishing cloth down beside her glass, picking it up every now and then to swish it over the surface. When I let a drop of wine hit the gloss, deliberately I might add, she's there at once. She doesn't fit the usual *Join Me* profile. I was expecting a laidback sort of person; flighty and careless. Perhaps I can come up with an idea on how to track such behavioural patterns. But then, perhaps it doesn't matter.

'What does Roger do for a living?' We swap vacuous anecdotes. She doesn't dwell too much on her children, perhaps in deference to my apparent childlessness but I suspect more that she likes to forget about them when they're safely in someone else's hands.

'A solicitor. Works all hours. What about Jason?'

I lie and say he is an aspiring artist. I enjoy the subterfuge. My fibs have become second nature. She doesn't seem particularly interested and lets me talk on while she goes and turns the heat up. Self-obsessed, bored and spoilt is my summation of Susan Harper.

'Sorry, carry on. I am listening. I need to turn the heat up. It's freezing.' She shivers, moves to the wall and twiddles with a thermostat. It's her chicken-like bones, she must feel the cold. I'm sweltering but don't want to take my sweat top off as that would hint I'm getting comfortable and there's only so far I want to go today with the charade.

Once we've polished off the bottle of wine, she shows me round the house before I leave. The back has been extended and the kitchen now leads into an obscenely large conservatory where frameless sliding glass doors open out onto a slick designer patio. The grassy area has been eaten away by huge russet-coloured sandstone slabs. It certainly has the 'wow' factor. Susan is delighted when I use the word 'wow'.

Her sudden excitement complements the unease that accompanies her OCD. She beams, self-congratulatory with her choice of new friend. I wonder how soon it will be until she needs to unburden herself about her new male friend, Vince; some guy she was meant to accompany to the zoo. She'll weigh me up over the next few weeks as she becomes increasingly desperate to open up to someone. Building a friendship, becoming her trusted confidante, is part of my plan. She's naïve enough to get sucked in.

When we reach the front door, she tells me how lovely it was for me to pop by. She misses the 'pop in' sort of friends.

'It's so boring around here.' She entices me to look round the cul-de-sac. 'You never see a soul.' She puts her hand over her mouth, patting it back and forth faking an exaggerated yawn and grins.

'It is rather quiet,' I say. 'Perhaps we'll do lunch another time?' I do a little hand wave as I pick my way back down the drive. I imagine her smile of assent behind me.

'That would be nice. Bye.'

An old lady opposite is positioning a couple of potted plants outside her front door. We nod politely as I stroll back down the street, leaving the dead end behind. I must say I prefer our long road, extending into unknown worlds at either end. It offers so many more possibilities.

Poor Susan. Her perfect kitchen and marbled grandeur have already swallowed her up. She'll soon think Vince is the answer.

11

SUSAN

Monday 10.45am
Two for one at the zoo Friday next week. Are
you up for it? Vince
Tuesday 12.00pm
Special penguin display, tiger trail, gorilla
mating?? Can even sleep out by the lion enclo-
sure! But perhaps that can wait. Go on, what
do you think? Vince
Wednesday 5.00pm
Last chance! I'll bring a picnic if you say
the word? Honestly, don't worry if you can't.
Just thought it might be fun. Vince

I am rereading the emails from Vince. It is one week to the
day since we met up in London. It is now Friday night and
the clock has struck nine, the monstrous wind-up mechanism
clonking through the deathly hush. The early weekend wine
magnet has sucked me in, helping me to relax and mellow the

anxiety. I browse the pictures of animals slumped in corners of caged enclosures with a gnawing empathy. They are all trapped, having surrendered to the imposed limits with inevitable resignation. I find myself wondering if the cage door were accidentally left ajar whether the lions would spring to life and wreak their revenge. Perhaps while they're sleeping, they keep one eye on the gate.

I've logged on to *Join Me* to check for new messages. Apart from the three from Vince, there's a new one from a group leader, Troy 900, inviting me to join an organised outing to the zoo; from one fellow animal lover to another. There are already twelve enrolments but I delete the message. Troy 900 reminds me of a left-wing leader of Save the Amazon Rainforests or, with his goatee beard and wire-rimmed glasses, he could be leading the interminable battle to Save the Whale. I take a sip of cold wine which glides effortlessly down my throat, each mouthful imbuing me with increasing recklessness. I click on Vince 666's profile and notice he's added a couple of new photos which showcase him skydiving and windsurfing. Each pose looks as if it has come from the portfolio of a professional photographer. My phone beeps and makes me jump.

Hope all ok. Kids in bed? Finishing up shortly. Looking forward to the weekend!! Rog xx

The screen is accusing, flashing brightly as if reading my thoughts.

Yep. All quiet. See you soon. X

The weekend will be spent packing, sorting out shirts and ties with matching shoes and socks. The kids will pester their father with wish lists of gadgets that only New York has to offer.

They will use the chance to blackmail him for their own gain, pulling at his heartstrings, manipulating as only children can. Roger will be flattered, emotionally brainwashed and miserable at having to leave home for a week. But he'll go anyway. It's his job after all and he'll not look back, locking the door behind him.

I turn the green bottle at an angle and notice that there's only enough wine left for one last glass. I greedily dislodge the dregs. I'm not quite ready to embrace my cage with its stifling claustrophobia. Instead I take the plunge and finally reply to Vince. Perhaps I knew all along that I would. The alcohol has only precipitated the action.

> Might be able to make next Friday. Hope ok to let you know nearer the time. Susan.

I read and reread the message, still sane enough through the drowsy haze of alcohol to keep it brief and avoid anything flirtatious. A trip to the zoo next Friday might give me something to look forward to. That's how I sell it to myself anyway. My finger hovers over the send button but I know that any more pretend prevarication is futile. My meeting in London with Vince has produced a stubborn little scab, which my mind has been picking at for over a week. Hell. Why not? I drain the glass. Why shouldn't I have some fun?

I'm about to shut down the screen, prepared to deal with any reply on Monday, when a message bounces straight back. Shit. It's ten on a Friday night. How is this guy not busy, out having fun, or drinking with mates? Can he have been on *Join Me* at exactly the same time? I'm not a fan of coincidences.

> Perfect! I'll keep the ticket for you. What fun. Have a great weekend. Vince x

PS We'll make arrangements nearer the time.

I log out, once again frantically clearing my browsing history, and close down the laptop before shutting it away in the desk drawer. I turn out the lamp and wander over to the window, pausing for a glance through the slit in the curtains. The street lights around the close are all turned on, each one emitting a dusky orangey hue. Bob and Olive Thompson are to be complimented on their insistence with the council that turning alternate lights off might save money but that in doing so residents can't see a 'bloody thing'.

I watch Olive wander round the close clutching what seems to be a pile of flyers, leaflets of some sort. She is huddled up under a thick old person's woollen coat. Style has flown along with youth. A dark thick hat sits jauntily to one side of her head as a token reminder of a sixties fashion statement and I can make out a long gold pin protruding from the top. She is strolling up each driveway in turn, popping papers through letterboxes. I wonder if I'll care about such matters when I'm her age. Perhaps I'll have sleepless nights over dog fouling, street lights and double parking, but I doubt it.

As I draw the curtains tightly together, a rogue thought takes hold that maybe I need to make more of the present. This offers me comfort and justification for the small drunken step I've taken on the road to God knows where.

Deep down I've been expecting some sort of emergency to spring up, offering me an excuse to duck out from this afternoon's trip. Yet the last few days have passed by without a hiccup and unusually, nothing untoward has happened all week. Tilly and Noah have bounced off merrily to school every day with none of the usual sneaky attempts to avoid education with bogus upset stomachs or fever. There seems to be a conspiracy, or some particular alignment in the stars that is propelling me to the zoo and a second meeting with Vince.

I've cleaned the house from top to bottom, making meticulous lists of chores that need to be tackled. Kitchen cupboards and drawers; sorting Roger's socks and underwear; bathroom cabinet cleaning and de-cluttering; clothes clear-out for the charity shop. I've kept adding to the list with frantic compulsion. In reality I've been desperately filling time all week until this morning.

Standing in my underwear, I'm faced with the clothes conundrum of what to wear. Dressing for a date would demand subtle seductive outfits but a random trip to the zoo for a day of wandering around animal enclosures is proving bizarrely taxing. The rain's still falling, smearing the windows with dull wet blobs but the noise is strangely soothing.

I wash my face three times, a rigorous morning ritual as my skin has become increasingly irritated by dust mites which lurk in the night. Roger bemoans the red splodges caused by the scrubbing and berates me for my obsession. He tells me I have OCD; obsessive compulsive disorder.

After an hour of prevarication over what to wear, by eleven I'm finally ready. Designer jeans and a warm angora jumper will play down hints of provocation and sensible flat boots will dispel notions of flirtatious motives. I spray a little perfume onto each ear, to mask the earthy animal stench then slather my hands in hand cream against the elements and touch up my lipstick in the hall mirror as I do every day. I kid myself that this is another normal day, albeit it with the addition of an educational outing to Regent's Park. Bizarrely I make a mental note that it is Friday the thirteenth.

I see him long before he sees me. I'm one of those early people. He is sauntering along towards the park entrance casually glancing behind him every few seconds. The umbrella offers me camouflage from my viewpoint across the road but the steady stream of London traffic randomly interrupts my line of vision. I remember standing outside Nick Logan's house, twenty years ago, staring up at his bedroom window willing him to spot me. I planned the pretence that I was randomly passing, taking a detour home, when he would ask why I was in the neighbourhood. I did this twice a week for two years but he never appeared. The flashback is unsettling.

A car suddenly splatters dirty water all up over the pavement and I jump back. The driver's head turns towards me and I notice the upturned smirk.

Shit. Shit. Shit. 'Pig!' I yell after him. The umbrella flails backwards and I feel cold water splash against my trouser legs. I look up, pulling my shield back over my head but I'm too slow. Vince has seen me. Hesitant, I wave back, the opportunity to reconsider and slope away long gone. I move towards the crossing and wait for the green man as Vince walks over to meet me.

'Hi,' he says. 'Jeez you're soaked.' At first I think we're going to shake hands but instead he leans in and kisses me on the cheek. It seems the most natural thing in the world, as if greeting a long-lost friend. He's wearing aftershave, something musky, to mask the smells. We've had the same thought.

'Hi. Yes, I was a bit slow. The driver went through the puddle deliberately.' I shake my umbrella closed. The rain is easing off but I'm also not ready to share the enclosed space under the spokes with this stranger.

'It's good to see you. I wasn't sure if you'd make it.'

We move slowly, side by side, towards the entrance and I'm mesmerised by Vince's easy manner. It's as if I've known him for years.

'Touch and go but here I am.' I feel flustered, weirdly tongue-tied as I watch him present the tickets and make pleasant small talk with the man in the kiosk. Vince hands me a map and asks where I'd like to go first, what my favourite animals are. His grin makes fun of the pretence that I'm an animal lover as he takes my arm and propels me towards the monkey enclosure.

The park is strangely peaceful as we amble from one captivating sight to the next. As the monkeys swoop high from branch to branch, mocking the rather sparse smattering of humans with their cackling squeals, I start to relax, falling into step with Vince who seems to know his way around.

'You've been before, haven't you?'

'Once or twice I must admit. It's a great place to escape. I think I prefer animals to humans. Less complicated. You?'

'No. First time. I fancied doing something completely different.' I wonder if he knows I'm lying and that the zoo was last on my wish list until I read his profile.

We are only feet away from the penguins, leaning over the railings, both of us gripping a small bag of fishy treats, when the heavens open and a torrential downpour sets in. A penguin slithers down a slope and disappears under the water, followed by a steady stream of friends.

'Here. Let me.' Vince takes my umbrella and re-fixes a stray spoke back into its slot. 'Let's go for a coffee and get warm.' He holds up the umbrella and pulls me in to his warmth. I'm too cold and wet to protest. I feel like the penguin, diving deep until the danger passes, ignoring lurking predators in the temporary safety of the underwater confines.

The coffee shop is bright and welcoming. Once inside, we take our coats off and shake them down, dripping wet globules onto the floor. Soon I'm aware of a young waitress staring at us; at Vince, to be more precise. He is unbelievably handsome, even more so than last time we met. *Too good to be true* pops into my mind. Although the room is warm, inviting, I feel uneasy as I sip my latte.

'Tell me about yourself,' he says.

'Not much to tell really.' I feel awkward and wonder why I don't tell him about Roger and the kids. They're my life after all. 'I live in North London. What about you?'

'You don't get off that easily. Come on, give me something more.'

'What like? Why don't you try to guess?'

'I get the impression you don't work; lots of spare time to tone up at the gym. Perhaps you like shopping.'

'Don't all women?' I make light and we laugh together. 'You're obviously self-employed otherwise you wouldn't have such ridiculously large gaps in your week for these leisurely trips,' I fire back at him.

We bandy to and fro meaningless chit-chat. Vince is a consummate listener, laughing on cue with his perfect mouth and dazzling teeth. What big teeth you've got, Grandma. Noah had made me read it three times last night, cowering under the bedclothes every time Grandma got close to Little Red Riding Hood. Vince is like the wolf; magnetic and dangerous.

It is almost four o'clock when we decide to take a last stroll around the lion enclosure before dark finally closes in. Vince points out the huts where you can spend the night. I turn my collar up against a chill wind, and Vince reaches over and takes my hand as if it is the most natural thing in the world.

'Here. Just round the corner you'll see him sleeping. Simba, he's called.'

I can't see anything. I can feel, but not the cold; rather my heart beating erratically. A strange excitement churns in my stomach as I'm led further into the enclosure.

'Look. There. Can you see him?' Vince points with his left hand and when I don't answer he turns towards me, and time seems to stand still as he pulls me gently into him. As he kisses me, my eyes automatically start to close but I can make out the lion over his shoulder. The animal is staring straight back at us, his eyes wide open. He gets up, slowly, and with measured pace moves forward.

Perhaps tonight the people will leave the gate open and he will escape. Perhaps he's imagining the wild plains from whence he came. My eyelids clamp shut and it's too late. I am lost.

12

SUSAN

ONE WEEK LATER

'It'll only be a couple of days.'

'But you've only just got back. Why can't someone else go?'

Roger has taken the coward's way out and is telling me over the phone that he has to fly to Paris this time. I can hear a soft hum of conversation in the background and imagine him in his slick mahogany office, books lining the walls all the way to the ceiling; thick important tomes. His personal assistant, Mrs Fitzpatrick, will be hovering nearby.

'By Easter things will get back to normal.' He's talking quietly, letting me know that he's not alone and that making a scene would be futile. 'The High Court battle starts on Tuesday and it should all be over by the end of March.' It's some high-profile celebrity divorce apparently but for me the details aren't important.

I'm dressed ready for the gym, armed with a weak-willed determination to get back to classes and some sort of routine. I've no choice but to say I understand and that it's fine, I can hold the fort a while longer. I have been planning dinner parties, couples' outings and neighbourly soirees in an effort to pull myself back from the brink of a looming disaster with Vince. I'm trying to ignore his pleading emails but with a somewhat flimsy resolve. Roger's return from New York was meant to propel me back to sanity.

'It's fine. I can manage, don't worry. I'll see you later.'

'Thanks. I'll make it up to you. Promise. Love you.' The last is said in a very faint whisper. I imagine Mrs Fitzpatrick, with her sharp beady eyes, eavesdropping behind the door, feeling momentarily downcast. I've always suspected her devotion to Roger might not be entirely to do with proving her organisational efficiency.

'Love you too.' I listen to the phone die on the other end before I replace the handset. It's too late to go to the gym; Pilates will be over. I wonder at what stage people embark on affairs. It all seems rather random. I can hear the well-worn adage of *My wife doesn't understand me; things haven't been right at home for some time. My husband never gets back before ten o'clock* sits aptly alongside *He's much too tired for romance.*

Decision making has become more and more impossible and I feel like everyone is pulling me along, dragging me in their slipstream and I've no real purpose of my own. Of course I have the children, Roger, a beautiful home, and money for all manner of indulgences. But it's not enough. I need something for me other than cleaning and tidying. Without Roger's presence at home, time has become enemy number one, with endless stretches of hours to fill. *Join Me* was meant to help me get out and about, escape the boredom, but instead it has presented me with a nightmarish conundrum.

I'll meet Vince one more time and tell him it's over. I've made the decision. I'm not sure what is going to be all over but since the trip to the zoo, I've had the most lurid fantasies and longings which Vince is feeding with ever-more-persistent messages. Perhaps this is what the beginning of an affair feels like. I desperately need to nip it in the bud before it takes deeper root.

~

The traffic is snarling up and down the Archway Road and I find myself wondering at the ugliness of the venue which Vince has suggested for our meeting, especially after the peaceful tranquillity of the zoo. The air is filled with black exhaust fumes, and irate drivers hang dangerously close to the cars in front, hooting their horns in frustration as the queue snarls slowly forward.

I stand outside the tube station and check Google Maps on my mobile before heading towards the traffic lights at the corner of Shepherds Hill where I turn left down towards Crouch End. My unease abates as trees line the road and residential houses replace the aggressive drabness of the main thoroughfare. Perhaps Vince lives nearby.

I wander slowly down the hill, keeping my eyes peeled for his car. It's a red Audi coupé apparently, hard to miss. He said he'd be waiting in the first vacant parking slot. It is ten minutes past midday and I'm wondering why I decided to be fashionably late. It's not a date after all but a chance for me to 'call it a day' and end the madness. Vince suggested a lunch meeting to try out some traditional English pub food, now that pie and chip venues have suddenly sprung up as places to visit on *Join Me*. The more basic choice of venue somehow seems less threatening than an upmarket gourmet restaurant. However, I do wonder at the interminable lightness of tone in his messages and his uncanny ability to make everything seem genuinely fun and innocent.

I shiver and pull my coat tighter as the chill air pinches at my ears. I reach a bend in the road halfway down and realise there are lots of vacant parking spaces on both sides of the road and no sign of a red Audi coupé.

'Boo.' I jump backwards, tripping on a loose paving stone and momentarily lose my balance. Vince has been spying on me, hovering behind a hedge.

'Shit. I didn't see you. I've been looking for your car.'

'I know. I've been watching you.' He bends over to kiss me on the cheek while steadying me with his arm. He hesitates as I brace against him but he doesn't comment and discreetly pulls back. I smell his scent, musky and distinct, and once again I'm stunned at his uncanny ease of manner as we stroll side by side down the hill.

'The Bird in Hand. It's my local.' He points to the pub which sits across the main road at the bottom.

'That's why you didn't drive,' I say. I don't ask where he lives; probably too close for comfort, but I sense he wants to tell me, let me know things about himself. I loosen my scarf which is constricting my windpipe and I battle back the panic. I have to remind myself that *Join Me* has enticed us to share experiences, enjoy ourselves. Perhaps I've been overreacting. As if he can read my mind, he continues.

'I thought we could try some good old-fashioned pub grub. Pie and chips here we come!' He pulls me back as I'm about to step out in front of a car, again putting his arm protectively around me. I laugh nervously as he leads me across the road and in through the main entrance.

The pub is dark inside, heavy wood panelling coating the walls. There's a jukebox in one corner and a couple of one-armed bandits lined up against the wall. An old man is pulling one of the handles down and in between times sipping beer from a tankard.

'I could get used to this,' Vince says as the waiter sets down our food. I'm drinking again, to give me Dutch courage. A couple of sips and I'm already thinking that I could also get used to it as I begin to struggle to remember why I'm here. I warily eye the stodgy fare.

'If you can't eat it all, don't worry. The portions are huge.' He knows my stomach is in knots and I'm mesmerised by his ability to read my thoughts. I wonder if he knows I came intending to put an end to our meetings. He leans across and tops up my wine glass while I toy with a mouthful of food.

'Is this really your local?' I ask. Perhaps he comes here all the time, lives nearby, and that's why he's so relaxed. I flick my hair back, toying self-consciously with the ends, realising it's a flirtatious gesture.

'Yes. I can walk here in about fifteen minutes downhill. Twenty minutes going back up.' He smiles, his eyes twinkling, sucking me back into his web. I push the sloppy mess of meat and pastry round on the plate. I don't want to eat. I perspire, small beads of sweat collecting under my armpits. Again he senses my struggle and leans across and brushes his lips against my cheek while resting a teasing hand on my thigh. I don't move it away.

'Do you live alone?' I want to take it back as soon as I ask.

'Most of the time. You?' He's toying with me, waiting for me to speak. Sitting here, his body achingly close, we both know that it's all about the moment. Neither of us wants to spoil the romance with real-life meaningful conversation.

'I'd rather not talk about me.'

'Shall we stick to the weather? Probably safer.' He laughs, knocking back his pint before wiping his lips with his thumb and finger. His hands are so perfect, his nails neatly clipped, and as he places one on top of mine, we laugh at the identical shapes. For a woman, my fingers are unusually long and I avoid growing or painting my nails so as not to draw the eye. But today I'm not embarrassed. They match Vince's exactly in length.

'You see. We're clones of each other.' I withdraw my hand and lift my wine glass. What am I doing? Why is he sitting here with me? I'm not sure whether I want the moment to end and never see him again. Perhaps it is my own insecurities that make me wonder why Vince would want to spend his time with me but something doesn't feel quite right. I can't put my finger on it but at this particular moment I don't really care.

The old man has put a coin in the jukebox and Elvis Presley's dulcet tones purr out 'The Wonder of You'. Vince moves closer and sings along. I laugh, letting the tension explode in a bizarre wave of giggles which border on the hysterical.

'Do you fancy going into Crouch End for a coffee? Somewhere quieter. It's a bit too noisy, don't you think?' He puts his hands up to cover his ears after he has pushed his empty plate to one side. He knows I'll say 'yes' and although a warning voice tells me this is because he is a master in seduction, I'm powerless to refuse. The wine has loosened my thoughts again and is letting the truth seep out. I need more of this guy.

13

SUSAN

I'm not sure how we've got on to the subject of money. The coffee shop is warm and cosy, the windows steamed up from the heat, and there's a gentle buzz of conversation going on around us. We've so far managed to avoid talking about personal matters, laughing conspiratorially at how we've skirted round emotional issues like men at a football match. While I'm relieved that I don't have to lie about being married with two children, I feel it's odd for him not to pry.

'I'm into investments,' he begins. He talks about the money markets, sugar and coffee share prices and property bonds. I don't really take in what he's saying, as I sip my coffee letting the words waft over me, content to be sitting beside him, our thighs dangerously close. I tingle inside every time his body touches mine and electricity courses through my veins.

'It's a great opportunity but such a pity.'

A bluebottle seems to be taking its last breath as I watch it buzz frantically against the misted windowpane. Noah told me flies only live for three weeks and I am about to share this fact with my companion when I'm aware he is looking at me, waiting for an answer.

'Sorry? What's a pity?' I straighten in my chair, trying to sharpen up and make sense of what he's been talking about.

'The investment. It's a property block in Canary Wharf and promises returns of up to fifty per cent.' He takes my hand, willing me to feel the importance of what he's saying and to get sucked in by his intensity and enthusiasm. 'I can't meet the minimum amount.' He slumps back in his seat, withdrawing from me, moving his thighs away and lets out a long, measured sigh. 'That's life, I suppose,' he says in a tone of resignation. He's waiting for a response. What does he want me to say? It takes a minute or two for the realisation to sink in. The bluebottle is on its back, all hope gone. It does a little death shudder and lies still.

'How much are you short?' He waits a respectable time before he sits back up and leans his hands across the table, placing them firmly on top of mine this time.

'Five thousand pounds. It's not a lot considering the size of the investment but the brokers won't budge. There's a minimum sum which can be put in to each bond.' The hum of conversation in the shop has died down. I imagine the school run has probably kicked in and that quite a few of the customers have gone to pick up their children. I look at my watch and realise Tilly and Noah will be getting out soon. I should make a move.

'Do you need to go?' he asks as I cover my watch with my sleeve. Although he seems relaxed I sense a touch of finality in his tone. He motions for the bill and the waitress nods at the handsome customer and indicates that she's onto it.

My motive for being here, for putting an end to any more meetings, has become blurred as a premonition tells me I needn't have worried as Vince seems to be cooling off. A weird illogical panic hits that he might not want to see me after today.

'Maybe we'll meet up again soon.' His voice lacks conviction.

He stands up and moves away from the table and I sense a definite hint of closure in the statement. I watch him smile at the waitress who turns pink from the attention. I remember the girl at the zoo. He knows his throwaway comment has hit the mark. I now have the *get-out-of-jail-free card* that I wanted. I can hop back on the tube and tell myself nothing has happened. It will all have been a mirage. However, as I hesitatingly pull on my coat over my flimsy top, watching Vince draw his wallet out of his pocket, I'm hit with the terrible realisation that I can't walk away. I want to see him again.

It has nothing to do with not loving Roger. This guy has sucked me in with his animal magnetism. Perhaps one afternoon of unbridled passion would be enough; then I could settle down at home, having escaped my humdrum existence for a few hours. It must be the alcohol talking because from somewhere far off, I hear myself speak.

'Vince. Sit down a minute. Listen...' but he knows what I'm going to say. He's watching me, listening, all ears, waiting for the words to spill out. 'I'll make up the shortfall for your investment. I'll let you have the five thousand. Let's call it an advance. When you make your millions you can pay me back.' He'll have to meet me now at least one more time.

I can still feel his hard body as he pinned me up against the large oak tree on the way back up to the tube station. He told me that he's starting to need me, badly. I close my eyes as the train rumbles on towards my stop, remembering the urgency with which he pushed his hips towards mine. We laughed when a couple of passers-by looked askance in our direction but he carried on kissing me, letting his tongue tease me further into the abyss. It had nothing to do with the money. He wouldn't have been able to play-act such feelings, such passion. That was surely something that couldn't be faked.

As I walk back up Riverside Close towards home, the afternoon chill has become more biting. The lights are on downstairs in our house. Tilly and Noah will be back from school and will scream 'Mummy' as soon as I open the door.

I pause outside the Thompsons' house and see Olive standing by the window, her aged back stooped. Her husband is by her side, handing her a glass of something. I smile acknowledgement. The alcohol is steadily draining through my system, leaving in its wake a bad taste in my mouth. It's the poisonous fur of deceit, of adultery, and as I put the key in the lock, I have to remind myself that I've still done nothing really wrong and it isn't too late to turn back. As I go to close the door behind me, I know this is a lie, that it might be too late to turn back.

I cross the threshold into the hall and am aware of someone watching me. I glance over my shoulder and see Olive Thompson in her front living room, face pressed up hard against the window, staring in my direction. She's like a motionless silent statue and even after I close the door, I can feel her eyes boring through my soul.

14

ALEXIS

I don't know why I'm shocked at where Gary lives. He's the young rookie private investigator I met in Luton and he's renting a room in a terraced house in the middle of a long rambling road off Green Lanes, near Turnpike Lane tube station.

I double-lock the motorbike, chaining it up against a rickety set of railings. I wander up and down the street, trying to find a number on any of the houses. About halfway up I spot the number twenty-seven painted on to a wooden sign hanging off a door frame at an angle; the digits are barely decipherable through the rotting wood. I pick my way through a mass of debris littering the front path. Empty beer bottles are stacked randomly in a blue plastic container outside the front door and I have to bang hard against the cracked frosted glass to be heard. A disused brass bell hangs from an exposed wire to the right of the door.

'Hi. Come in.' Gary's face pokes out round the door. He invites me in to step over more litter. Unopened envelopes are strewn across the floor along with piles of free newspapers. 'Excuse the mess,' he says as he leads the way upstairs to his room. The trail of clutter continues into the bedsit as he ushers me through a strange green gunmetal door and proceeds to pull open the curtains to admit daylight.

'Coffee?' he asks pointing to a kettle, powdered milk and a half crumbling packet of Jaffa cakes.

'No thanks. If it's okay with you, I'd like to get down to business.' I peel off my leather gloves and stack them inside my crash helmet. Although Gary looks like a teenager and desperately in need of a good meal, logic tells me he's in his early twenties. There's something innocently likeable about him as he fidgets around clearing a place for me to sit. I scour the room for traces of a female presence, glad that he appears to live on his own. Male mess is everywhere: clothes littering the floor and empty beer cans on the coffee table, and I've an urge to help him clear up. A large poster over the bed depicts an early eighteenth-century map of London and underneath there is a torn picture of Marilyn Monroe; a strange pairing.

'I've something I'd like you to do for me. It's personal.' I blush and wonder why. My leather trousers are sticking hotly against my legs and I have to unzip my jacket as the room is stifling. A small blow heater is whirring full blast in the corner. 'I wonder if you'd follow someone for me, take some photographs.' It all sounds a bit sad and seedy as I say the words out loud but I don't really have a choice. I justify my methods as being in keeping with my new career challenge. The truth is I want to catch Adam in the act and then make him sweat. This time he'll pay. I need proof before I can confront him. Although I have a grainy video recording of him entering Waverley Mansions with a bunch of red roses, I need clearer photographic evidence of him up close and intimate with Debbie. A good divorce settlement will depend on it. Adam will fight to the bitter end and deny anything untoward without evidence to prove it. I know him too well.

'I don't have a car,' Gary says. 'I'm sorry but I can't afford one. The course in Luton took all my cash. I saved for weeks. A car's next on my list though,' he offers eagerly, willing me to accept his story. He has a strip of determined acne running down the centre of his face, red aggressive spots being fed from a dirty fringe drooping across his forehead. His nose is worst affected, an angry zit sitting proudly on its tip.

'Don't worry. That's not a problem. This is how it'll work.'

An hour later we set off up Wightman Lane snaking through the back streets of North London towards the hospital. Gary clings on for dear life to my leather-clad torso, squealing in delight every so often as we weave in and out. I suspect he hasn't ridden pillion before and certainly never behind a woman.

'Shit!' he yells when a black Rastafarian driver winds down his window and gives us an aggressive two-finger sign. 'Up yours!' Gary shouts in response and we laugh together as I over-take on the inside, raking up the High Road and leaving the queue of cars behind. When we finally reach the hospital car park I drive slowly past the visitor bays until we spot the staff parking at the far end. I turn my head, lifting the visor, and point out the blue Mercedes.

'That's it; AM 2456 number plate.' We circle round to the far side of the car park and Gary dismounts while I keep the bike ticking over. He unfastens his rucksack and slings it casually over one shoulder. I point him in the direction of the main entrance. 'There's a coffee shop on the ground floor. Adam's due to finish around five. Keep your phone on and I'll text with any updates. You do the same,' I say, giving him the beady eye. 'Keep me posted.'

I watch Gary walk towards the main entrance. With his

loping gait and rounded shoulders he doesn't stand out from the crowd. He's perfect. I think I'll make a good PI with Gary as a willing sidekick. There's something vulnerable about him and I realise he reminds me a bit of Trent.

My phone pings a message at around four thirty. It's from Adam. I'm biding my time in a dark dusty pub a couple of streets away from the hospital. My collar is turned up and I've slunk to the corner of the saloon which is deserted apart from a couple of old men drinking pints. I'm sticking to water.

> Hi. Sorry still operating. Will be later than usual but will txt when leaving. Adam xxx

I'm about to text back, when another ping announces a message from Gary.

> He's getting into car with blonde nurse. I got a couple of pictures. Now waiting outside. G

I text Gary to tell him I'm on my way and ignore Adam's message. He can wait. One of the old boys looks up from his pint and whistles through gaping gums, winking as I push my way through.

Outside the rain is falling again and rush hour has begun. I kick-start the engine into life and realise London traffic never stops; it's just heavier in rush hour. The beating heart of the capital doesn't rest. I remind myself of the need for caution. Trent's words 'it's not a toy' ring loud in my ears.

I make my way round to the hospital and spot the Mercedes slide out of the car park as I turn in. Bastard. Debbie's touching up her lipstick in the mirror and Adam is laughing at something. A big mistake. Up ahead, I see Gary standing out in the rain and I'm impressed that he isn't sheltering under the entrance canopy.

I think he wants to impress his new boss. He steps forward when he sees my approach and hops up behind me. He points after the Mercedes and I nod acknowledgement as we set off on its tail.

We only ever see what we're expecting. Adam has no idea that I'm onto his tawdry little tryst and as I follow tight behind, trailing close to the driver's side, I can see him looking back at the unknown motorcyclist. He'll be getting irate. He hates tail-gaters but I enjoy irking him, baiting his blood pressure. Gary shouts over the incessant traffic noise for me to pull back. He's getting nervous and is clinging ever more tightly to my waist.

When we draw level with the entrance to Waverley Mansions, I lift up my visor and point a leathered finger towards the entrance. 'That's it. The one with the orange Fiat outside.'

I drive round the corner, pull in to the kerb and wait for Gary to hop off again. He removes his helmet and tucks it into the box attached to the rear of the bike and pulls his hoody up over his head and winds his scarf tightly round his neck. He then puts on a set of dark thick-rimmed glasses which he's taken out of the rucksack. The glass lenses are large and cover at least a third of his face. With his hair scraped in to a ponytail, no one will give him a second glance. His facial features are well and truly hidden.

'Mr Kabal's finest,' he laughs.

I laugh with him. This might work.

I'm getting ready for bed when Adam gets home. I've bathed and dressed in a new silky see-through negligee. It's a peach colour, soft and luxurious. I've washed my hair and fluffed it up. I have two personas now. I will overdo the feminine allure so that there'll never be an inkling that I'm connected to the dark leather-clad motorcyclist who races round the maze of London streets on covert missions. The scented body lotion feels soft against my skin and I've dabbed Adam's favourite perfume behind my ears; Poison. I lighten my voice.

'Hi. Upstairs!' I yell down. He'll hear my happy mellow tone as he unpeels his overcoat and hangs it up behind the front door. He'll be breathing more easily, contented and smug that his home life is intact and he's got away with his peccadilloes once again. He thinks he knows me. He always thinks he's one step ahead of the game and that he's clever in the extreme. His arrogance is spawned from a background of privilege. A medical degree, first class honours and years of dedication, have coated him with a layer of armoured invincibility. I tease my hair once more with the comb and decide to wander along the landing to meet him. He does a double-take on the stairs.

'My. You look gorgeous.' He smiles. It's a tired smile, subtly manufactured to warn me in advance that he's had a very busy day. I want him to remember this moment, remember what he has thrown away and the cost of his deceit. He's going to find out soon what a fool he has been.

15

ALEXIS

Today is Adam's birthday. I have everything planned. It'll be our last birthday together so I want to make it special. It'll be very special. He has warned me on more than one occasion that there are to be no surprise parties but he should perhaps have warned me against all surprises. He's in for such a treat. My anger has made me brave, determined.

It's seven o'clock by the time I've prepared all the final touches to the table. I've stuck with a red theme; harlot red. Scarlet serviettes are neatly tucked inside the large wine glasses and a very expensive bottle of St Emilion Grand Cru red wine is open and breathing in the centre of the table. Tonight is about his favourites. He'll remember the details later, my perfect and successful husband.

I've treated myself to a figure-hugging red dress which nicely complements the serviettes. I've lost a lot of weight, through all the activity and angst. I'm wearing Pacific Island oyster pearls, a present from Adam on our first wedding anniversary. I sit gripping a large glass of champagne, waiting for him to get home, my nerves jangling. Anticipation of his reaction is playing havoc with my insides.

Adam is usually self-contained, not prone to emotion. When I miscarried the first time he took control, relief seeping out through insincere words of comfort. There'll be a next time, he assured me, saying that perhaps we weren't ready to be parents. He was let off the hook a while longer but when I announced pregnancy the second time round, I watched the slump of resignation in his shoulders. I still haven't forgiven him for opening a bottle of wine, purely for commiseration, when a small red blob of blood hit the toilet bowl for a second time in the same year. All hopes of parenthood were flushed away in a chink of glasses which was meant to ease the pain. Men are not meant to cry but Adam had nothing to hold in; except relief. His eyes stayed dry.

The close is very quiet. I've lit several candles, placing them strategically round the room and have turned off the centre light, leaving only a single lamp on in the corner. I hover by the window. There's an eerie stillness outside. There's no through traffic; no passing cars or lorries. Only silence. A bright light is on in the Harpers' kitchen. Susan will be awaiting Roger's return to help with the bedtime stories. I no longer want to trade places. It's too late.

As I drain my second glass of champagne, I notice Olive by her window. She'll be making notes in her diary, logging the silence. Perhaps she'll record Adam's time of arrival and will proudly show me the activity log for the close in the morning.

The key turns in the door at exactly seven thirty. I don't move but can't control the stiffening of my body. My teeth clench and I have to consciously unclamp my locked jaw. I flick my hair back and check my outline in the window. I don't recognise myself. Olive waves to confirm she's seen me.

'Hi. I'm home.' Home. What a strange word. It's where the

heart is, or so they say. It's where you can close the door and escape from the real world; feel secure and safe inside. That's always been my understanding anyway.

'In here,' I chirp. My lightness of tone rings false but Adam will be more shocked by my appearance and will rightly put down my apparent merriment to something more devious. He'll suspect that it is that time of the month when attempts at baby making might prove fruitful. There'll be panic in his eyes.

He pokes his head round the corner of the dining area, sheepishly pushing open the door against the dreaded appearance of friends and acquaintances who might raucously appear from behind sofas and curtains screaming 'happy birthday' in unison. His smile is fixed. He looks like a doctor who is trying to dampen a terminal diagnosis. He waits until I see him visibly unwind when he realises that we're alone. It takes a further couple of seconds for the baby-making scenario to cross his mind.

'Wow,' is all he says. It speaks volumes.

'Happy birthday!' I raise my glass, wander over and kiss him lightly on the lips before handing him an already filled flute. Adam is the consummate professional. The terminal diagnosis can wait, as he loosens his tie and decides that partying might not be such a bad idea. A birthday only happens once a year after all.

'I'll go and get changed and,' he says as an afterthought, 'thanks.' He smiles, making no mention of the provocative red outfit.

I smile back. 'You're welcome.' With that, he disappears upstairs.

I've cooked his favourite meal. Veal escallops lightly coated in rice flour and then pan fried in a rich Marsala wine, and have covered my expensive outfit in a 'kiss the cook' apron. It was a Valentine's Day present when I first invited him round for dinner. On that occasion we also had veal. Tonight my apron will help him to relax as the overt sexual innuendoes are camouflaged for the time being. I am a cook, housewife and partner until supper is eaten. He'll deal with the sex issues then. Perhaps the wine will mellow his mood and make children seem not such a bad idea after all.

Adam reappears in jogging bottoms and T-shirt, in what appears to be a deliberate attempt to divert the emphasis away from sexual overtones. I watch as he pours himself another drink and realise I feel no guilt at what I'm doing but do wonder how long it's been since I felt any affection for him. Before I sit, I ask him to top up my glass as I move to close the curtains. Nothing outside has changed and Olive is still looking.

I extract a small neatly wrapped package and what looks like a large birthday card from the desk by the window. Adam's watching me; I can feel his eyes on me. He'll be thinking that he didn't do so badly for himself after all. Perhaps he's regretting Debbie at this moment but it's too late and any regret would be short-lived.

'Happy birthday,' I repeat and set the parcel and envelope on the coffee table. 'For afters.' He pulls me down onto his lap and tries to kiss me. I pull away.

'Thanks,' he says. 'For everything.'

If I was going to feel remorse this would be the moment but I don't.

'I'll put some music on and you can tell me about your day,' he suggests. I think he's wondering whether to give in to the moment and make love to me by the hearth in a devil-may-care fashion, like lovers in a cheesy romantic movie. He's so sure that he's in control.

I sway my hips in time to the music, drunk from all the champagne and shimmy with abandon. Adam picks me up, swirls me round and pulls me towards him before running his hands over the sheer fabric of my dress. A zip runs all the way from top to bottom. He toys with it for quite some time, slowly undoing it notch by notch, teasing me with his patience. I plan to stop him when he reaches my coccyx.

'What's that?' Adam spits out the question.

'What's what?' I play along. He turns away and snaps the main light on. He points down at my lower back.

'Shit, Alexis. Is that a tattoo? What the hell?'

'Don't you love it? It's a detective with a magnifying glass. I thought it perfect.' I spin round, drunk on wine and adrenaline when the realism of what I'm doing warns me to sober up.

'I think that's a bit over the top. You know I hate tattoos and they're a medical nightmare to remove.' He assumes I'll want to remove it and he will be responsible for the procedure. I manage to pull the zip up again, relieved that the sexual pantomime at least is over.

'Let's forget it for now. Here, calm down and open your presents.' There's only one apparent present but the large card envelope contains something much more exciting. I move to the chair opposite, no longer at ease on the sofa beside him, as he rips open the small package. The box is dark green and hints at something expensive; jewellery, a ring perhaps. He's trying not to look excited as that would negate his irritation over the tattoo. A stern upper lip is his choice.

At first he's not able to make out what the cufflinks represent as he peers down at the silver accessories but eventually realises they are exact replicas of the tattoo on my lower back. A picture of a detective with magnifying glass is embossed onto each small square of sterling silver.

'They're not expensive but it's the thought that counts,' I say.

He doesn't know what to say. That works for me.

I then hand him the white envelope, having dulled the mood sufficiently for the final blow.

I must say Gary is very good. The black and white images could be Andy Warhol originals. They're evocative, sensual and vivid. Debbie is curled around Adam with her legs high in the air in the first photo. In the second, their lips are locked, tongues slithering in and out the wet crevices. The third one is the best. It was taken from the street outside Waverley Mansions with the long zoom lens and shows Debbie's naked breasts pressed hard into Adam's bare torso.

Suddenly there's a knock at the front door.

There it is again, persistent; louder. Before Adam has time to speak and stop me, I move past him towards the hall, relieved of the distance presenting itself between us. I unfasten the latch and pull the door open. It's Olive.

'Hello, love. I remembered you said it was Adam's birthday, so I baked a cake. I could see you were at home so thought I'd drop it over.' Olive beams proudly down at her creation. It is covered in blue and black icing and there's one candle in the centre.

'I didn't like to ask how old he was going to be,' she whispers. She hovers on the doorstep, waiting, hoping to be invited in. I take the cake and thank her, saying that we're in the middle of dinner but what a lovely thought.

'Thank you, Olive. Adam will be delighted. He loves cake,' I lie.

Olive turns to leave, visibly disappointed at not being invited in, but she understands. She has been watching us.

'My pleasure,' she says before winding her way slowly back down the path.

16

SUSAN

I stand on the scales, after wiping them furiously first to clean the surface. Roger's wet feet have left behind huge dirty webbed outlines. I look in the long mirror and don't recognise the person staring back. Although the image is skeletal, it's still too fat. Perfection requires dedication, self-control. I grit my teeth before I dare to look at the numbers which slowly flicker to life. I am two pounds up. I decide to try again as I know I didn't eat any of the calorific canapés and starved myself all day yesterday. The bottle of wine on its own surely couldn't have inflated the figures by so much.

Since I've been trying to control my weight, aiming at perfection, I'm eager to watch other people overeat. It makes me feel good, strong and superior. The cholesterol buttery-filled offerings which I prepared for the ladies last night were calorie laden but they were all eaten. This memory calms me down. My hands are shaking, with a persistent tremor, and I scrub them clean while I wait for the scales to reboot.

I've become increasingly gaunt but Roger doesn't seem to notice my demise and diplomatically avoids the subject of my appearance by telling me I need more fresh air. I pinch my cheeks until they redden and notice a very small broken vein on my left cheek. I follow its line with my finger which comes to rest on a small cold sore on my upper lip. I should be ecstatic that my weight has dropped so much in the last few weeks but I don't feel particularly healthy, wondering when the dizzy spells will abate. I know my strict regime needs me to cut back on alcohol but it's my comfort blanket; it helps me cope.

I dress quickly, scrunching my hair back from my forehead. There's an eerie silence about the house. I go downstairs and remember the relief, peace and quiet I had felt when the kids first started school. Whole days of nothing beckoned to be squandered at will: shopping trips, languid lunches with the girls or a game of tennis. I grip the banister to steady myself from the dizziness. Tilly has dropped 'Beanie' on the stairs. I pick up the tattered bear, smelling its dirty scent, sweet and familiar.

The safe is located in the understairs cupboard, right at the back. It's bolted in to the floor. Roger is determined that no one will ever touch anything that is his. He thinks I am his. The cupboard is cramped and I bang my head on the overhead beams. My knees bend further and further down as if I'm sinking into a quagmire, until I'm crawling the remaining few inches to the corner. The code to the safe is Noah's birthday. Tilly questioned why it wasn't hers. Our next safe will have her unique code which she'll choose herself and not share with anyone else. Secrets are such fun.

I pick up the torch beside the mat which covers the top of the huge dial and illuminate the space. The mess disturbs me. I frantically move odd shoes and tatty files around in an attempt to create a semblance of order. I stack the files and scrabble around for matching shoes. Tomorrow, not today, I'll clean out the cupboard. The thought makes me panic as my list of cleaning and household tasks is becoming too long. I've no time for what needs to be done to bring order back into my life. I make empty promises to tackle fruitful activities. Perhaps this task tomorrow will delay the early glass of wine.

There are several large brown envelopes in the safe. I take the first one, the one on top of the neat pile. Roger keeps our documents meticulously filed and the cash envelopes are carefully labelled in black marker pen. Five thousand pounds will not be missed. He squirrels money away more readily than he spends it. Roger will not be near the safe until the end of next month and then I'll offer to hide his petty cash for him.

Sweat is streaming down my forehead and small strands of hair have worked their way loose. My fingers are dirty, and dust motes attack my eyes and make me sneeze. The explosion echoes in the dark as I fiddle with the dial. A large black spider scuttles out from under the skirting board and I bang my head again, screaming in the silence. I wonder at my fear of the spider. It is ugly but harmless. Tilly shares my phobia. It has something to do with the animal's speed and dark hairiness. Noah happily pulls their legs off if he's clever enough to catch one and taunts us with his prize, seizing on the pleasure of hard-earned control.

The clock in the hall has started its hourly wind-up sequence. I don't need to be told the time. I'm living in a new dimension where I can hear the seconds, minutes and hours tick by. I count them, willing them to pass, until I can meet Vince again. Although deep down I know survival depends on crushing my animal instincts, I'm unable to quell the all-consuming obsession which is controlling my life.

I crawl backwards away from the safe and slam shut the cupboard, locking it behind me. My knees ache from kneeling; there's no flesh to pad out my bones. I put the key back in the small bureau behind the door and pick up my handbag.

The phone in the lounge rings but I leave it. I need to get

going; Vince will be waiting for the promised bank notes. As the clock chimes its last stroke, I exit the front door and step out into the afternoon sunshine. I scan the circle of our cul-de-sac, an almost-perfect ring. I'm scared people might be watching and someone might guess what I'm up to. I scrunch up the plastic bag containing the wad of notes and stuff it into my handbag, wishing I'd done this inside away from prying eyes. The claustrophobic enclosure of the houses makes me feel as if I'm encased in the glass bulb at the end of a thermometer. My skin is see-through and fragile.

Lara, a neighbour on the other side of the close, is in her garden and she waves. Did she see the carrier bag I was holding as I left the house and is she wondering where it's gone? I spot Olive Thompson, in the house next to Lara's, sitting by her window, net curtains veiling her ghostly form. She makes me uneasy. Lara is trying to coax her dog into her car, probably to walk it through Porters Wood, and this gives me the chance to hop into my own car and start the engine. I need to get away.

As I drive round the circle to get out the other side, Lara waves merrily in my direction. I wave back before putting my foot down hard on the accelerator.

A week has gone by since I handed across the clean crisp bank notes in the Waitrose carrier bag but the disappointment that there have as yet been no strings attached is gnawing away. We met on Hampstead Heath and walked round the lake. After I had handed over the money, Vince told me he couldn't stop for long as he had to make the trip into London to deliver the cash. However, true to his word, he texted back the next day and promised that today's treat would be on him. At the end of his text he mentioned casually that he's been offered more investment opportunities and can't wait to tell me about them. He thinks we're sharing them together. For now I'm managing to put the unease at the amounts involved to the back of my mind. All I seem able to think of is ways to keep on meeting him.

I'm back on the train rattling towards London with my nose pressed close against the glass. Outside, the lush green countryside has given way to a concrete jungle. The train is chugging between stops and we pass characterless tower blocks, apartments defined by individual rows of washing trailed across steel-rimmed balconies. Potted plants are sporadically threaded through ugly railings. I wonder where all the people are, the inhabitants of these hideous shells. *Windy Pines*, our brightly named home, suddenly seems palatial, belonging to another world.

Perhaps if the train had carried on as far as Brighton or continued westwards towards Somerset or even as far afield as Cornwall, I might have stayed aboard. But the London terminal called a screeching halt to such wild imaginings and after a short tube journey in the bowels of the earth, I find myself in some back-street mews not far from Hyde Park Corner, again trying to get my bearings.

'Can I help you?' A tall suited gent stops and offers encouragement. He probably thinks I'm a tourist and I'm tempted to shrug, feign a language barrier and scuttle away.

'Burton Mews. It doesn't seem to be marked on the map,' I say, keeping my head down. I turn the map towards him, wishing I didn't have to say the street name. He might be a witness at some future date, telling Roger that he did indeed talk to me on the day in question at the junction to Burton Mews. The hammering in my chest is threatening to break through the walls and I can feel a random bout of tinnitus ringing in my ears.

'It's down there on the right. I'm walking that way. I'll show you.' He takes the lead and I follow in silence a couple of paces behind. He halts and points down the small cobbled street indicating my destination. 'Here you are. Have a good day.'

'Thanks.'

I immediately spot the restaurant sign hanging up ahead, swinging merrily in the sunshine above a small intimate-looking bistro. When I reach the door, I stop and peer in through the frosted glass. I can make Vince out standing by the bar, talking and laughing with someone at a nearby table; a woman on her own. I experience the most excruciating pang of jealousy. His image is distorted but his manner is evident; flirtatious and assured despite the vaguely grotesque outline. I think of Dorian Gray.

I gingerly push the door open and Vince's attention immediately transfers in my direction.

'Hi,' he says. 'Susan.' He raises his hand in greeting and moves towards me, quelling any romantic notions the lone woman might have been harbouring.

'Hi. Hope you haven't been waiting too long. I got a bit lost,' I say. I struggle in the heat to get my coat off when a waiter once again appears out of nowhere to help. Vince leans over and we kiss lightly on the lips as the cheek-to-cheek custom no longer seems apt. The lady at the table returns to her menu.

'Come. I've booked us the best table, over there by the window.' A waiter leads the way and asks Vince how he's been keeping. Perhaps it's a stray polite enquiry but my neuroses make me wonder. I'm unable to decide if it is Vince's easy manner that fuels random conversations but the waiter seems particularly respectful as if he's serving a regular customer deserving of special attention. It's a recurring pattern.

17

SUSAN

'Vince.' We've finished eating and the plates have been cleared away.

'This sounds serious.' He purses his lips with mock gravity and opens his eyes wide.

'Can we talk?' I ask. I need to hear his angle on what's happening, to help me sort out a way forward. 'I don't think this is a good idea anymore.'

'Why? I thought we were having fun.' He takes my hand and looks into my eyes as if searching for a clue. I'm momentarily thrown off tack by his apparent surprise at the opening.

'We are. It's...' I don't really know what to say. I'm not prepared to own up yet about Roger and the kids. It somehow seems wrong, tarnishing any good impression Vince might have of me. This still strangely seems important.

'Listen. I understand. It's that I love being with you and thought we might have something special going on,' he says. It sounds like a corny line from a movie. I think of film stars, play-acting, while the cameras roll. 'If it's the money, I'll give it back to you. I promise.' He moves slightly away. I again experience that sick feeling of loss.

'It's not the money. Look.' I bend down and extract a cheque-book from my bag, keen to show him that I'm willing to trust his investments. 'Ten thousand pounds. I've already written it out. I don't know much about property bonds but I trust you. This is it though. There's no more.'

'You're a star. You won't regret it, I promise. We'll double our money, I'm certain.' He leans across and pushes a strand of hair away from my eyes. 'Thanks.' He takes the cheque and folds it in two before slotting it into his wallet. For a bizarre moment I feel like I'm paying for his services rather than investing in some potentially profitable business scheme but his use of the word 'our' offers me some security.

'I've left the name blank. I couldn't remember the name of your broker. You can fill it in. Is that all right?'

He nods before sharply flicking his fingers at the waiter who appears instantly alongside.

'A bottle of champagne, please. We're celebrating.' He turns to me, smiling, once more entwining his fingers with mine and says, 'You're not in a rush, are you? Let's talk over a proper drink.'

I have a list of questions. Why me? Are you married? Do you have kids? What about your past? Have you always lived in North London? What about your parents? But I don't ask any of them. Instead we let the bubbles go up our noses; laugh and joke at the motley selection of passers-by who motor past our vantage point by the window and let the sexual tension build up between us until it becomes unbearable.

One hour later we leave the restaurant side by side like a couple of merrily drunk young lovers but the cold air outside sobers us into an awkward silence. We both know what's going to happen but only Vince knows where. I let him lead the way, blanking rational thought from my mind, letting the champagne work its anaesthetic magic. I know I'm at that point of no return as we blindly push past people and shops. I spot the hotel, discreetly tucked between two large private residences, before Vince points it out.

It is exquisitely chic adorned on either side of the entrance with vibrantly filled flower pots. A red, yellow and purple display fruitlessly vies for my attention. The ringing in my ears is back, the incessant cacophony of sound blocking out rational thought.

I hover behind as Vince walks up to the reception and collects a set of keys. The woman behind the desk has been expecting him. This should make me uneasy but I don't care.

'Let's walk. It's only on the second floor.' Vince takes my hand and leads me towards the stairs away from the lifts in the foyer. I feel like a child being led away by a stranger, someone magical and intriguing, to a special place somewhere far off that will be festooned with treats and rewards. I choose to forget the dangers of accepting sweets from strangers.

Once inside the sumptuous bedroom, my senses become weirdly over-heightened. I bounce ridiculously up and down on the bed. I'm waiting, unsure of what to do next, while Vince locks the door behind us.

'Come here, you.' He stretches out his arms and pulls me off the bed towards him. The waiting is over. 'You're so beautiful,' he moans as he gently unbuttons my blouse, slowly unpeeling the silk from my shoulders and slipping his strong fingers under the flimsy strap of my camisole. I can hear his heavy breathing, but perhaps it's my own. We are moving to become one.

He tells me again I am beautiful and I choose to believe him.

When he lifts his own shirt off over his head, his muscles ripple. His body is smooth and tanned, and I'm so desperate for him to be inside me that I pull him down onto the bed so that he's on top of me.

I cry out and in the distance can hear the gentle rhythm of the headboard beating in time to our lovemaking. Vince clings on to the bedstead, steadying himself, moving with measured thrusts until he shudders and falls spent beside me. My own cries shriek above the silence.

I can hear a trolley being wheeled along outside in the corridor; room service or the cleaners. The faint creaking sound breaks the trance. Vince lies very still, spent from the exertions, and lets his arm flail loosely across my body.

'Would you like a drink? Tea or coffee?' He asks turning to look at me. 'There's a kettle over there.'

'No thanks.' I then blurt out, 'That was ten thousand pounds well spent.' My voice sounds vicious and aggressive although my intention is only to put some levity into the situation.

'Hey. What's up?'

It's as if someone has poured ice-cold water over me. It must be the shock realisation of what we've done. I gingerly get up.

'Come here.' Vince holds out his arms, smiling, reassuring, and tries to coax me back down beside him. He watches as I gather my clothes together before he stands up also. I sense him hovering behind me.

'I need to go,' I say, not daring to look at him.

'Susan.' The one word, however, gets my attention. When I turn round, he looks downcast and forlorn and for a minute, I regret the quip about the money. For some kooky reason, Vince seems to have fallen for me. I need to bury the niggling self-doubt that his charm offensive has increased since he received the payments.

He waits a moment before he asks, 'When will I see you again?'

I desperately try to unravel my blouse; the sleeves have become tangled inside out, and I'm suddenly embarrassed by my pale freckly skin. I manage to pull the blouse over my head before zipping up and straightening my skirt. I don't know what to say but I know I need to leave.

'I'm sorry, Vince. I can't see you again.' I clutch my handbag and coat and slip my feet into my shoes. 'I'm sorry.' The tears well up as I try to open the door. Vince leans across and releases the catch but doesn't speak.

He understands. He knows what my problem is. He has no doubts about his prowess but will have concluded that I'm married.

'Kiss me,' he says, 'even if it is goodbye.' He waits a moment and adds, 'I'll call you.'

I hurry along the corridor and take the stairs again rather than wait for the lift. I run, pounding downwards over the echoing fire well. In the foyer I look left and right. The concierge smiles.

'Good day, madam.' I ignore the plastic grin and hurry out into the street, tears streaming down my cheeks as I head towards the station. I will the throng of faceless people to swallow me up.

The train back up to Hampstead is busier than it was earlier and as it chugs out of King's Cross for the return journey north, darkness is drawing its cloak over the drab north London land-scape. Hazy lamplights flicker on and off in the concrete tower blocks. I stare out the window, imagining the small claustrophobic lives within but nothing appears to have changed since earlier. A tiny ray of hope pricks through the doubts.

As the miles pass and the minutes tick by, I dare to let myself think that maybe it doesn't matter so much after all. Roger need never find out and life will carry on as usual, as it does everywhere. I won't ever see Vince again. If he persists in contacting me, I'll tell him the truth. The time for games is over. When I tell him I'm happily married, he'll understand.

I alight from the train and stroll along the platform, up the stairs to the High Street and home. Home. It's where Roger and the children are. I realise I'm looking forward to getting back; suddenly normality is welcoming.

As I walk up Church Street towards Riverside Close, I plan to forget this afternoon ever happened. I need to bury my dark little secret. I must be meticulous in this regard.

18

ALEXIS

Perhaps we don't really know anyone until they are pushed. I'm in the bathroom, breathing deeply, playing for time. The door is locked, offering illusory safety. There is no noise from the bedroom but I'm sure Adam hasn't gone back downstairs. I pin my ear to the door and listen, not daring to breathe. The silence scares me and I'm sweating in my tight dress. Something stops me from taking it off; undressing would leave me more vulnerable and perhaps taunt him one step too far. I need to stay calm, remember that I'm not the one in the wrong. Adam will twist things.

After Olive left, Adam fell dangerously silent. He stopped talking, narrowed his eyes and watched me. I knew better than to carry on speaking but decided to go up and change.

'Not so fast. Where do you think you're going?' he hissed.

I made the top of the stairs before he had time to register where I'd headed. I managed to run through our bedroom and make it into the bathroom before he appeared.

I had heard his feet pound up the stairs, two at a time and I only managed to lock the door before he rattled and rattled at the handle. 'Come out, you bitch.'

It's only now I remember the severity of the black-eye incident, the endlessly recounted tales of walking into a glass door. Silly me! I hadn't seen it, there were no markers announcing its presence. It was an invisible danger; like Adam. I now wonder if I have used the Debbie affair as my way out. She has provided me with a good reason to leave when I should have done so long ago.

Half an hour must have passed. There's still no noise and I think Adam must have gone downstairs again. I creep to the door and try to unlock it as quietly as possible, tentatively sliding open the tiny bolt. Adam never locks doors in the house; that is not what marriage is about. He has always been so confident in assuring me that he is trustworthy, open and solid.

The black eye and the glass door incident have lain dormant, buried in my memories. Adam carefully covered up the event with wine and roses, a trip to Paris and a gold necklace. He spent freely to buy back my trust and silence, and he thinks he was successful in dispelling any doubts I might have harboured in thinking it more than a one-off aberration. I must admit, while he clasped the gold necklace round my neck, I believed it wouldn't happen again. I lied to myself.

The bedroom is in darkness. I thought I'd left the light on but instead I tentatively make my way, keeping close to the wall, towards the switch. Instantly a hand is round my throat, constricting my windpipe. The other hand is pushing my body, face forward, into the wall. He's hissing words of venom and the wet spittle is closing in on my ear.

'Fucking bitch,' is all he says as he squeezes tighter. I try desperately to kick up with my feet which are now free from the patent heels but he knows that he's in control. This is all that'll ease his battered psyche.

'Why?' his dark voice snaps. 'How did you find out? If you've sent photos to Debbie, I'll kill you.' Her name fuels my determination but I don't answer. My anger is as great as his but not my strength. I need to be careful.

'How did you find out?' he repeats, spitting his words. 'I'm listening.' The menace in his tone has escalated and he turns me round to face him. I'm not ready for it. I think that by facing him he'll not seem so savage, that his face will become familiar, respectful and safe. I am wrong. He hasn't turned the light on so I can't see the intent in his eyes, but I sense it.

His left hand is too quick. It slaps me on one cheek, then the other and back again. My head flails from side to side and through a thick fog, I feel the sting of the black eye. I won't lose consciousness. Not this time.

When he has finished with me, I'm lying on the floor unable to get up, barely conscious. He gives me a final kick in the thighs, one blow to each side, before rampaging down the stairs and out the front door. The neighbours will hear the bang echoing in the night air.

I'm not sure how long I have been lying here but I think I might have passed out for a few minutes. It's already gone midnight. I manage to haul myself up onto the bed. Adam will not come back tonight, I'm almost certain but a doubt lingers.

I somehow drag myself down the stairs, gripping the banister rods to stop me from tumbling and eventually reach the front door. I double lock the mortise and pull the safety chain across. I leave my keys in the door so that I'll hear any warning of his return, enough time to call 999. My mobile is gripped in my hand.

There is an eerie silence in the house as I crawl from room to room, fearful that Adam might jump out from behind a door. Dark shadows filter through the open curtains and I freeze when I hear a rattle outside. I think it might be Adam. I stay very still and look out through the dining room window, too scared to move. I watch the neighbour's dog, who has escaped from its own claustrophobic confines, bound across the close. It's running wildly from side to side, glancing over his shoulder every few seconds to see if its owner is following. Although the dog is free, it's dependent.

I now know I need to break free and become independent. I stay where I am for at least ten minutes until I'm certain Adam hasn't come home and finally inch myself, step by step, up the stairs to bed.

Without daring to turn on the lights, I fall into an exhausted sleep.

19

ALEXIS

There is an incessant banging from somewhere far off but I can't wake up. I feel as if I've been drugged. I glance at my phone. It is 8am and light outside. I can't move but hear small sharp raps at the window; as if a ricochet of bullets is hitting the pane. The curtains are still open. There had been no need for Adam to close them last night as the lights had been off and the room in darkness the whole time. For a moment I can't remember exactly what happened until the memories filter through.

'Alexis.' I can hear someone calling my name from outside. Adam has returned. Perhaps he's managed to locate a florist in the middle of the night, or perhaps he's bringing chocolates, planning a grovelling apology. I lie still, close my eyes and will him to leave. Someone's talking to him.

The neighbours will be embarrassed, unwilling to get involved but Adam will tell them he has forgotten his keys and has been operating late into the night. That's why he's throwing small pebbles up at the window. Another emergency, he will be saying. He probably slept in the car. Debbie's husband will be sharing her bed and panic has propelled my husband back to his senses.

I can hear a muffled conversation and am glad that I didn't give the Harpers a spare key. Their aloofness made me hesitate. I manage to crawl to the window, my body feeling as if a lump of concrete has been dropped on it, and tap on the windowpane. Adam is talking to Olive. She has wandered out in her dressing gown and is standing beside him. She knows what's going on and for once I'm grateful for our little cul-de-sac whose homes share the intimate space. Olive, with her arthritic little hands and wizened face, appears like a talisman in the street below. She smiles up at me.

'I'll be down,' I mouth through the glass. She is my witness. She will see the bruises and will log them in her diary. The date will be important, and as I make my way slowly down the stairs, I wonder if she remembers any other battered wives in the close.

I don't want to let Adam in but I know he'll otherwise stand and keep knocking, assuring the neighbours that I have become an increasingly heavy sleeper. He'll be assuming that I haven't called the police and in the cold light of day also assume I will realise we had nothing more than a domestic tiff. The absence of a police presence will confirm I've taken the matter no further.

I go to pull back the chain. Perhaps I should call the police but I'm sure Adam will play the apologetic contrite card rather than resume the violence. He knows the neighbours are watching, so cautiously I open the door. I don't feel strong enough, mentally or physically, to confront him yet or to plan the exit from our marriage but the latter will need all my strength.

Adam is in quickly, panning Olive off with bright and breezy platitudes, and closes the door behind him. He stares at me, trying to work out how I can look so battered. He reaches for my hands but I ignore him and instead begin the painful walk towards the lounge.

'Let me bathe those wounds,' he says. The doctor's caring façade makes him feel better. He wants to soothe my injuries as if they were inflicted by someone else.

'They're not as bad as they look,' I lie. I need to get rid of him. I pretend my injuries don't matter that they were a deserved result of my subterfuge. He will naively believe that one bad deed led to another and now we're all square. He doesn't know I have photographed the bruises, noting down the date and time. This is my detective brain thinking ahead, gathering the evidence for the right moment. I would prefer a more amicable separation, two adults accepting the marriage is over, rather than dragging our dirty linen through the courts. I might still have to reveal his true nature but for now I'll go through the motions and hope that Adam's desperation to avoid public or professional humiliation will simplify a divorce. However, I've saved the pictures in case.

He thinks everything is as it was before and he will, of course, tell me that he'll never see Debbie again. That is the least he can do. What he has conveniently forgotten is that his physical attack is the only unlawful deed that has been carried out. His affair, my confrontation with the facts and sadistic birthday pantomime will not warrant prison sentences. He seems to think I won't realise this but in my fragile state, my fear doesn't let me voice such knowledge. Silence is my best weapon for now.

I can hear him put the kettle on in the kitchen, take down a couple of mugs from the cupboard and then make a phone call. He tells the hospital that he has had a minor family crisis and will be delayed in getting to work but he should be there by ten. I am a *minor* family crisis. If he had used the word *major* I wouldn't have mellowed but might have at least talked to him. The word has become the final nail in his coffin.

'Here.' He hands me a mug of sweet strong tea. He's put

sugar in to help with the shock and sweeten the blow. I see Olive through the window and Bob is by her side.

'Bloody snoop,' Adam snaps, pulling the curtains across. He has to curtail his anger which is still simmering near to the surface. I think for the first time he is questioning the wisdom of moving to Riverside Close. It was his choice but might turn out to be my saviour in the end.

'I'm sorry,' is meant to make it all right, together with the sweet tea. He needs to get to the hospital, it's a life-or-death thing, but he can't go until he knows I'm okay and he's forgiven. I don't say that we are long past forgiveness but the only way I can get rid of him is to pretend.

'Go to work. I'll be fine.' I sip the warm tea and don't look up. I feel so cold, shivering in my red dress which I still haven't taken off. He runs upstairs. He's late for work, and comes down again holding up one of his large woollen jumpers. It makes him feel better as he watches me pull it over my head. He thinks we're still together, a team, helping and sharing items, and assumes we'll move on from this, like other couples who have had marital contretemps. Adam is desperate to nurture the world's view of him as a successful respected physician. Divorce wouldn't suit his image. His untarnished reputation is crucial to his survival.

He leans over and kisses me on top of my head and repeats, 'I'm really sorry. We'll talk this evening.' Then he'll give me his diagnosis. He's desperate for forgiveness so we can carry on as before. He doesn't yet know that this won't happen and he's had his last chance. I need patience. I will him to leave but he hovers as if trying to decide what else he can do.

'Go on,' I repeat, smiling through gritted teeth. 'I'm going to have a shower.' I pretend for now that I don't feel too bad and that the day will carry on as normal, as it does every day. He seems satisfied. He slips me a couple of strong painkillers from a half-full plastic bottle, assuring me they'll help ease the worst of the pain, then lifts his briefcase and puts his fingers to his lips and blows me a farewell kiss.

'Take a couple every four hours and you'll not feel a thing. I won't be late. Promise.' With that, he's off back to his godlike role of saving lives.

Olive appears at the front door once Adam has gone and his car has disappeared from view. I hobble over and let her in. She hugs me but doesn't speak. There's no need. She feels my body shake.

'Olive, I need to get the locks changed; straightaway. Maybe you can help.' I frantically begin to search for local locksmiths on my phone. Filled with purpose, Olive starts to jot down possible contact numbers in a small black notebook which she has produced from her pocket. She touches my arm in a comforting gesture of support.

'Leave it to me, love. I'll take care of it.'

I then phone Gary and tell him he needs to get to me as soon as he can and to bring his overnight things. I say I'll pay double if he spends a few days with me. Olive goes upstairs to dig out some bed linen and get the spare room ready for the new lodger.

I somehow manage a hot shower and although the heat stings the bruises, I feel refreshed and more positive. The stiffness in my limbs is abating as well as the searing pain which has effectively been dulled by the painkillers.

The locksmith is coming in an hour and Gary's on his way, more than happy to oversee the installation of the new locks. I decide to get out of the house and clear my head before Adam discovers what I've done and tries to batter the doors down.

～

'Hope you don't mind.' I smile as I let Gary in. He doesn't comment on my black eye but laughs nervously when I joke that I walked into a door. I don't expand on what happened with Adam, having told Gary the gist on the phone. I had to tell him as I desperately need him in the house. If he has any doubts about helping out, he doesn't show it. 'I'll make it up to you, I promise,' I say.

'No worries. I'd do the same for any of my mates. Also this looks a lot more comfortable than my bedsit.' He wanders from room to room and I tell him to make himself at home.

'I'm going out on the bike for a couple of hours to clear my head. I'll be back before Adam gets home.' I feel an urge to hug Gary but instead pat him on the arm and repeat how grateful I am.

'Go on. You might need to bang hard on the door when you get back as you'll not have a key to get in,' he jokes.

I let myself out, get into the car and head for the lock-up. As I drive towards Camden, I remember how burning up the open road used to blow the cobwebs away. Today it'll help release the tension and prepare me for the battle ahead. I'm not thinking of the heavy London traffic with its incessant aggression and hidden barriers to speed. The enticement of escape is what motivates me and a desire to forget, even for a short time, my marital nightmares.

But Adam didn't warn me of the drowsy side effects of the medication and that I shouldn't be driving. It all happens so fast. The last thing I remember is the bike spinning in an uncontrolled three hundred and sixty degrees. After that, the world turns black.

20

ALEXIS

A FEW HOURS LATER

It takes me a while to work out where I am. There's a low buzz and bright lights flicker overhead. I become aware of someone holding my hand and coaxing me gently back to consciousness.

'Alexis? Alexis? Can you hear me?' Why is Adam wearing a green gown and talking to me gently and kindly? Something tells me he should be shouting at me, swearing and hitting me instead.

'Where am I? What's happened?' I can hear my voice from somewhere in the distance, a soft croaking whisper. A small Asian nurse is checking my pillows, straightening them behind me. Adam thanks her. He's a doctor and he's in charge.

'You came off a motorbike,' he smiles or is he sneering? The nurse hovers and I don't want her to go. 'I hear it was a wet patch of road.' He knows about the bike. What else does he know and what am I trying to hide? I can't remember. Everything's a blur.

'Please may I have a glass of water?' I ask the nurse, knowing that this will bring her back, delay time alone with Adam. What has he done? I can't remember. I ask for a mirror; it's an automatic request now I'm in public. My hair is wild, caked in dirt and my lips are cracked. I watch the doctor pull the curtain round my bed once the nurse has gone. He makes sure it shuts out the rest of the ward and then he comes in close.

'Where the fuck did you get the motorbike?' He's spitting in my face and holding my hands down tightly against the bed. I can see a red string dangling by the side of the bed, an emergency cord, but it's too far away. What would be the use? I'm with a doctor already. I'm not completely sure where I got the bike, I can't recall. That's what I'm going to tell Adam as I start to remember the wet surfaces round the back of Highgate. But everything's fuzzy and I feel so groggy. I think a small black cat appeared out of nowhere and I vaguely remember spinning up onto the pavement.

'What bike?' I close my eyes. The nurse will be back soon. I realise my left leg is in plaster. I must have broken it when I crashed into the fencing. The pain, I can remember the pain shooting through my body before I must have blacked out. The nurse returns and gently pulls back the curtain, setting a water jug and plastic cup beside my bed.

'Can I get anything for you, Dr Morley?'

Adam's mask is in danger of slipping; that perfect manufactured sincerity that accompanies his bedside manner. I can hear him over the dinner table belittling his patients, making fun of their distress and telling our friends humorous little anecdotes pertaining to their various conditions.

'No thank you, sister. I'm fine. I'll be over to theatre in five minutes.' I keep my eyes tightly shut but hear him lift the water jug and pour me out a glass.

'Here. Open your eyes. A glass of water will help.' He forces me to sit up, pushing the glass to my lips. The cold liquid spills down the front of my gown before I manage to swallow. 'I'll be back.' With that he pours the rest of the iced water over my face out of view of the retreating nurse.

I've been sleeping on an off for a couple of days but am finally wide awake. Adam brings me some magazines and a couple of newspapers. I think he's testing my faculties, attempting to draw me out. I'm seeing more of him than I have over the last six months. He's putting on the act of caring professional and the ever-devoted husband. It is all for show. There's been no sign of Debbie, not even a fleeting image. If I were her I would be curious to see the spurned wife but perhaps her lover has told her to steer clear.

I toy with the possibility that she has finished with him but it is more likely that he won't want her now he's been found out. The clandestine nature of the affair was the attraction, of that I'm certain. It's so much more exciting having an unsuspecting wife at home and a similarly married lover who is not expecting a future. 'No strings' will have been the attraction. Adam is a complete bastard.

I am now in a private ward. Adam has used his influence and fast tracked me away from the other patients. It suits him as he knows I can't go anywhere and we can't be heard. I want to get back home and as far away from him as possible. Gary is still in the house and the locks have been successfully changed. He has sent me various texts, keeping me updated and I've asked him to stay there and not let anyone other than Olive over the threshold.

After the accident, Adam kept clear of the house apparently, once he discovered the locks had been changed. He is waiting until I've recovered. He knows better than to create a fuss in front of the neighbours and won't want to go to the police to gain access as he's well aware of the visible effects of his attack on my body. The nurse commented today on the bruises on my face and thigh, making small talk and commiserating over my dreadful accident. I had a lucky escape.

My phone has reappeared by my bedside. Adam, no doubt, has been through my contacts and messages looking for something to pin in my direction. I call Olive. She will help.

She picks up immediately; she has been waiting.

'Olive?' She listens silently on the other end. 'I'll be home on Friday around 3pm. Would you come over for a cup of tea? I need someone with me, and Gary desperately wants a break away from the house.' She understands. She will watch for me from her window and come straight round.

Perhaps cul-de-sacs were built to bring people together, to manufacture communication between taciturn occupants. Today I'm glad we moved to the close as it will work in my favour, hampering Adam's attempts at invisible suppression and imprisonment. Olive is my infirm elderly weapon with the mind of a vibrant twenty-year-old. It lifts my spirits when she tells me she has baked another cake. She also tells me Gary has been working hard on his laptop, ordering pizzas and Chinese takeaways.

Olive coughs down the phone and I can hear a chesty wheeze as she tries to catch her breath.

'Take care.'

Adam arrives as I click the 'off' button.

'Who was that?' He demands, mellowing his tone when he hears the nurse following behind.

'A friend.' I won't tell him that Olive will be there when I get home. He'll wait until he knows I'm back before he makes his move. Gary hasn't seen any sign of him for the past few days, not since he tried unsuccessfully to gain access the day the locks were changed. Adam will have worked out that I've had enough and, as far as I'm concerned, our marriage is over.

I expect though that he'll try to maintain the marital façade for his work colleagues and will insist on driving me home himself when I'm discharged. But I'm prepared. Olive will be waiting and won't leave before him. She has a well-matured stubborn streak. Also Gary's promised he'll come back immediately should we need him. He'll keep his phone turned on at all times, waiting for the emergency call.

The nurse helps me swing my legs round to the side of the bed and hands me the crutches. I have a couple of days to master their use so I can hobble around with the cumbersome plaster cast. She assures me a broken leg will heal. The accident could have been a lot worse, she says, encouraging me to pull myself up in readiness for the work ahead.

21

CAROLINE

The ten thousand pounds has hit the bank account. It's so easy. *Join Me* has turned me into my husband's pimp. I scroll down the online bank statement. In such a short time my slick duplicitous husband has doubled our turnover with his increasingly regular encounters. We play-act that the sex means nothing, that it's an integral part of the scheme's success. Not talking about it is supposed to emphasise its lack of importance. Yet in my nightmares I see him, sucking them ever deeper into his sleazy web, using his taut tanned body to tease them further and further into frenzy. I try to forget that I was once such a victim.

I wonder how he became this person. While I can fathom my own insecurities and obsessions, I question Jason's readiness for sex with random women; albeit for money. Although he doesn't open up, it's in his past. I'm certain. One day I'll dig deeper. One day when the answers won't be able to hurt me.

He's going out tonight. I hear him upstairs getting showered and dressed. I've left out his Italian chinos and pale cream linen shirt, carefully creased and pressed to perfection. We are team players in the game of deception; a skilled double act. I pretend to myself that the money eases the pain and that it's a shared ruse we've concocted together. I kid myself that if I let him have enough treats he won't ever feel the need to leave me and I'm certain enough, at the moment, that he wouldn't ruin what we have for Susan Harper. She is turning out to be a wise choice of companion with plenty of spare cash.

I force myself upstairs and into our bedroom. I sit down on the edge of the bed and watch while he adds the finishing touches to his appearance.

'How do I look?' He twirls around, pirouetting on one foot, unbelieving in the luck that allows him to date beautiful women with the full blessing of his wife. Such a beautiful wife too, he teases, leaning across to kiss me. 'Come here, gorgeous.'

He's mad, or perhaps I am. I wonder at the egotism that allows him to prostrate himself in such a manner. He's like a beautiful teenage Adonis who has no idea how perfect he is. As I neaten the collar of his shirt, I have to remind myself that he is in his thirties and time is on my side; not his. His looks won't last forever.

Queenie, our white long-haired Persian cat, strolls into the bedroom and rubs herself up against his legs. She flirts, teases him and then turns her back and walks away. That's what I should have done but it's no longer possible.

'Shit.' Jason frantically picks hairs off his trousers as white stragglers have stuck furiously to the creases. I smile, turning away from him and look out the window. Queenie has come back. She is a minx, as sure of her appeal as my husband is of his. Perhaps if we had children I wouldn't need to fill the house with cats.

'Where are you taking her tonight?' I ask, without looking at him. I watch the car headlights stream past and busy passers-by rushing to unknown destinies. Our road is long and impersonal, comprised of 1930s bland middle-class semi-detached homes. Only the location has made their blandness desirable.

Jason is still picking hairs off his trousers and has kicked Queenie into touch. I like to think he's not perfect, to have evidence of weaknesses and things that might one day kill off my obsessions. His occasional taunting and cruelty of Queenie give me hope. These and his map of Brazil are slim pickings.

'We're meeting in Covent Garden, outside the Opera House,' he says, always careful not to mention a name. He still tries to save me from hurt which he's right to suspect lurks close to the surface. I fear my jealousy might be fuelling his passion rather than dousing it.

Down on the street below, a pair of young lovers passes the gate, laughing, holding hands with a shared umbrella shielding them from a light drizzle. I am starting to long for the years to pass so that the passion will all be over and the sexual desire will be replaced by something more solid, meaningful and deep-rooted.

I turn to face my lover, my husband, my tormentor and my obsession. I take his hands, intertwining my fingers in a loving gesture, and kiss him gently on the lips. He pulls me in. I can feel him hard against my body. I want him to think of me when he is on top of her. Yet deep down I want him to be revolted by what he is doing, to tell me he loves me and that he will never be unfaithful again; that we don't need the money, after all. 'Why don't we sell up and move to the country or Spain perhaps?' He might ask. 'Our London pot could set us up in style.'

Instead he picks up his jacket and says goodbye. I realise this is never going to happen. He will always be a player, and unless I'm prepared to let up, I have to find another way to keep him close.

I follow him downstairs and when he has gone I go and pour myself a drink. I take it over to the computer and sit down in front of the screen. I spend an hour trawling the latest list of enrolments on the website, making notes and researching candidates. I need to stay one step ahead of the game, not letting things spiral out of control. I'm checking out who my husband might be drawn to next and those that I need him to avoid. At least we have agreed all companions must be married.

I'm drawn to Susan 789's profile again. Susan Harper. At the moment she is putty in our hands. I have to constantly remind myself that her bony freckly body and obsessive neuroses are unlikely to captivate my husband. Meeting her in person offered temporary relief but it has been short-lived. The gnawing doubt grates on, like a rat's teeth against bone. Perhaps taunting her with more measured punishment might give me some relief.

22

ALEXIS

Susan Harper has invited me across the road to one of her ridiculously labelled *Friday Fizz* events. These are all-inclusive drunken evenings apparently for lady friends and neighbours. I think we're all supposed to bitch in confidence about our husbands and unfulfilling sex lives. Anyway I'm glad of the excuse to get out of the house.

I find myself hunched down low by the log burner, desperately willing the itch inside my leg cast to abate. Surreptitiously extracting a thin pointed knitting needle from my handbag, I steer it down the gap between the plaster and my calf scraping the skin to find relief. Susan teeters across the room in three-inch heels, holding a bottle aloft.

'Here, let me top you up, Alexis.' She bends exaggeratedly low to refill my Prosecco flute. 'Poor you,' is tossed through the air loudly enough for everyone to hear and to admire her concern. She wants to be liked.

The oven emits a bright ping. The canapés are done. Mini quiche, mini pizzas, mini sausage rolls and a plethora of other mini delicacies. Susan parades back to her spotless double-fronted glass oven. It is all for show, like the three-inch heels.

The fizz and the claustrophobic heat are making me woozy and I feel slightly nauseous. Perhaps the mini delights will settle my stomach. I hear my phone beep. It will be another message from Adam. I wonder if the text will be contrite, aggressive or accusatory. He's varying his tone with fierce determination, trying to decide which tactic will work best in his defence and get my attention.

I plop my encased limb awkwardly back from the heat and wonder if my inclusion into this Friday session of alcohol-infused merriment might have something to do with my shattered left leg; a sympathetic gesture perhaps.

However, I feel Susan's insistent invitation might have had more to do with intrigue following Adam's apparent absence from our home. He's been gone too long for it to be a business trip. She will have told the other guests, behind closed doors and in the strictest of confidence, that Alexis and Adam Morley, the new neighbours to the close, seem to have split up. The lump of plaster cast is hiding my slender legs and my lack of make-up renders me downtrodden, defeated. Pity has most likely helped to propel my sudden invitation into the event.

I scratch frantically at my left eye which has come alive. It is the Siamese cats; expensive, sleek and showy. One of them is rubbing itself provocatively on my cast which is so cumbersome that I am unable to politely nudge the animal away.

Caroline Swinton has now been announced as another new member of the Friday drinks club and as I blink, violently trying to clear my vision distorted by the allergens from the felines, I watch her arrival. The other guests squeal in delight, welcoming her with platitudes and air kisses.

She is heavily curvaceous and the skin-tight cut of her clothes accentuate a large bust and ample backside. Shoulder-length blonde hair is brashly highlighted in bleached tones and brightly red manicured nails draw the eye. However, there is something about her manner that makes me think her painted exterior hides a more steely substance. First appearances can be deceptive, and when she speaks I have the feeling that she is playing to the crowd. She is offering herself up to the bored housewives but doesn't quite fit the mould. It's a feeling; my detective's brain in overdrive.

'Hi,' she says in a quiet voice. She is uneasy at being centre-stage. She uncoils a silken Hermes scarf from around her neck and lets her eyes wander. Susan, as the hostess, is given special attention and is kissed confidently on both cheeks. I try to stand up, pushing the Swedish designer chair away from my body and stumble against the log burner.

'Ouch,' I scream. It is scorching hot. All eyes turn in my direction.

'Oh no. Are you okay?' Susan exclaims. 'Here let me help you.' She is by my side immediately, anxiously concerned and bordering on the manic. I say I'm happy where I am but she insists.

'You'll be much more comfortable up here. Come on.' She leans over, proffers her arm, and guides me to the kitchen bar, a large slab of shiny black granite. The ladies are lined up on swivel stools, and Susan's keen for me to be involved. 'Also you'll be able to join in the conversation better.' She helps me up to sit on the end of the counter, next to Caroline.

'Caroline. This is Alexis. Our very own private detective,' Susan announces as she agitates to get me involved in proceedings.

'Hi,' says Caroline. I think she already knows that I'm a PI as she doesn't pass comment. I imagine Susan has read out snippets from each of the guests' individual CVs, sharing backgrounds and personal information, when extending the invitations to each lady in turn. I'm wondering what Caroline's story might be when my phone pings again. She gives me a knowing smile when I ignore the alert. Perhaps she's surmising that I don't have children otherwise I would have worriedly extracted my phone immediately to check the message.

The Prosecco flows and as my mood mellows, I become less aware of my red eyes and itchy calf. One of the cats is perched on top of my foot which is encased in a sensible flat pump. The animal appears to be avoiding the other drinkers. The ladies all seem to be married but my marital status isn't discussed and there seems to be an unspoken acknowledgement in the air that I'm living alone. I wonder how much they already know, and if our hostess suggested beforehand that prying might not be a good idea. Adam's name isn't mentioned.

Susan darts around the kitchen, cleaning, lifting and tidying while she tosses meaningful little conversational questions and asides up into the air. Her OCD is hiding something and her borderline anorexia is highlighted by a refusal to taste her own food. On the other hand she is drinking copious amounts of alcohol.

Before long I'm wondering how I am going to extricate myself from the situation. It's not going to be easy jumping up and disappearing to the toilet, reappearing with coat and bag at the ready to make an early exit from the party. The cat on my foot has fallen asleep and is purring loudly. I reluctantly accept a top-up, allowing the excessive bonhomie to help stave off my unease. Our house has become bizarrely quiet without Adam around but deep down I'm filled with dread. Although he's always worked long hours, there's a threatening silence about the rooms without his usual presence.

I watch Caroline out of the corner of my eye. She is sitting primly on the end of the counter, drinking but not eating. There's something controlled about her under the heavy make-up and bright lipstick. She doesn't fit the usual bored housewife mould and isn't adding anything of substance to the conversation. There's no mention of a husband.

I finally push myself up off the stool and sympathetic eyes follow my struggle to the toilet. Offers of help abound but I politely decline steadying hands. On my way back, heading for the front door, I feel a soft tap on my left shoulder.

'Here. Take this,' Caroline whispers, thrusting a business card into my hand. 'Call me, please.' She nudges on past towards the cloakroom, having being careful that no one has seen the transaction. She needn't have worried as the other ladies are not looking, continuing their steady buzz of conspiratorial gossip.

'Here. Let me help,' Susan says, as she opens the front door wide to let me out. 'Thanks for coming.' She kisses me goodnight, shivering suddenly from the cold invasion of night air. 'When does the cast come off?'

'A couple of weeks still. Sorry I've been such a nuisance, but it was lovely to get out. Thanks a lot.'

'A pleasure.' Susan gently closes the door behind me once I've assured her I can make the short walk home.

The night air is sharp, crisp and bitter. A deathly hush covers the close like a heavy blanket. The night has closed off our dead end from activity other than its own. I glance back over my shoulder at Susan's house which is bright and brimming with life and false merriment but across the street our own home is in darkness.

I hobble warily on the crutches, trying to avoid any invisible patches of black ice. My head swims, my eyes itch but relief at escaping from the overpowering atmosphere is welcoming. The sky is clear and cloudless and millions of stars glisten overhead. I grip Caroline's card, desperately trying not to drop it on the ground as I manoeuvre my leg one inch at a time. I manage to pocket the card, gingerly sliding it into my coat, as I reach the front door. I'll phone her in a couple of days to see what she wants.

The house is very quiet. The little red light on the answer-phone in the hall is flashing and, leaning the crutches up against the banisters, I delete the six messages which I know will be from Adam. I'm no longer interested in his edgy pleading. The anger and venom have started nudging back to the fore, swallowing up his early insincere apologies.

23

ALEXIS

I boot up my laptop in the lounge, not ready to go to bed. I turn the wooden blinds halfway so they are neither open nor closed, and turn on the side lamps.

Riverside Close is not yet asleep. The lights blink on and off in the neighbours' homes. Blackness envelops the empty house for sale at number four. It is sandwiched between Susan's house and one similarly constructed 1950s property on the other side. It's only been on the market a week but it is eerily haunting with its black eyes and empty soul.

I shiver and look at the small white envelope which was lying on the mat in the hall on my return. My name is scribbled in Adam's near-illegible handwriting. He will have popped it through the letterbox when I was at Susan's; more vitriolic ranting no doubt. I tear it up and throw it in the bin before pulling ajar the door on the little mobile fridge which is neatly slotted under the small console table. Gary, bless him, brought it over. It's on loan from his bedsit so I wouldn't need to hobble to the kitchen for emergency supplies and a nightcap.

I pour a small measure of whiskey malt, filling the glass with ice, and settle back in the chair. It's hard to believe that it was only a few weeks ago that Adam and I moved to the close together and introduced ourselves to the neighbours. Yet now I am alone, dreading him coming back. But I know he's waiting.

Adam doesn't know that Gary has popped back to his own flat for a few days. He was furious that I had taken in a lodger. Deep down, he knows I installed Gary both for my own security and to act as a potential witness should Adam go on the attack again. My husband is playing for time, methodically trying to inveigle his way back into my good books, assuming that I will eventually capitulate as he thinks I don't have any other real options.

The first email in my inbox is from Adam. Rather than texting he's assuming the formal approach is more likely to get my attention. He's determined to talk, force me to listen. Ignoring him might not be wise, but until I'm mobile again I can't risk a face-to-face confrontation, certainly not on my own.

Alexis. We need to talk. I've said I'm sorry but I'm not going to crawl through any more hoops. I'll keep coming round until you let me in. Changing the locks was childish in the extreme. You can't keep me out of my own house. I notice he doesn't use the word home. His tone has hardened. I'll be round tomorrow so you'd better let me in. Adam

My inbox alerts me that I have two messages on *Join Me*. I log in. I have been flitting between Facebook, Twitter and *Join Me* to stem the boredom since coming out of hospital. The random flyer through the letterbox was intriguing enough to pique my interest and has helped me pass some time. **Where Would You Like To Go?** is a smart tagline.

Hi. What's new?

The first message was left at 8pm. It's by a guy called Eddie 300, the number part like an alias surname. He's in Manchester tonight apparently but the weekend conferences will not last much longer, he tells me. He's trying to persuade me to take a riverboat trip on the Thames. We've both put it on our 'to do' list. He seems determined for me to join him. The second message had been sent only fifteen minutes after the first one.

I'm back next week if you fancy it? If you'd rather meet up first to introduce ourselves, let me know. Eddie

I check out his profile again as I sip the warm malt, and wait for its soothing effect to take hold. From his profile pictures, this guy is unbelievably handsome. Although I only joined up to while away the time and plan some fun trips around the capital when Adam has finally gone and my life has to move on, it's hard not to be personally interested in this guy. I zoom in on his face and increase the image size, drawn to his dark piercing eyes. His lips curl with a hint of sarcasm, showing off a row of perfect white teeth.

I envisage Adam's crooked front set which cause him to talk with a slight lisp when he gets angry; an endearing trait when we first met. Now all I see is the angry spittle that escapes past the uneven bite in my direction.

Suddenly a loud squeal from outside breaks the silence. Something is being attacked. A cat will have trapped its prey; most likely a bird or perhaps a fox is the predator. The sound of pain is unbearable. I will the noise to end and suddenly, as quickly as it started, the silence returns. Something is dead, killed by a strong determined enemy. I reach for my jumper, pulling it on over my head. The heating has cut out and the temperature is plummeting.

While I am mulling the possibility of meeting up with Eddie when my cast comes off, my inbox pings again. Spam offers of gadgets I don't want vie with communications from online companies pestering me for custom. Through the flow of rogue emails the name Caroline Swinton floats by in the ether. I leave *Join Me* to check what she wants.

As I lean across to close the slats on the window blinds, I hesitate when I notice that one of the close's residents has arrived home and is staggering around outside their house. A light snaps on upstairs as someone runs down to let them in. I don't really know the neighbours apart from Susan Harper and Olive from next door but decide to leave the blinds open, letting the outside world keep me company a while longer.

I open up Caroline's email and read.

Hi. It was lovely to meet you tonight. Sorry if I acted a bit strangely. I wonder if we could meet up. I need your help. It's rather urgent.

The word *rather* hints at politeness, eager not to pressure but the word *urgent* gets my attention. She's emailing me in my role as PI, of that I'm certain.

Are you around tomorrow? I could pick you up at the Post Office in Church Street around 11am? I'd be really grateful. Best regards, Caroline Swinton

She hasn't told Susan, is my first thought, otherwise she would have offered to pick me up from home. Something tells me that she doesn't want to be seen with me donned in my private detective's hat. I wait a minute and then email back, smiling to myself that I might have found a paying client. I'm a busy sleuth working into the small hours. Dad would be proud.

```
Hi Caroline. Yes, nice to meet. I should be
fine for tomorrow at 11. I can't go far with
my leg in plaster but should be able to hobble
as far as the post office. See you then.
Alexis
```

I sit for a few more minutes, finishing my drink in the gloaming, and swill the melting ice cubes round my mouth. I can get back to Eddie another time. There's no urgency until I'm more mobile.

Once I close down the computer, I feel the shadows lurking in the corners of the room but remind myself that the unsettling night-time fears are a small price to pay for Adam's absence.

The Harpers must be asleep as their house is at last in darkness. The empty house alongside is no longer alone in the gloom but sits in companionable silence with its neighbours. A faint night light next door glows dimly at the Thompsons'. Olive doesn't sleep and says it's her arthritic pain that keeps her awake. She comes down in the night.

I join my neighbours and finally turn out the lights, glad to be sleeping downstairs. It'll only be for two more weeks until my leg is free again. The silence is deafening but oddly comforting as I stretch out on the sofa bed.

My mind is alert in the dark, and gradually ghostly images invade my imaginings. Adam's laughing at me but when I get a better look it is Eddie. He's not laughing. He's smiling. It's a trick of the light. Caroline is dressed as a nurse, drinking champagne and grinning. Her glass is raised in celebration. It has been achieved. She smiles as she produces a bottle which she's been hiding behind her back and lifts it high in the air. The shattering of glass outside awakens me with a start and breaks the nightmare. The cats are out prowling again.

24

ALEXIS

THE NEXT DAY

I see Caroline's car sitting twenty or thirty yards up from the post office. She told me to look out for a red Audi sports model. I notice its engine is still running as I hobble along, cautiously steering my crutches over the wet pavement. She waves out the window with an elegantly gloved hand.

'Hi.' I tap gently on the window when I come alongside. She leans across and opens the passenger door and motions for me to get in. If we are trying to be discreet, this is rendered difficult by the manoeuvring of my cast into the cramped space of the sleek two-seater.

'Ouch.' I grimace. 'Bloody thing. Only another two weeks,' I say once I'm safely ensconced on the heated seats.

'How did you do it?' Her disinterest is palpable. She concentrates on guiding the car out into the road, checking all mirrors several times. Perhaps we're being followed. I'm unsure if her agitated scrutiny is necessary for the few cars that drive along Church Street.

After a short journey, when conversation is limited to small talk about the weather and climate change, we end up in a café in Golders Green; an odd out-of-the-way place down a back alley. Our meeting seems strangely covert.

'Here, let's sit by the window,' Caroline suggests enthusiastically as if we are being offered an interesting vista of a fountained piazza or a chic designer precinct full of busy interesting shoppers and ladies who lunch. Instead the window backs out onto a side street, dull and dingy, with grey rubbish bins lined up along the kerbside awaiting collection.

She orders coffees and launches without preamble into why we are here.

'Jason and I've been married for nearly three years. Jason's my husband, by the way.' She relaxes, relieved, I think, to have got started. 'He's charming, good-looking, extrovert, caring and successful. Women are drawn to him.' I try to visualise her husband. I once thought Adam was all these things. Infidelity, however, soon chips away at perfection. He now seems rather pathetic, and his ineffectual attempts to inveigle his way back into my life are pushing me further away and making me immovably judgemental. I no longer want him back. I wonder at Caroline's loyalty.

'Since we got together, he's had a few casual affairs. Nothing serious, a couple of one-night stands but I've turned a blind eye. What's the alternative?' She drops her eyes, the lids of which are heavily coated with russet-coloured eye shadow, and stirs her coffee. She's in love, in thrall to her husband. I think she's trapped between a rock and a hard place, desperate to hold on to an errant partner when letting him go doesn't seem to be an alternative.

Her earrings are large expensive gold hoops. I admire them while I finger my simple silver studs, before asking, 'Is it different this time?' She looks up with doleful eyes. I'm not fooled. Behind the windows of her soul lies a steely resolve. Caroline's no pussycat.

'I'm not sure but that's what I want you to find out. I'm certain he's seeing someone new.' Outside, the view is dark and depressing and reflects our mood. As a light rain begins to fall, she drops her bombshell.

'I think he's seeing Susan. Susan Harper. I'd like you to follow them.'

25

CAROLINE

I squirm into my black satin dress and slip on the patent red stilettos. Tonight I'll be his prostitute again and he'll remember how it used to be; the erotic role-playing that once turned him on. It's our third wedding anniversary and tonight I won't be sharing him. 'Hi.' I sidle provocatively into the kitchen. I spot the red roses before he spots me. They match my shoes.

'Caroline. Oh my,' is all he says. He's shocked by my appearance. I can't tell if he's happy or disgusted because Jason doesn't do emotional displays; years of practice. I move up close to land a kiss, pushing my breasts into him and bend my left leg nimbly in the air behind me. I strike a pose. The false posturing sums up our life. His body tenses. He doesn't respond but pushes me gently backwards.

'Doesn't it bring back memories?' I put my leg back firmly on the ground, waiting for a reply which doesn't come. I turn away, biting my lower lip hard in an effort to control the hurt. I hear the pop of a champagne cork behind me and feel his arms circle my waist as he hands me a bubbling flute filled to the brim.

'To *Join Me*,' he says. There's a false ring to his tone. The omission of *to marriage* hangs ominously in the air.

'To *Join Me*,' I say and clink my glass against his. As we down our drinks, I try to relax. I remind myself that his forte is to ignore potential contretemps. I wonder at his shallowness but underneath fear hidden depths. I never delve too deeply but tonight we need to talk.

'I'll go and change,' I say. 'I was only having a bit of fun.' Prostitute and wife are an oxymoron; like a dead life or an honest liar. I live the former and he is the latter. I go back upstairs and come down some minutes later wearing twinset and pearls. My newly switched outfit screams sarcasm but it's meant to reflect the anger and hurt. Jason won't comment. He'll avoid rocking the boat.

The bistro in Hampstead is cosy, romantic and dimly lit. A warm smell of garlic and rosemary pervades the room and candles complete the stage set for the night. We came by taxi as I want us both to drink. It'll loosen our tongues and I've planned the conversation.

'I've been thinking,' I begin. Jason is not like other men; he's not threatened by female conversations and takes them in his stride. He never gets goaded to debate or be divisive. I fool myself into believing that he agrees with everything I say, that we're kindred spirits, but I know it's more likely because he doesn't care too deeply about things other than his own basic needs.

When we started dating, quite some time before we tied the knot, he told me he had no real desire to work. A proper job would bore him to distraction. He likes the finer things in life, he told me; a hedonistic lifestyle. Funding such a lifestyle didn't seem to be an issue. I didn't like to ask where the money came from and I didn't really care. Being with him was enough.

'All your ladies need to be married,' I begin. Susan Harper flashes before my eyes. 'The intention was always to avoid the single ladies.' He doesn't know Alexis is newly single but I'll come to that. 'Blackmail will only work on the married ones.' I raise the wine glass to my lips and wait.

'That's fine by me. That's always been the plan, hasn't it? I'm not sure I've had many invites from single ladies anyway.'

'Jason,' I say. He flinches at the imperativeness I imbue by announcing his name in isolation and then by hesitating. He senses gravity.

'I don't want you to see Alexis 201. She's separated and thrown her husband out. I know you've been communicating with her but there's no future in it now.' He won't know I've engaged her to shadow his movements and that she's a private investigator. Employing her will kill two birds with one stone. She can report back on my errant husband and I can keep an eye on her movements. I've indicated to Jason that she can't be blackmailed and therefore a waste of his time. Is he happy with these arrangements?

'It might still be worth it especially if their marriage gets patched up.' It makes marriage sound like a quilt, something easily sewn back together. 'Perhaps one meeting,' Jason suggests. He doesn't like to be railroaded.

'Also I think it's time to put the pressure on Susan 789.'

'How?'

'She's not going to hand over any more money for investments. She's given you plenty already.' I steady my voice. 'A final bit of blackmail should finish her off.' I sound as businesslike as possible, suppressing my inner loathing. I don't want Jason to feel my jealousy or suspect I'm struggling with her image. He doesn't know I've befriended her but that will be my secret for now.

I then deftly change the subject. I wait until the coffee arrives, small strong espressos which will spike us back to the real world. The candle flickers on the table and our romantic interlude is coming to an end.

'Also, I meant to tell you that there's a house I'm going to look at. I think we can afford something bigger. It's in a little cul-de-sac not far from us and it's ready to move into. It's in Riverside Close.' I don't tell him the house is located next door to Susan Harper and that a faked interest in its appeal might enable us to extort a last obscene payout from his neurotic mistress. I can imagine her slitting her wrists, taking an overdose of parac-etamol washed down with cold Chablis in her perfect marbled kitchen. Perhaps I'll help her end it all.

I hang my twinset and slacks neatly back in the wardrobe, resting the pearls beside the bed. They're not the sort of clothes a man rips off. My red chemise clings sadly to my heavy breasts. The television has gone back on. Jason will expect me to join him on the sofa, for a nightcap. We'll snuggle up together, like a contented husband and wife. He has willingly agreed to every-thing I suggested. He lets me believe I'm a smooth operator who manipulates our success with skilled acumen.

I think he plans on leaving me.

26

SUSAN

Perhaps if everything wasn't carrying on quite so normally, the simple rhythmical pattern of family life ticking along like a steady metronome, I wouldn't have time to wallow in the invasive lustful thoughts. It's been six days since Vince and I consummated our passion and until yesterday morning, I'd managed to ignore his persistent attempts at communication. I've tried turning my phone off, keeping away from my laptop and have instead concentrated on housework and pounding the treadmill at the gym.

It's all been a charade. I'm pretending that a one-off sexual encounter can be brushed under the carpet, written off as a careless transgression in an otherwise blemish-free existence. When I read Vince's text yesterday I realised I've been kidding myself.

I'm missing you, badly. Please call or text. I'm waiting.
Vince xx

Logic is no longer working. I'm unable to quell the longing. I've decided to meet him today, one last time, and tell him the truth. I'll beg him to be strong for both of us and tell him that me leaving Roger and the children will never be an option. I'll tell Vince how fond I am of him and how much I've enjoyed our dates but it needs to end here.

∽

I tick the tube stops off one at a time. I'm back in the deep underbelly of the earth being propelled along by something that is outside of my control. A young man is staring at me, or perhaps it's through me. I'm not attractive enough to warrant flirtatious stares today and am more worried that I might look a bit deranged. I certainly feel it. My hair is flying wild, frizzing all around the edges and I notice my reflection bouncing back at me in the glass pane opposite. I don't recognise myself. I close my eyes, count the stops, and try to calm my breathing.

Self-justification has become an art. Since I first met Vince, I try to explain everything I'm doing with logical reasoning. Roger takes me for granted. I pass the blame his way, tell myself that I'll go mad if I have to stay at home and clean one more surface. I don't tell Roger how bored I am but instead play the game of good and dutiful wife. I owe it to him, considering how hard he works. I also realise that carrying on as normal should help divert any untoward suspicions that might arise.

I remind myself that meeting Vince was only meant to be a bit of fun; that's what *Join Me* sells: fun outings around London, albeit with strangers. Even Roger wouldn't begrudge me that. I try to imagine what I'd do if Roger was sleeping with a member of the typing pool, the group of young well-groomed legal secretaries who frequent his offices, but then I know for certain he isn't. How can I be so sure? I'm sure because Roger is a good man; he's old-school, the hunter-gatherer type whose main role in life is to look after his family and he adores the kids. I put the unsettling thoughts to the back of my mind and open my eyes as the train pulls into Green Park.

The underground station provides a modicum of respectability. Smartly dressed ladies and gents who were sitting, quietly contained, unfold their legs and stride elegantly to the doors. I follow behind. I'm one of them. That's how it looks anyway and isn't that enough? Appearances. I can hold my own in that regard. Roger's income allows me to clad my body in designer clothes and expensive accessories. I drape my silken pashmina shawl loosely round my shoulders and pull on my calf-skin gloves. I prepare to join the suave travellers as they battle up towards the ticket gates.

The art gallery is buzzing. It lures me in with its sophisticated frontage. I see Vince straightaway. He stands out from the other attendees in all his perfection and is drinking champagne. I flinch at the expense and grip my bag tighter. Two attractive young women are fawning over him. My insecurities give rise to a rogue thought which makes me wonder why he so quickly excuses himself from their company when he spots me and heads in my direction. I'm not giving him any more money, so I try to push the paranoid thoughts to the back of my mind. I hand my coat to a hovering attendant but keep my gloves on, strangely unwilling to unveil the freckly backs of my hands.

'It's so cold,' I lie.

'Hi, gorgeous.' He smiles and instantly I know why I'm here. Perhaps snatched moments in time are all there is. My stomach lurches and in this one instant, my resolve and good intentions melt away. Sexual longing takes hold. The girls are pretending to look at the paintings, bizarre coloured shapes with ill-defined outlines. The girls are giggling behind their hands, sly unbelieving smirks painted across their perfect faces. Vince hands me a glass of bubbly and leads me to a small display of portraits on a lower level.

'Gregor Mantova is the artist,' Vince tells me as he puts his hand gently across my lower back to propel me along the wall. I'm not interested in the paintings and can't take anything in. I start to believe that the recent addition of fine art to his *Join Me* profile might have been genuine as he shares previously undisclosed cultural enthusiasms.

'He's from Croatia, from a peasant family. One of fifteen children. Imagine,' Vince continues, proud to display knowledge outside of the bedroom. I think I'm being unfair. I'm judging the book by its cover again. I don't like him having extraneous interests although it should make me feel safer. Instead I start to feel smaller, inferior, as he continues his monologue about the history of the Mantova family.

I tell myself that I have Tilly and Noah; they are my family and my biggest achievement. However, I'm unable to care. We mingle with the suited gents and glamorous ladies and watch the gallery owner proudly attach round red *sold* stickers next to the blobs of colour. There are certainly harder ways to earn money, and as I look at Vince, I realise he might have found an easier way to line his pockets.

I start to perspire, overcome all of a sudden by paranoia that he might be using me. Perhaps his investment schemes are a ruse. Perhaps he sees me as a job. But I'm not sure and does it matter? I can always ask him later. For now, all I know is that I'm on a train with faulty brakes, hurtling into the abyss.

'Shall we go?' He smiles, his winning smile. It's warm and familiar. Why shouldn't it be? But the thought of Jekyll and Hyde crosses my mind. I think he always knew I'd meet him again and he's assuming nothing has changed since we last met. He knows I can't resist his charms.

'Yes, let's.' I nod, eager for the inevitable.

The hotel is a couple of streets away and we stroll silently along, our fingers entwined. He kisses me every few yards, pulling me in towards him, as if to reassure me of his feelings. My body is shaking as he leads me blindly once more into his lair.

The passion is all over so quickly again. The climax has teased me with its coming for days and the aftermath of the desperate deed is staring us once again in the face. Vince is relaxed though. He makes tea, boiling water in the tiny kettle, and offers me shortbread.

'I love hotel rooms, don't you?' he says flippantly. I realise that I've most likely footed the bill. I decline the shortbread. 'Shall we have a shower together?' He tries to reawaken my enthusiasm by maintaining the shared intimacy.

'No thanks. I'll pass.' Tears stream involuntarily down my cheeks, large wet silent rivulets. My mascara is running. I don't need to look in the mirror. I want this ghastly moment to stay in my memory; the disgust, the loneliness, the fear. I'm like a heroin addict who has paid for their fixes. In the aftermath of anti-climax, the reality hits home again but this time everything seems worse than before.

'I can't do this anymore,' I sob. I wait for him to throw me a crumb but he stays silent. 'I thought I could.' It suddenly hits me. Sex, no strings attached, isn't possible. Not with this guy anyway. I start to panic. I need to get out of here and not look back. There can't be a next stage; this has to be the end of the road. We're trapped in our own personal cul-de-sac.

'Why? We both need each other.' It feels like a lie. Why does he need me? I cling to the faint hope that it's not about the money. Roger wanted me after all and still does. It's not a total impossibility. Vince comes and takes my hands. He tries to push me back onto the silken sheets. They have an expensive sheen.

'No. I'm going. The children will be home soon; and my husband.' There I've said it. I'm married but Vince knew anyway. He doesn't comment. He doesn't have children, I'm sure. He's too caring and thoughtful to be playing around if he had children dependent on him. I'm almost certain but don't voice my summations. I don't need to know. It won't help.

Vince turns and walks over towards the window as I put my clothes back on and something about his measured stance alerts me that he's going to say something, something of import. Perhaps he's going to open up. I wait for him to speak, not sure what to expect.

'I met your husband on Tuesday.' Vince carries on looking out through the glass, his voice an ominous monotone. It doesn't sound like him. 'In a small wine bar in Lincoln's Inn. He was with a pretty little thing; his secretary, I think.'

The tiny window overlooks a small park and I can see past Vince's body at the neatly manicured gardens down below. He is fully dressed again, armoured in his designer gear, his hair teased to perfection. I can't take in what he's saying. Why was he meeting Roger? Everything's shrouded in fog. How did Vince know I had a husband and where he works?

'Sorry?' I ask. 'What do you mean?' I'm finding it hard to get words out and I can't think straight. He turns back from his vantage point and smiles at me. Although he's smiling with his usual charm offensive, there's a hint of threat in his manner.

'It was all a bit of a coincidence,' he carries on while simultaneously ruffling his hair in the bedside mirror with his fingers.

I don't want to hear. I suddenly think I'm going to be sick. I don't speak but instead lurch towards the bathroom and lock the door. I retch into the toilet bowl. I slump on the cold floor and lean my head against the lid.

'Are you okay, Susan?' Vince sounds concerned. He tries the handle but I don't answer. I need time to think and to get out of here, back to my children and husband. I throw water on my face, scrubbing the make-up from my cheeks and soaping the black mascara smudges away from under my eyes.

After what seems like an eternity, I come out.

'I've got to go,' I say. I move to unlock the bedroom door. Vince must have pulled the chain across when we came in but I don't remember. Although he's done it before, I'm not sure whether he was locking us in or intruders out. I can hear him behind me, teasing with plausible explanations.

'I didn't say anything. I promise. I was interested to meet him, see what he's like. Aren't I allowed to be jealous?' He advances slowly towards me and I fear I'm going to throw up again.

'I'm sorry,' I say as I finally manage to wrench the door open. I don't look back, scared of what I might see. Jealousy, lies, desperation or scorn all seem likely. I need to escape before my whole world crumples to the ground. I career headlong over the empty carpeted landing and on down the stairs into the foyer.

As I exit the hotel, I manage to breathe again, expelling the trapped air from my constricted lungs. I push my way through the heaving throngs back towards the train station and let myself be swallowed up by the seething masses.

27

CAROLINE

It's strange that Riverside Close seems to be at the centre of events unravelling around our lives. That is, my life and Jason's life. It's a strange artificial little enclave. There never seems to be anyone about and the emptiness of traffic and people gives it the feel of a ghost town. A constant buzz of traffic can be heard in the distance but life seems a long way off.

Everything has been cleared out. All the furniture, fixtures and fittings have been removed and a weird echoing presence follows our footsteps from room to room.

'The potential is unquestionable,' the estate agent begins, referring to his clipboard for dimensions. 'You could knock down this wall.' He points, indicating where a stud wall has artificially cut off the kitchen from an L-shaped dining area. Mr Herriott is a slimeball, greased black hair slickly smoothed down against his scalp and his lips are non-existent. There is a slit somewhere near his chin which displays artificially large capped teeth. His smile is robotic, fixed and insincere. Shiny black shoes with sharply pointed toecaps, click click click across the bare floorboards.

'The patio is divine,' he gushes, throwing open the sliding

doors to reveal a marbled landscaped area showcased by an impressive water feature. A large wet concrete ball has water cascading over its surface which I imagine might be tantalising in the heat but at this particular moment makes me freeze as cold air assaults my senses. I wonder if the feature continually streams water, winter and summer, or if Mr Herriott switched it on for effect before my arrival, as if it might clinch the sale.

I'd parked my car a couple of streets away and walked the few hundred yards to the close. I've not yet decided at what point to confront my new best friend, Susan from next door, that I'm considering buying the adjoining property. Perhaps I'll pop in after the viewing. Jason has no idea that I'm here but then he doesn't need to know.

The oil slick of an estate agent guides me through the rooms and eventually leads me up to the master bedroom. I'm excited by my plan of pretending to buy the empty house beside Susan's. Once she hears that we're interested in the purchase and realises who my husband is, Jason and I should be able to extort a final substantial blackmail payment. At last all my planning could be coming to fruition.

'Hey presto!' Mr Herriott throws open the door leading to the en suite bathroom which adjoins the master bedroom. A huge free-standing bath is positioned in the centre of the room and a large walk-in shower extends all the way along one wall. When I gasp and use the word *fabulous*, I can see he is already counting his commission.

Looking out from the upstairs bedroom window, I spot Susan arrive home. She isn't seeing Jason today. Well, he hasn't put it in the diary and he promises me he is meticulous in this regard, although I still wonder. However, with Susan, I think he's been methodical in his loggings. He feels no emotional connection to her. She's much too skinny, and white freckly skin and red hair are not his thing. We laughed last night about this while drinking Dom Pérignon and counting our ill-gotten gains. I can, for the time being at least, ignore the images of intimacy. He would never fall for Susan in a serious way. She's far too easy, and Jason thrives on challenges.

'Thank you, Mr Herriott. I've enjoyed looking around. I'll get back to you.' I tease him with interest but he doesn't let it rest.

'Shall I call you in a couple of days? Perhaps your husband might like to come with you next time.' Herriott is grasping at straws. He's worried that he's not done enough. Perhaps he should have worn the black pinstriped suit to lend him a more professional air and imbue his tour patter with authority. He straightens his pink tie and glances at himself in the mirror on the stairs as we glide past.

On the front steps, he continues selling me the property, expounding on the desirability of living in such an upmarket cul-de-sac while at the same time tries to secure the mortise lock. I ignore the well-rehearsed spiel and simply smile along. He's reluctant to leave me on the driveway but eventually gives in and hops into his saloon, waving with manufactured bonhomie out the window, and snakes his way round the circle and out the other end. I hesitate, take a deep breath and head straight up the neighbouring path and ring the bell.

I hear her footsteps before she opens the door.

'Susan. I hoped you might be in. I've been looking round number four.' I nod towards the *For Sale* sign.

'Come in. Come in.' Her voice is excited and screechy, and grates through the air. 'Great to see you,' she enthuses.

I think she's regretting not looking through the spyhole before letting me in. She wants to be alone, with her thoughts. She's going through the obsessive compulsive stage which accompanies her newly awakened passions. Yet she's desperate to talk to someone, someone anonymous, who doesn't know either Roger or Vince. Somewhere in the back of her mind, she will house the faintest suspicion that I might be that person; the person to whom she can unburden her load.

She leads me into her bright pristine kitchen and reties her long straggly hair back from her face. Sweat glistens through her ghostly white make-up.

'Have you been to the gym?' I wander through the conservatory towards the patio doors which lead into her compact garden. It's the mirror image of number four but without the shiny marble slabs and water feature. Thick Indian sandstone paving leads down to a small hedged planter. There's a dining table covered in black canvas, sitting out the winter months.

'You're thinking of buying the house next door? How exciting.' She sets down two black mugs neatly side by side and starts up the coffee machine. 'Cappuccino?' she asks. I don't turn but continue to look outside at the garden. There's a small gate at the far end. I think there's a similar one in the house I've just viewed.

'Yes please to cappuccino and yes to thinking of buying the house. Where does the gate lead to?' I ask. Susan is distracted and is trying to gather up coffee beans that have spilled from the packet. 'The gate at the end of the garden.'

'Oh that leads out to a small wood with a river running through it. It's what clinched the sale for Roger. Sugar?' She promises to show me out the back after we've had our coffee.

'No thanks.'

We sit at the table rather than at the breakfast bar. It's lower down and it feels like we're about to start a meeting with a set agenda. She describes Roger to me. He's a solicitor working out of Lincoln's Inn, earning lots of money. She pauses, sipping slowly on her coffee, while clasping the black mug. Her knuckles are starkly white against the dark china and her bony hands are those of a skeleton. I prompt her to continue.

'How's Jason?' she asks in an attempt to divert attention away from her husband. I tell her he's working on a small exhibition of paintings; portraits in oil, I lie. I confide that he's waiting for his big break. She's too nice or too disinterested to pry into the financial implications. She's not interested in where our money comes from or how we could possibly afford to purchase the house next door. Her mind is taken up with Jason, or Vince as she thinks of him. It amuses me to consider that it could be her money that would afford us the theoretical deposit. While we've no intention of buying the house, Susan needs to believe we have serious intent. The blackmail payment needs to be substantial and the possibility that we might become her new neighbours should help snare the prize.

It takes about thirty minutes before Susan contrives an opening to steer the conversation on to a more intimate level.

'Marriage isn't easy,' she says. 'It seems ages since I was single and having fun. I love the kids but they're hard work.' At this point she stands up, excuses herself and heads off to the toilet.

'Won't be a minute,' she calls back through the open door. I check my phone. Jason's called twice but I'm keeping it on mute for now. I watch Susan also check her phone which is sitting on the hall table. I know from her anxious expression that Jason will have texted her recently and she's most probably reading his message. I suspect this was the real reason for the trip to the bathroom.

'I know what you mean about marriage. It's bloody hard work.' I carry on once she's come back. 'Ever been tempted to have an affair?' I get up and move away from the table and perch high at the breakfast bar to be nearer my hostess who is flitting skittishly round the kitchen.

Susan doesn't answer at once then suddenly stops and looks at me. 'Yes. Actually I have.'

She leads me out into the back garden and through the small wooden portal at the end. The sun is trying to poke through the clouds which are moving steadily across the sky. I shiver. A ghost is passing overhead. Susan lifts the latch which squeaks loudly and she bemoans how Roger never fixes anything around the house or garden. She'll find the oil later, once I've gone, and loosen the hinges herself.

The riverbed is wider than I'd imagined and the stream babbles actively downstream. The undergrowth all around is wild and untamed. We stand for a moment or two and then decide to turn back. Next time, perhaps when we are neighbours, we'll laugh, we'll wear our boots. As she recloses the gate and secures the latch, she turns to me with a wild look in her eye.

'His name's Vince, by the way.'

28

CAROLINE

A WEEK LATER

We've been invited out for dinner, like a normal married couple. It's been in the diary for a few days and I've been so looking forward to it. Jason's wearing navy slacks and a Ralph Lauren polo shirt. We went shopping earlier, splashing out using our ill-gotten gains and treated ourselves to new wardrobes. *Join Me*, and of course Susan Harper, has afforded us such luxuries.

I'm tired of her sad invitations of friendship and her neediness is driving me mad. The sooner she becomes *finished business* the better. She's started opening up about her secret double life, a life which, unbeknown to her, includes my husband. Vince is so handsome, unnerving, cool and passionate that she can't help herself. She's floundering.

Watching Jason splash aftershave on his perfect face, I cringe at the knowledge of mine and Susan's shared desperation. The only difference is that I got there first. On paper, Jason belongs to me. Susan told me last week, in the strictest of confidence, that Vince is into lucrative investments and needs extra money to secure a deal. She has helped him out.

She embellished her story with untruths for my benefit and

ones she is desperate to believe. Vince will be paying her back, in regular monthly instalments, offering up a healthy interest rate. He wants to share his profits with her and she trusts him completely. I asked about the amounts involved, feeling compelled to check that Jason isn't squirreling away surplus profits for himself. I needn't have worried. The amounts tallied and he seems to be sticking to the agreement of an open and honest sharing of our dirty money.

Susan confided that Vince has met Roger near where her husband works and she's worried it might not be a coincidence. What should she do? I wonder why she's asking me. She wants my approval and any suggestions I might have to help deflect guilt off her own duplicitous skin.

I sat while she scoured her kitchen tops and listened as she prattled on about her secret lover. My eyes were drawn to the plethora of fridge magnets spoiling the perfection. Mickey Mouse and Winnie the Pooh hold in place Post-it notes of significant dates and events. She doesn't need to leave them there and could clear the shiny silver fridge door of all the paraphernalia. But they're left there as an overt display for visitors, and probably for Roger, to show everyone how busy and fulfilled she is with motherhood and family life. She needs to feign chaos now that her OCD symptoms have reached psychotic proportions. She lives in a land of make-believe, a land of Winnie the Pooh and Disney fairy tales, but underneath a dark discontent and passionate frustration are channelled in my husband's direction.

'How do I look?' Jason asks. He knows. I don't need to tell him. His appearance is our job. He says I look lovely and takes me in his arms. I can smell his aftershave, *Muscle*. We chose it together.

'What time are they expecting us?' Jason lifts a soft dark cashmere sweater from the bed and ties it loosely round his bronzed neck; a casual perfection. I lift my jacket from the wardrobe, navy satin, and pull it on over my skin-tight dress. I'm wearing seamed stockings and Jason teases me by saying they make me look like a policewoman. That'll do. Later I'll wait for him to rip them off and tell me he still loves me. I'll believe him until the moon shines through the window and he is fast asleep while I lie awake and count the stars.

Jason has never been to Riverside Close before. I tell him he'll like the Hunters. Sandra, as I pretend my new friend is called, is the typical bored housewife and Robert is her wealthy successful husband. I don't use their real names in case he smells a rat and Hunter as an alternative surname to Harper sprung to mind. Afterwards I'll joke how dreadful he has always been with names and how I can't believe he didn't twig on to my little ruse.

As we sip an aperitif before leaving, I start to enjoy the game I have concocted. I watch as he sips a gin and tonic, oblivious as to what is about to unfold. He will be amused and afterwards we will laugh together at the ridiculousness of our hosts in their phoney make-believe world of lies and deceit. But for a moment I waver. A fleeting doubt casts a shadow. His unfettered enthusiasm to our plans so far has encouraged me to have some fun at Susan's expense but as we haven't come this far before with any of the other ladies, an inner voice is warning me to be careful.

We decide to walk. This means we can drink too much and fuel our enjoyment of the evening. We've always drunk too much when we are together. The heady cocktails feed our games. The night air is crisp and Jason asks me if I've been to this Sandra's house before.

'Yes. I've been round for coffee. You'll like her,' I tease, anticipating the shock that's to come. 'She's tall, longish hair.' I don't embellish the details and leave out the fiery red colour and pale mottled skin. 'A bit skinny for your liking,' I add. I take his hand as we walk along, strolling through the sleepy London side streets, like a couple of young lovers, uncomplicated and together. Only age and the passing of time will dim our passion.

Children might have lifted our love to new heights, or so I've been told, but this won't happen for us; it's not an option.

I grip his hand tighter.

'Let's walk a bit faster. It's bloody cold,' he says, pulling me along. 'Didn't you look at a house for sale near these guys?'

'Yes. The house next door to Sandra's is on the market; number four Riverside Close. I was being nosey.' He knows if I'd been viewing with intent, he would have been invited along and eventually battered into submission if I had fallen in love with it. He doesn't yet realise the real reason for my viewing. Later on I'll own up. We'll plot together the charade of a potential purchase and endeavour to extort one final hefty payout from Susan 789. Jason's meeting with Roger in London was only the beginning. I intend for us to turn the screw much tighter and what better way than by pretending to move next door.

As we start the walk up the close towards the 'ass-end', as I call the circular bulb at the top, my heart starts to thump. I glance at Jason, wondering what he's thinking. These sorts of events are not his thing but he likes me to be happy and it's only for a couple of hours after all.

The straight stretch of road leading into the cul-de-sac feels normal, like any other anonymous London street that keeps moving at either end. The houses here are semi-detached, 1950s brick built with smart neat gardens. They are bland, functional and forgettable. The only detached houses are in the sac at the end where the pretention begins.

Monstrous 4x4 cars block the driveways and a small black Mini sits in the house opposite to the Harpers. Alexis Morley appears to be at home. What a double shock if she were to appear. A pale light peeks through her downstairs curtain and I wonder for a moment at her broken leg. I don't think she told me the truth of how it happened. I'm her new client. While she's tailing Jason, I'll be watching her. Next door I see someone sitting by the window; two people. It looks like an old couple sharing cups of tea. Their curtains are wide open.

'Which one?' he asks, hesitating by the *For Sale* sign. 'Is this the house you looked at?' It's a rhetorical question. It's the only house visibly for sale. 'It's not bad.'

'Here. We're going next door.' I unlink our hands and straighten my dress. I take the lead and walk purposefully the few steps to the front door. Excited children's voices can be heard shouting from within and I raise my eyes heavenward so Jason can note my derogatory reaction. I expect Susan will chase the children upstairs when her guests arrive, shooing them away with extravagant sloppy kisses on their warm bedtime bodies for all to see. She thrives on overt displays of affection and showy concern.

I press the bell and move back down next to Jason who tries to stay one step behind me. He is showing that he's only present by dint of being Caroline Swinton's other half. He's more than happy to tag along and be second fiddle; it's less effort.

The wait is interminable and I hold my breath until Roger opens the door.

29

SUSAN

I've been looking forward to this evening. It has given me something to concentrate on, being a good wife and hostess. I feel calm as I stir the casserole and then put it back in the oven. It is exactly eight when the bell rings. I wonder if it will be Caroline and her husband whom I'm dying to meet or perhaps it will be Roger's partner, Lucas, and his dull appendage Imogen.

I let Roger go and answer the door. I'm surprised how much I've enjoyed my day, shopping, preparing and tidying. I've managed, for the time being, to push aside thoughts of the recent mayhem torturing my psyche. Tilly and Noah have been blackmailed with all manner of treats and have scurried upstairs to start attacking the mammoth bags of sweets and chocolates. Roger has put *Home Alone* on in the children's DVD player and all is as it should be.

I see Caroline first as she crosses the kitchen to embrace me, her new best friend. I turn away from my culinary preparations, waiting as she prepares to introduce her husband.

'This is Jason,' she says, not offering anything further in the way of explanation, purely extending an arm in his direction. She stands aside to let him step forward to meet me; he has been lingering behind and suddenly appears out of the shadows. I proceed to wipe my hands on a dishcloth before I look at him.

'Hi. Nice to meet you,' he says, extending a hand in my direction. A weird sensation suddenly hits me and I feel my knees give way. I have to grip the marble top to regain my balance. This guy is the spitting image of Vince. My first thought is that he might be his double, or stranger still, his twin brother. I hear a buzzing in my brain as I try to focus and collect my thoughts.

'Are you okay, Susan?' Roger is moving towards me. He realises something is wrong and possibly thinks I'm having some sort of an attack; perhaps it's my heart. In the distance I hear the doorbell ring again.

'I'm okay. I'm feeling a bit hot,' I lie, wiping sweat that's gathered across my brow. There's a faint sheath of steam coming from the oven which is clouding my vision. I blink furiously to help me see straight. 'Can you let Lucas and Imogen in,' I hear myself speak. Caroline takes the initiative. She leans across and kisses me on both cheeks, hugging me tightly as befits a greeting from a new best friend. She's waiting for me to acknowledge her husband.

'Jason. This is Susan.' She smiles, waiting for the stranger and me to make physical contact in the way of a hug or a handshake. I extend a hand and feel Vince's firm dry grip. I realise immediately that this guy is no twin or double. He's the man I've been sleeping with.

'Hi,' I say. I'm having trouble staying on my feet; my knees are knocking and my head is spinning. I sit down on one of the high stools while Vince, or Jason, or whoever he is, offers me his hand by way of assistance. I'm frightened I might be suffering a full-blown panic attack. Perhaps I'm dreaming and will wake up any minute, jolted violently back to reality. There's a pounding in my ears; my heart is thumping as it tries to break out. Roger returns with the newly arrived guests and asks again if I'm okay.

'Are you sure?' He looks concerned and pours me a long glass of cold water. 'You don't look well,' he says, putting the palm of his hand on my forehead to check for a temperature. 'You're definitely feeling hot.'

'Honestly, I'm fine. I came over a bit strange but I'm okay now.'

Lucas proceeds to step forward and kiss me, followed closely by his wife but I can't concentrate on what is being said. I need to get a grip. Suddenly Tilly screams down from upstairs and I push past Roger.

'I'll go,' I say. 'You stay with the guests. I'll be back down in a minute.'

'If you're sure,' Roger replies, concern etched on his face.

I climb the stairs and put my head round the bedroom door. Noah has fallen asleep, slumped on top of his sister who is desperate for him to move.

'Get him off me, Mummy,' she demands. The popcorn cartons are empty with rogue traces of the sugary husks strewn over the bed cover but Tilly is still eagerly chewing her way through rainbow-coloured sugar shapes. I sit down and pull her close, squeezing her so tightly that she yelps. 'Ouch, that hurts,' she protests. I gently lift Noah up and place him in his own bed next to hers, pulling the duvet round his tiny body.

'Just ten more minutes, Tilly, and then lights out.' I close the door behind me, leaving it slightly ajar but I can't go back downstairs yet. Instead I go into the bathroom and lock the door. What's Vince doing in my house? Why is he with Caroline? He can't be her husband, surely. He's not married. Or is that how I had willed it to be?

My neck is exuding salty sweat which makes the back of my hair stick together in clumps. I stare at my face in the mirror. My eyes are enormous, bulging out of their sockets, giving the illusion of insanity. Perhaps I'm hallucinating through the first signs of madness. I hear a gentle rap at the door. It's Roger.

'Susan? Are you okay? I'm worried about you. Open the door, please.'

I hesitate because I can't decide what to do. Perhaps Roger can sit round the table on his own, entertain the guests until the food is finished, and then make excuses to cut short the evening. But I know he won't do this. He's too kind and caring to leave me on my own, especially if he thinks I'm not well.

In a hoarse whisper, I tell him I'll be down shortly.

'Turn the oven off, please, I'll be fine. I need a moment.' Why am I lying to Roger? He's the only one I can trust.

I throw water over my face and drag a brush through my hair, reapplying lipstick and a couple of blobs of colour to my cheeks.

Everyone is talking quietly, sitting by the open fire and drinking Prosecco when I reappear. Caroline is the first to speak.

'Are you okay? You look dreadful. Is it flu?' She seems genuinely concerned. 'Listen, we'll go. You look as if you need to get to bed.' She's a good friend or is she? What isn't she telling me? I don't know anymore. What hasn't she told me? That her husband is unbelievably handsome, like some James Bond stand-in? What did I expect her husband to look like? I don't know but certainly not like Vince. I wasn't prepared for him to be Vince. I got to him first; I found him and he's my lover, not hers.

'I'm fine, honestly. Just a hot flush,' I announce, putting an end to possibilities of their early exit. I want to find out what's going on. I go back to the oven and busy myself with culinary preparations. The conversation behind me has started up again and levity has entered the proceedings, everyone relieved that the hostess is feeling better.

Out of the corner of my eye, I can see Vince (I can't bring myself to call him Jason) standing beside Imogen and jealously notice her rapt attention as she coquettishly hangs on his every word. I haven't yet dared to look properly at him. Lucas, Imogen's husband, with his balding pate and thick-rimmed glasses pales into insignificance beside Vince. The kitchen feels unbelievably hot in the enclosed space. Caroline hands round the canapés in deference to my dizziness and then lifts the avocado and lobster salad starters on to the table. She asks me for matches to light the candles.

'I love the smell,' she enthuses as she bends over to light the wicks, inhaling the vanilla aroma. I watch her, relaxed, helpful and unconcerned, as she moves round the room and I'm momentarily startled at the similarity in her manner to that of Vince. Perhaps marriage has helped clone their personalities.

The dining area is soon in darkness apart from the candles with their romantic glow. Roger wants to turn the lights up, 'See what we're eating.' He laughs companionably with Lucas. Imogen is clinging like a limpet to Vince's side. The lights stay dimmed as we sit down at the table. The place names now seem ridiculously pretentious in their solid silver holders, an ostentatious attempt to showcase my worth as a hostess.

'Sit where you like,' I say. Vince's place name is next to my own. Seeing the word *Jason* makes my stomach churn. I remember I felt excited to be meeting Caroline's husband for the first time. I'd heard so much about him. Or had I heard anything? I can't remember. Vince sits down, checking his name in the holder and smiles at me.

'Jason,' he says. 'That's me.' He frowns in my direction, owning up to the little white lie. But it wasn't a little white lie. It was an enormous whopper of deceit.

'I'm beside Susan,' he says, pulling his chair out. 'Perhaps she'll give me seconds.' Everyone laughs on cue. The drink is relaxing the mood but as I glug from my glass, I fear it might push me dangerously close to the edge. What's happening? I can't work it out.

'Bon appétit!' Roger raises his glass, takes a sip, and waits for me to sit. I can't eat. I push the delicacies round my plate, scared to put anything into my mouth.

'Aren't you hungry?' Vince turns, encouraging me to relax and for one bizarre moment I think he might be in on events. But why? Why would he come along and risk blowing the lid off our affair unless he and Caroline are in on the ruse together? Caroline and Jason? Bonnie and Clyde? This is too preposterous. Roger has switched the music on in the background. Chopin nocturnes float softly through the air as a gentle hum of conversation fills the room.

'I didn't know,' he says. Vince can read my mind. My initial instinct is to look over at Caroline but she's talking to Lucas, engrossed in anecdotes pertaining to the legal court system; juries versus high courts. She isn't looking at us. 'I promise,' he continues. I believe him. I'm jealous of his ability to eat. I watch his strong brown hands with their perfectly manicured nails work the food on his plate, cutting delicate mouthfuls one at a time. He finishes before I have started. Perhaps his ability to eat with such relish is a clue.

'That was delicious,' he says for everyone to hear. I catch Caroline's eye. It's a fleeting thing but she's definitely been staring at me, watching my reactions.

'It's strange,' Roger says when there's a momentary lull in the conversation, 'but Jason and I met only a week or so ago in Lincoln's Inn. By pure coincidence.' Roger's putting his last mouthful of lobster to bed and is looking at Jason. 'The City Flogger pub, I think it was,' he says. Roger glances from one of us to the other. Is he jealous of Jason? Does he suspect? Or is he purely making polite conversation?

I think in my earlier shocked state, I vaguely remember the two men laughing at how they had already met. What an amazing coincidence. They had been sitting at adjacent tables in a pub, Jason waiting for a friend when he had joined in a conversation Roger had been having with his secretary about the cost of living; fresh produce as opposed to ready-made meals. He had joined them in a drink.

Caroline is unusually quiet and doesn't partake of the conversation. I wonder why. She's keeping quiet in deference to Jason but it seems out of character. She is very verbal when we are alone.

I insist everyone stays at the table while I tidy up and serve the main course. I want the evening to be over, I need to think and work out what's going on. Vince doesn't obey my wishes but follows me into the kitchen.

'Here. Let me help you.' He brushes up close and I feel a desperate longing. I stand by the oven, close my eyes and imagine him hard inside me. He stands behind and teases me with his presence, coming back and forth from the table laden with dirty dishes. Perhaps we could escape unnoticed and have wild abandoned sex in the eaves of our attic. The thought makes the panic return.

Roger is soon pushing his way between us. 'Jason. You go and relax and top up your glass. I'll help Susan.' Did Roger notice? What was there to notice?

He isn't encouraging anyone to have a nightcap like he usually does. He asks me as soon as the dessert course is over how I'm feeling. He senses that I'm still not great and asks the guests if they would mind calling time as he thinks I need to get to bed.

'I'm sorry,' I manage. 'I've not been much of a hostess but I'll be better next time.' My smile is weak, perpetuating the myth that I'm coming down with some seasonal virus and as everyone gets up to go, I watch Roger direct Caroline to the cloakroom.

'Susan.' Vince is beside me, and for a few minutes we are alone. 'I'm sorry,' he says, gently putting his hand on my back. I feel the jolt of electricity. 'I really didn't know. You do believe me, don't you?' He's looking at me, staring into my eyes or is it through me? I can't be sure. I wonder what he didn't know. That he was coming to our house for dinner? That Caroline knew me and Roger?

'It doesn't matter,' I reply. 'I don't know who to believe anymore.' I see Roger return and glance over in our direction. Vince has moved his hand from the small of my back and I'm worried Roger might have noticed. I move quickly into the hall to collect the coats and hear my voice, loud and chirpy, belying my supposed sickly demeanour.

'Thanks for coming,' I say. I tense, waiting for the goodbye kissing ritual.

Vince hangs back and waits for the other guests to cross the threshold into the night air. I close my eyes as he leans in to kiss his hostess on the cheeks. His smell is so familiar, strong and musky. He grips my arms and whispers in my ear. 'I'll call you.'

Caroline is watching. I can see her, over the top of Vince's shoulder, as she rubs her hands together with the cold. Or is it in victory?

Suddenly Roger is by my side, extending his hand towards Vince. 'Goodnight.' There's a sense of finality and coldness in Roger's tone.

'Goodnight, Roger, and thanks for a great evening.' Vince turns his collar up and accepts Caroline's outstretched hand as he catches up with her. For a moment I wish I was the one walking away with him.

The house seems strangely empty now the guests have left. Roger tells me to leave the clearing up until the morning after I've had a good night's sleep. We go upstairs together and neither of us speaks until Roger finally makes a comment.

'It seems a bit of a coincidence that I've met Jason before.' Roger is brushing his teeth and spitting words out between strokes, using the activity to augment his air of indifference. White globules of toothpaste splat into the sink. 'They're a strange couple, don't you think?'

'In what way?' I'm eager to hear his opinions; get an objective viewpoint. Perhaps he'll be able to shed some light on Caroline and Jason's relationship. Roger is astute. Also I've a faint inkling he might suspect something, but I can't imagine what he could have gleaned from the evening's events.

'I think she wears the trousers. He seems rather weak and a bit vacuous.' Roger wipes his mouth vigorously with a hand towel.

'What gives you that idea?' I don't see Vince as part of a couple. Roger does.

'She does most of the talking and he doesn't add much. What does he do for a living? I don't think he said.' Roger looks at me as if I'll know the answer.

'I've no idea. Banking or something, I think. Caroline hasn't talked much about him.' This is true. I still have no idea what he does for a living, apart from investing in lucrative schemes with my money. I want Roger to stop talking but he carries on like a dog with a rat in its mouth.

'He doesn't half fancy himself. He looks as if he does nothing but work out and lie in the sun.' Roger replaces the towel on the rail and straightens it neatly, rounding off the belittling finale with, 'I suspect Caroline is the one with the brains.'

I lie in bed watching as Roger gets into his pyjamas and wonder how we might have appeared as a couple to Vince. Who does he think rules our roost? Roger climbs into bed and turns to kiss me as he does every night before clicking off the bedside lamp.

'Goodnight. A great meal by the way.'

Five minutes later, he's fast asleep, letting out gentle contented little puffs of air. I lie on my back and stare at the ceiling. Will Vince be snoring alongside Caroline or will they be making love, rounding off a romantic Saturday night?

As I lie next to Roger's slumbering form, a dull wave of depression washes over me. He's my partner, not Vince. I should be grateful for my lot but instead feel an overwhelming sadness that I've reached the future too soon.

30

ALEXIS

Although I'm moving with measured care, getting the cast off yesterday has lifted my spirits and I'm starting to feel more confident about attacking the future.

My first trip across the doorstep is to visit Olive, who has been watching over me from her vantage point by the window. I hobble down our driveway and up the short pathway leading to the Thompsons' house. I relax when I reach the front door, lean against the frame and put all the weight on my good leg. I peer through the glass panels and press the bell. Olive usually comes on the first ring, spritely, eager for company, but today I watch as her frail body inches its way along the walls. She stops every few steps to catch her breath.

'Coming. Just a minute.' Her voice is faint and a hacking cough suddenly wracks her body. There doesn't seem to be any sign of Bob. His car's not in the driveway.

'No rush. It's only me, Alexis. Take your time!' I yell back, cupping my mouth close to the glass with my hands.

I pull back while she unlocks the mortise and unfastens the chain.

'Come in,' she whispers, her smile weak, through dry cracked lips. 'I hoped it was you.'

'Oh, Olive. You look dreadful. Here let me help you.' I step inside and taking her arm, we shuffle back towards the sitting room.

'You need to see a doctor. That cough sounds as if it's lodged in your chest. Let me go and put the kettle on. Is Bob out?'

'He's gone to the pharmacist to see what they'll give him. I hate doctors. Lots of hot liquids should do the trick.' She slumps into her chair and closes her eyes. Her eyelids twitch. I head for the kitchen but hear a faint mumbling sound behind me.

'Listen, don't try to talk. I wanted to pop by, now that my leg is out of plaster. It's such a relief to be out of the house.'

Olive doesn't answer but her laboured breathing filters through the quietness.

I return and set down a mug of tea beside her when suddenly she stretches out a frail hand and places it on top of mine. Her beady little eyes poke out from under the heavy lids.

'Don't worry about me. I'll be fine. You need to take care of yourself.' She looks at me, unblinking. It's a warning. 'Make sure Gary stays with you as long as possible.'

'He's promised. Well, at least until he has to go to Spain in a couple of weeks. He badly needs a holiday.'

'I've been watching out for you. I've seen Adam lurking around when you're not about. Be careful. That's all I'll say. Stay alert.' Wet pus oozes from the corners of her eyes, the left one red and swollen from an infection. I want to hug her, tuck her into bed and look after her. She's like the mother I no longer have. She closes her eyes and seems to drift off into an uneasy slumber. It's my cue to move nearer. I whisper very gently, 'I'll be careful. I promise. Get some sleep and I'll check in on you later.' I kiss her soft downy head before I thread my way, as lightly as my leg will allow, towards the hall.

With a glance backwards at her fragile body, I quietly close the front door behind me, reluctant to leave her but she insisted that Bob will be back soon and that he's good in a crisis. She tried to smile at this thought but the effort brought the phlegm back up.

I wave through the window from outside in the garden, pressing my nose against the pane in case she's watching but there's no movement from the chair. She's already fast asleep.

When I get back from Olive's, I settle myself in the study and prepare to spend the rest of the morning sifting through emails and reconnecting with the outside world. I want to move forward, get on with the new business and my own life. Adam has become less persistent in his attempts to communicate and I'm hopeful, though not convinced, that he might finally have got the message that our marriage is over and I won't be taking him back.

It's been a couple of days since I checked my emails and notice straightaway that there are several notifications from *Join Me*.

```
Hi. It's me again! I'm going up to London
tomorrow on business and thought it might be a
chance to meet up. Perhaps a quick drink at
King's Cross around midday — The Waggoner's
Arms? Eddie 300
```

A second email had come through ten minutes later. Both came through this morning.

```
Bring your diary and we can check dates for
```

that trip on the Thames, if you still
fancy it.

I reread the messages and wonder whether I should reply. The challenge of taking a train up to London is appealing and would give me a chance to get back out there, start living again. My mobile suddenly breaks the silence, fiercely accusing. Adam's name appears but I ignore it. The divorce papers will have landed on his desk and automatically I glance outside to check that he isn't back, lurking on the doorstep.

The postman is walking around the otherwise-deserted close, dropping bills and circulars through letterboxes and his presence offers me a weird sense of comfort. I'm about to call Gary to find out when he'll be back from the lock-up when a ping heralds a voicemail.

Have received the divorce papers. If you think I'm going to sign these you're well off the mark.

Adam's tone is calm and monotone but with definite threat in the delivery.

Olive has somehow managed to reach the front door again to collect her letters from the postman. This is a ritual every morning as she watches out for him. In her left hand, she's grasping her little black diary and she manages, ever so slightly, to lift her arm in the air and wave across at me. I'm on her mind and she is keen to remind me.

I leave a voicemail for Gary, asking what time he'll be back and as I end the message, my phone vibrates. Adam. I turn it off and instead begin to type.

Hi Eddie. Thanks for the message. I've had my
leg in plaster for a while (long story) and am
just about mobile again. Could perhaps manage
the length of King's Cross but a river trip is

```
definitely not on the agenda. Where's The
Waggoner's Arms?
```

A reply bounces straight back.

```
At the end of the station concourse, next to
the sushi bar. Past the Harry Potter platform
(perhaps we could pop in there afterwards??)
```

```
Ok. One drink but Harry Potter's definitely
not my thing. See you around midday. Alexis
```

~

I'm very early. It's only eleven when I step onto the platform at King's Cross. I check my phone, nervously, every five minutes. It's automatic.

Adam went suspiciously quiet last night and I couldn't sleep imagining him hammering on the front door in the small hours or climbing in through some casement window, forcefully prised ajar. Although Gary snored loudly on the other side of the wall, it offered slim comfort. I doubt he would have woken even if there'd been a monumental earthquake. He sleeps like a child.

Today Adam will be in touch again. I'm certain. He doesn't like being ignored but I'm not sure what his next move will be. A couple of hours away from the house should bolster my confidence and help put paid to the macabre imaginings.

As I hobble along the walkway and scan the coffee franchises for possible sightings of my online contact, butterflies in my stomach hint at misgivings. I remind myself that the public nature of our arranged meeting, in broad daylight, should allay the fears, but it is hard not to wonder at the sanity of meeting up with a complete stranger.

I pass a mirror outside an accessories shop and am glad that I underdressed. I tousle my short hair, spiking the ends upwards, and straighten the collar of my beige leather jacket. It feels great to be back in jeans and although it was a struggle with footwear, I've managed to squeeze my swollen left foot into a flat brown ankle boot.

In the mirror, over my shoulder, I spot him. I'm sure it is him. He stands out from the hoard of travellers snaking back and forth from the trains as he casually picks up a paper from a kiosk. He is wearing a pale-yellow jumper and even from this distance I can see the expensive cut of his clothes and the glowing suntan. Two teenage girls nudge each other as he passes by. I'm tempted to hop back on to the train when my phone rings. It's Gary but I decide to listen to his message later and shove the phone back into my pocket.

As Eddie moves on and exits the concourse, he turns right in the direction of the pub. I shadow him from a distance, keeping at least fifty yards between us. Suddenly pins and needles shoot up my left leg and an onset of cramp makes me wince and forces me to take a brief respite on a bench. I massage furiously until the pain abates, and when I look up again, Eddie has disappeared from view. The station clock is showing 11.45am.

31

ALEXIS

At midday on the dot, I walk into The Waggoner's Arms. A young woman is seated next to Eddie, smiling coquettishly in his direction, crossing and uncrossing slender legs while he appears to be captivated by her bubbly flirtation. He spots me and stands up straightaway, excusing himself and moving in my direction.

'Alexis?' His smile is bright and easy, and I find myself instantly questioning what his secret is. This guy doesn't need to invite anonymous people for sightseeing trips around London.

'Eddie?'

He offers his hand and we shake like business colleagues meeting for the first time.

'Come. Let's go through here. It's not as busy.' He gently puts his arm on the small of my back and leads me through to a snug in the far corner where there are two vacant seats. 'What do you fancy to drink?' he asks.

'White wine. Just a small glass please.'

'Coming up.'

As he goes to the bar to get the drinks, I feel uneasy at what I might have got myself into. Everything seems a bit surreal. There's a steady background hum of transient conversations as travellers while away the hours between journeys. I take out my phone, suddenly remembering that Gary left a voicemail. Three voicemails are blinking at me. I dial in to listen.

Alexis. You need to come home. Adam's here and has barged his way in. He's threatened me with legal action if I don't get out.

Alexis. I've had to leave. I've taken my clothes and things. Adam's gone mad and even swung a punch in my direction. You need to get back. Good luck. Will talk later.

Hi Alexis. I'm home. The last message is from Adam.

'Problems?' Eddie's hovering over our table as a waitress wipes down the sticky surface. Eddie is holding aloft two large glasses of white wine.

'Sort of,' I answer, snapping shut the cover on my phone. I'm anxious to go home but as Eddie sits down and sets the wine in front of me, I realise I need to finish my drink first.

'Cheers,' he says, waiting for me to lift my glass to his. I'm not sure what he thinks we're celebrating but the cold wine tastes good and it will hopefully calm my nerves.

'Cheers.'

Eddie bandies small talk about the weather, bustling train stations and unknown destinations. He grins teasingly into my eyes as he toys with the words 'unknown destinations'. He's flirting and I feel uneasy. Ted Bundy springs to mind. All the ladies he battered to death had followed him willingly to their fate; his looks and self-assurance sucked them easily into his lair.

'What about you? Don't you ever fancy hopping on a random train and taking off somewhere?' Eddie asks. This guy has the hallmarks of *too good to be true* tattooed on his forehead. He is certainly not my type; much too smooth and synthetic.

'Yes. Sometimes it would seem like the perfect answer.' I sip, self-conscious, unused to intense male scrutiny from someone other than Adam. 'Problem is, I'd probably not come back.'

Underneath the façade, there's something oddly childlike and uncertain about this guy. My detective mind toys with the idea that it could be the perfected mask of a prolific serial killer. As the wine takes the edge off my fears, I sit and listen, let him talk. Perhaps like me he craves a moment of escapism, a moment away from the real world.

I try to ignore my phone as it beeps again and Eddie raises his eyes in mock exasperation. He knows I have to leave and manages not to look disappointed or upset, rather understanding.

'If you need to go, don't worry. It's fine by me.' He smiles. 'Also if you want to talk about it, I'm happy to listen.'

'Thanks for the offer but maybe another time. I'm sorry but I do need to get going.'

As I stand up and down the last of my wine, Eddie lifts my jacket off the back of my chair and holds my jacket open. He's the perfect consort, smooth and considered but reeks of plastic. I think of Ken and Barbie dolls, the ideal prototypes of children's aspirations. Eddie doesn't seem real. There are no rugged edges.

'Thanks. Sorry again,' I repeat, uncomfortable at the impending goodbyes. I needn't have worried. Eddie leans across with practised aplomb and kisses me on the cheek. His subtle aftershave hums expense and as I walk away, his scent wafts after me.

I wave a nervous hand back in his direction. As I descend the steps from the bar back onto the main station concourse, I shiver. I don't look back.

Sitting on the return train to Hampstead, I look out the window and play over in my mind the conversation about running away and the lure of the unknown. I wonder what Eddie is running away from. Something about his physical perfection conjures up memories of the Stepford Wives, the perfectly formed robotic spouses with flawless complexions and faultless manners, created to pander to their husbands' every whim. Adam and I had watched the movie together and I remember his pointed asides about how he preferred the more human imperfections of a real wife. He was, of course, referring to me.

I slow down as I head back up Riverside Close and see the lights are on downstairs in our house. It's still our house; it's in joint names. I'm not sure why the lights are on as it is not yet dark. Perhaps Adam wants to welcome me back by pandering to my love of wasted electricity on romantic atmospheric lighting.

Olive is watching as I walk past. Bright yellow pansies in her front flower bed, which she planted a few weeks ago, herald the early onset of spring. I brace myself to walk the last few steps to our front door.

'Welcome home.' Adam has flung the door wide. The gesture is designed to reflect a mood of all-encompassing magnanimity. That's what it feels like. His muddy trainers have been neatly placed outside in deference to my constant carping that I don't want mud brought into the house. They're a visual conciliatory gesture which bolsters my confidence that he'll be in a mellow mood after a jog round the woods.

'Hi,' I say.

'I've put on the kettle. Green tea?' He waves at Olive. This is another obvious peace offering as he has made his dislike of our neighbour blatantly apparent since his birthday celebrations. He nudges the door closed behind us and we head towards the kitchen.

'Can we talk?' he begins. I fill a glass of cold water from the tap, looking out the back window towards our unkempt garden, unsure of where he wants to go with the conversation. 'It's all over with Debbie. I told her it's you I love and want to be with.' He is still after forgiveness and his plan is to make amends, make things better.

Without turning round, I decide to tell him it's all over and there's no going back.

'Adam. I want a divorce. I'm sorry but it's too late.' Although I'm scared of the physical assaults, his words can't hurt me.

He doesn't speak straightaway. I hold the rim of the sink which is wet where he has been cleaning round the surfaces and automatically flinch when he puts his arms round my waist and tries to pull me back towards him.

'I'm really sorry. I'll prove it; make it up to you. I promise.' A heavy stench of sweat oozes from his pores and the once-familiar earthy smell churns my stomach. There is no familiar hint of aftershave to woo my waning passions. I swallow the cold liquid and look out at the straggling weeds, noticing how they have attached themselves fiercely to the fence.

'The back garden needs clearing,' I say, changing the subject. His empty promises are too late but it isn't the time for confrontation. I need to be patient, work out a plan to get him out without more violence.

'I'll do it at the weekend. I promise,' he repeats. He fills mugs and jiggles teabags around before throwing them in the bin, dripping the wet dregs on the top. He thinks he can win me back with a few easy words and a cup of strong tea. Not this time.

'By the way, this envelope was pushed through the door. It's marked *private and confidential*.' I hear the barely concealed sarcastic tone as he hands me a large brown envelope, addressed simply to Alexis Morley.

Adam waits for me to open it but instead I turn and head upstairs, taking the envelope with me. I then proceed to move my stuff back into the spare room. He knows not to follow but he will hear the quiet determined movements which mark my departure from the marital bedroom. Gary, in his hurry to leave, has left behind a pair of shoes, and a couple of his T-shirts lie strewn on the guest room floor.

I close the door to the spare room around 10pm. Adam and I watched some television in silence, sharing a sandwich and glass of wine, before I made my excuses and disappeared upstairs. I turn on the bedside lamp and lie across the bed, trying to curb the anxiety that accompanies the presence of Adam back in the house. The brown envelope is sitting on the bedside table and I know it will be the photos of Jason Swinton, Caroline's husband. She promised I would have these by today at the latest.

I peel back the brown seal, intrigued to see what her husband looks like. It will be my first real job and as a cheque floats out onto the bed for three hundred pounds made payable to 'Alexis Morley', I realise I'm finally in business. I scan the enclosed pictures, six in total, and feel the weirdest sense of unease. I'm looking at Eddie. It is Ted Bundy in all his glory. In one picture he's standing on a beach somewhere far off and exotic, dressed in shorts and T-shirt, beaming at the photographer. There are sunglasses perched on top of his unkempt thick brown hair. In the second one he's at a writing desk, his head turned sideways, twiddling a pen between his lips. It's attempting to showcase another side of his personality. Then he's diving into a swimming pool, not looking at the camera but his perfect torso is rippling for the lens.

The pictures are trying to tell me a story. Caroline is desperate for me to understand her obsession. As I turn the pictures around and look through them again, I can't believe what I'm seeing. I don't believe in coincidences. That's the first rule of detective work. What am I looking at? Why have the pictures arrived after I've met up with Eddie, or Jason, as I now know he's called? The questions swim around in my head.

There's a gentle knock at the door. Before I have time to hide the photos back in the envelope, Adam's voice whispers through the barrier. 'Night, Alexis. I love you.' He's not stupid. He knows not to come in and when to back off. He thinks he's working me.

'Goodnight.' I wait for him to move away before I go to the window to draw the curtains.

The street lights outside are dim. They emit a faint orange glow which creates a hazy fog inside the circle. It's as if a warm suffocating blanket has covered the close; bright enough to illuminate the pathways and gardens but too dim to pick up detail. I'm not sure why I want the lights to be brighter. They were designed to be dim and unobtrusive and not to interfere with night-time slumber. I watch the cats prowling, stretching their limbs as they stalk the area like little sentries; stealthy watchmen of the night. I reluctantly close the curtains in desperate need of a good night's sleep.

32

CAROLINE

I don't think there is such a thing as companionable silence, of being so in tune with your soulmate that talking is unnecessary. As we walk away from Susan and Roger's house, Jason is several steps ahead of me, pulling further away and the unnatural quiet is deafening. This is not a companionable, but rather an accusatory silence.

'What's the hurry?'

He ignores me and speeds up, putting more and more distance between us. The night air is bitter and a chill wind is biting at my ears. Jason refuses to answer but continues on his mission. I decide to take my heels off and jog after him in stockinged feet. The icy ground turns my feet numb and I brace against the shock of pain but this is the only way I can think of to get him to slow down; to listen. He turns and looks at my feet.

'Christ. Put your shoes on. You'll catch your death.'

I slowly slip my feet back into my heels when I'm certain I have his attention and he won't run off.

'Hey. I'm sorry. Okay? I thought it would be a bit of fun, putting her on the spot like that. There's no harm done.'

Jason walks again, this time much more slowly but he's

trying to curb a seething anger that has taken hold. I can tell from his rigid gait. I know him too well.

'We agreed you'd go and bang into Roger, so what's the difference?'

His step falters.

I continue. 'Please talk to me.' I stop walking. I need to make him speak. 'If she freaks out a bit more, we'll get that one last payment. Then we'll let her off the hook. I thought that was the plan?' I stare at the back of Jason's head until he finally comes to a halt. I hold my breath.

'That wasn't about the money tonight though, was it? You wanted to humiliate her, put her on the spot. Well, it worked.'

Why does he care? I'm certain he hasn't got feelings for her. We are the partnership, the team. She is merely a pawn on our shared chessboard.

'Why do you suddenly care?' I don't want to hear the answer but carry on like a rat in a trap, up against a wall. 'Perhaps you do care. Is that why you're so cross?' I scream as he walks on. 'Stop. Answer me.'

Silence. He ignores my desperate pleas.

It takes us about twenty minutes to get home and I soon fall behind again, unable to keep pace in my heeled shoes but the fear inside me increases with every pace of his measured footsteps.

As soon as we go through our front door, Jason heads upstairs while I hover in the kitchen. I can hear him moving around in the bedroom. He's opening cupboards, drawers and I hear a distinctive thud on the floor. I know what the noise is but please God, don't let it be what I'm thinking. Please God, no. Don't let him be leaving.

I creep up the stairs, clutching the banister for support. I watch him from a vantage point on the landing through the bedroom door which is slightly ajar. He is neatly folding a jumper, patting down the sleeves before setting it carefully into the small suitcase. There's a pair of jeans and a couple of T-shirts on the bed and he's started to extract underwear from the bedside drawers.

'What are you doing?' I hold back for a second before I go in. I'm now scared I might lose it completely. 'Let's talk, please. Where are you going? Why?' Perhaps there is more to this than Susan Harper. It was meant as a joke, a prank at her expense but he seems to be taking it to heart.

'I need some space,' he says. He carries on with the packing. As he goes to zip up the suitcase, he looks at me and smiles. Jason doesn't do confrontation. His smile is his weapon when we argue. He knows it'll make me back off. 'Just for a few days. Don't worry, I'll be back. Promise.' With that, he heads into the en suite and picks up his toothbrush and other toiletries. I follow close behind.

'Why?' I don't understand. 'I've said I'm sorry. I'll fix it.' But I don't know how to put it right or what I'm supposed to fix. I hear the panic in my voice.

'I told you I don't like being tied down and I won't be used, Caroline.' His use of my name at this point terrifies me and when he turns round, the look in his eyes tells me what I already know. I've gone too far.

'You can't control me and, to be honest, I'm not sure how far I want to go with all this anymore.'

Jason has always wanted an easy life, the good things with no strings attached. Money without emotional upheaval has always been his driver, and my own insecurities have made me temporarily forget what makes him tick. I need to back pedal, give him some space and perhaps rethink our approach to the business. All I know, as I watch him, is that I can't let him go; not now, not ever. He zips up his case with a measured finality and lifts it off the bed.

'Where'll you go? Please don't go back to Francine,' I beg. Begging is my only option. If I shout at him he'll clam up before disappearing off into the sunset. Jason won't get angry; an argument will render him mute. His wrinkle-free complexion is due to a lack of emotion that accompanies an adult life free from all responsibility. Worries are brushed under the carpet like pesky dust mites. Money lets him do this and Francine and I have made it possible.

However, I need to know where he's going. He seems confident of another open door with a warm welcoming reception. He walked away easily enough from Francine, so why not from me? Perhaps I'm overreacting, being paranoid. We're married after all.

'Please. We can sort this out. When Susan pays up, we'll move on. Remember I'm only pretending to buy the house next door so she'll panic and then you won't have to see her again. It's a job, remember.' I hate my voice. It's become whining.

He sets his case down and walks across and takes me by the shoulders.

'I'll be back. Honestly. I'll probably kip at Francine's for a couple of nights till I get my head straight but I'll call.' He kisses me on the lips and holds me tight. 'It's not your fault. It's all getting on top of me. There's no such thing as easy money.'

I stand in the doorway, blocking his exit.

'You can't go. I love you.' My tears stream in torrents down my cheeks. He wipes the heavy wetness away and as he kisses me hard on the lips, the moisture mingles with the wet saliva.

'I know,' he says. He doesn't say 'I love you' back, simply that he knows. He knows I love him and that I'm at the place of no return. He lifts me roughly onto the bed and soothes my torment with the only way he knows how. This is his skill, his talent. As I give myself up to the moment, lying naked below him, the images of the numbered women scream past like haunting tormentors from hell.

I torture myself with the knowledge that the random women he sleeps with feel the same as I do at such a moment and that is why they hand over money readily, to ensure that he'll come back. My own desperation has led me to become a cheap pimp. It has usurped my role as wife and lover. But the new role is no longer working, no longer giving me control. I pray I can find another way; before it's too late.

Jason has gone. I am lying back on the bed; the silent heaving sobs slowly abating. I'm alone, my thoughts screaming in my brain. I don't think I can survive without him. He said he would be back in a couple of days and that I need to be patient.

I switch off the bedside light and let the darkness envelop me. I don't believe him. It will be longer than that. I think my husband is making a bid for freedom but that can never happen. There's work to be done and tomorrow I'll start to make new plans, plans that will never let him go away again.

After all, Jason belongs to me.

33

ALEXIS

'I'm not sure what to tell Caroline. It all seems too much of a coincidence. What do you think?'

Gary and I have tidied up the lock-up and made it into a usable office space. A couple of desks and filing cabinets have been the first purchases for the new business. The two small windows on the back wall are constantly cracked to filter away the rancid stench of caked grease. Bright overhead lighting to replace the dangling death wire has been our first major expense, but worth the outlay.

Trent's motorbike is back in the corner under its tarpaulin waiting until we have enough money to get it repaired. I've told Gary I'll treat myself when the divorce comes through but for now I know to keep it well hidden from Adam. He no longer mentions the machine, assuming it was scrapped after the accident. If he suspects otherwise he is not letting on. The lock-up is my secret.

'It definitely seems a coincidence that she asked you to follow Susan Harper and Jason, at the time you've met the same guy through this *Join Me* website, albeit under a fake name.' Gary is looking through the pictures which came through my door, before throwing out a barbed comment. His laptop is open at the *Join Me* homepage.

'He's handsome but what a prick.' Gary peers at the photos. 'He doesn't half love being in front of a camera.' Gary hasn't asked me what prompted my interest in the site but as his work for the day will involve probing deeper into Jason's habits, I suspect we'll get around to discussing the site's appeal later on.

'Should I tell her that Jason is using the website and that I've already met him? It's all so weird.'

It feels good to be working again, with the added bonus of being away from home. Adam demanded to know who Gary was and why he'd moved into our house. He rightly guessed that he wasn't a secret lover, surmising from his adolescent appearance that I wouldn't be that desperate. I told him the truth that we had met at a private investigator's conference and are working together but since throwing him out, Adam no longer seems to have any interest in Gary or his whereabouts. He won't be a perceived threat to his plans.

I still feel decidedly uneasy around the house. Adam is constantly trying to wear me down and I know he is banking on success and that I'll eventually let him back into my life and the marital bed. He has assured me, more than once, that he's ended it with Debbie, that she begged him not to leave her; it's only me he has ever loved. His mistress has reluctantly returned to her husband. Instinct tells me he's lying and Gary has it on his 'to do' list to dig for relevant information which might help me when our divorce reaches the courts.

Meanwhile I have a date with Caroline Swinton to tell her a few facts about her husband. As I pack up my belongings, Gary looks up. He has cut his straggling fringe in an effort, I suspect, to smarten himself up for his new job and the effort has helped to calm the acne. My summation that he might have an old head on his young shoulders is given confirmation when he speaks.

'Tell her the truth. She'll find out in the end anyway. She might already know he's using this website but you need to find out what she knows before you can get to the bottom of what the guy's up to. She probably won't like the truth but as long as she pays, do we really care?' He grins, crooked little teeth poking out through his moist lips. I like Gary. He'll become a good friend, already has.

Caroline is waiting. We are at the same café in Golders Green where we first talked. She is in the corner and the first thing I notice is that she looks different. Although she is wearing her usual caked mask of heavy make-up, her eyes look smaller, void of her trademark thick mascara. There are red raw circles underneath which thick powder is unsuccessfully trying to conceal.

'Hi,' she says, standing up as I push through the door. She seems to have shrunk and as she steps out from behind the table, I see she's not wearing her usual killer heels. Something is up.

We order coffees and settle down straightaway to business. It's only three days since I met Jason at King's Cross, believing at the time that he was an interesting stranger called Eddie.

'Did you get the photos?' I wait for her to continue. It's clear she has things she's desperate to say. 'He's handsome, don't you think?' This seems to be of overriding importance. Appearance seems to be her driver, her turn on. I smile and listen.

'The agenda has changed,' she begins. 'Jason's left me. I need to know where he's gone. I've no idea, he packed a suitcase and left.' Her eyes well up but she swallows hard to keep the emotions in check. 'We argued. It didn't seem important at the time, more the usual married thing.' I wonder what she means by *the usual married thing.* Another woman? Alcohol? Abuse?

Sexual disinterest? Emptying the dishwasher? The list is endless as my active brain weighs up the possibilities.

I was due to start trailing Susan Harper and Jason, following on from receipt of the photographs. That was the arrangement. Now things have changed and she wants me instead to find out where her husband is staying and with whom. At this point I decide to own up, tell her what I know.

'I need to tell you something, Caroline.' I watch her stiffen and take a tentative sip of coffee before I drop the bombshell.

'I suspect your husband is dating other women,' I begin. 'I have to own up I met him myself a few days ago under the online pseudonym of Eddie on a no-frills website called *Join Me*.' She doesn't flinch. Does she know? Is she playing me? It's hard to tell as she robotically stirs her drink. 'Have you heard of it?' At this point I'm concerned that Gary and I might lose our first paying client by dishing up unasked for dirt on her husband but something doesn't feel quite right. Caroline sits up, placing her cup back on the saucer with an audible clunk, and raises her eyebrows.

'What's *Join Me*? Is it a dating website?' I can tell she knows something as she doesn't seem that shocked. She looks at me with mild interest.

'No it's not a dating website as such. It offers people a chance to link up; to enjoy London's sights and experiences together, that sort of thing.' I sound like the advertising blurb. 'Actually I was bored after breaking my leg and it seemed like a harmless bit of fun.' I'm uneasy. I feel foolish as if I should have known better. 'A flyer came through the door.'

'When did you meet Jason? Where? How do you know it was him?'

'From your photos. I only realised who it was after I got back home from meeting him and found the pictures you'd pushed through my letterbox. It's such a coincidence.' I wait. She answers too quickly. The words have been rehearsed.

'Oh my god! I can't believe it.' She extracts a tissue which seems a weird reaction for such a monumental piece of information. I would have expected shock, anger but not instant tears. Crocodiles spring to mind; both for their tears and for their lethal bite.

'What do you want me to do? I can meet him again and try to find out where he's gone. That might be the easiest way. If I can't make him talk, I'll at least be able to follow him. My colleague Gary could trail him after our meeting, if you like.'

'Maybe that's how he met Susan Harper, through this *Join Me* website,' Caroline suggests, also too quickly. 'Can you find out if he's still seeing her too?' Caroline's grasping at straws, flitting from one thing to the next. I feel like a pawn in some game but try to keep it professional.

'Do you want me to meet him again? He's waiting to hear from me. That might be the best place to start.' A slight tic flickers under her right eye; a relentless rhythmical beat. I think it was the words *he is waiting to hear from me* that set it off. 'I'm sorry,' I say in deference to her obvious distress. It could be real or perhaps it's faked.

'Yes please. I need you to do it straightaway. I'll pay you well.' She takes out a cheque book from her bag and fills in spaces, not giving me time to respond.

'If you're sure then I'll contact him today. He seems flexible.' As soon as I've spoken, I regret the last sentence as being rather thoughtless. I take the cheque, caught between excitement at the welcome cash flow and unease at unfolding events which somehow seem to have unwittingly put me at the centre of someone else's story.

34

SUSAN

I keep the curtains pulled across, wishing Roger had closed the bedroom window when he left for work. He was in a rush as he agreed to drop the kids off at school first. He thinks I have one of my migraines and didn't question my reasons for staying in bed.

I can hear a delivery van being unloaded outside and the noise of merry chatter grates as I haul the duvet up round my ears in an attempt to block out the world. The sleeping pills have made me groggy and I drift in and out of sleep wishing it was night-time again.

It is around midday when I finally stagger downstairs in my dressing gown. It has been two days since the fateful dinner party and I feel I am waiting, waiting for a moment of clarity about what I should do next. Roger hasn't mentioned the Swintons again and I'm not sure if it is my current paranoia that makes me sense that he's deliberately avoiding the subject of our recent dinner guests or he may, of course, purely have little interest in them.

I boil the kettle, squeezing half a lemon into a mug and wander through into the study. Through the window I can see the sales agent who has a viewing on the house next door, his insipid estate car parked next to a sleek Jaguar. The lemon acid stings my throat as I remember Vince drives a red Audi. He told me to look out for it on the day we had lunch in Crouch End. The Jaguar must belong to someone else, someone as yet unknown; but not to Vince. It gives me slim comfort.

I'm battling the cruel realisation that Vince might have targeted me for money. The thought of blackmail is too horrific and the likelihood that I've been targeted by Vince, and perhaps by Caroline as well, can no longer be ignored. My future depends on it.

I open up the *Join Me* website to look at Vince's profile for one last time. While the computer boots up, I watch Mr Herriott through the window shake hands with a middle-aged grey-haired man who is looking round the outside of the house before he gets back into his car and drives off.

Across the road, Olive opens her front door and bends down to pick up milk left on the doorstep. She looks in my direction which makes me feel uneasy but then she coughs and I watch, transfixed, as her shoulders shudder uncontrollably for several seconds. She grips at the door frame with both hands until the fit abates before hobbling back inside. I should pop across for five minutes when I have the time. But not today.

Vince's handsome face is still smiling out from my computer screen and I wonder how many other women have fallen for his charms. Why did he pick me? Or did I pick him? I can't remember; it all seems blurred. Why did he want to meet me in the first place?

I type into the space below Vince's profile in the box high-lighted *make contact*. It will be the last time.

We need to talk. It's urgent. Susan.

My message sounds demanding, desperate, but I've no choice as this is no longer a game. I need my old life back which now beckons as a haven of security and stability. How could I have been so stupid? Was I really that starved of excitement?

I sit by the screen, unable to move, knowing that I'll stay where I am until a reply comes back. I find myself wondering how Caroline will cope when she finds out about us. I daren't believe she has known all along and perhaps together they've been using me.

When the phone rings, I ignore it, thinking it will be Roger wanting to find out how I'm feeling and if the migraine is any better. I glance down at the phone but don't recognise the number.

'Hello?' Vince. I swallow hard to contain the nausea.

'Hi. It's Jason.' He's no longer pretending to be Vince. The game is up. I look across and watch Bob, Olive's husband, lead her tenderly to their car. She's still in a dressing gown which is flapping round her bony ankles. He lifts her gently onto the front seat and, with the cough wracking her body, Bob hurries back to the driver's side and starts up the car. He wastes no time driving away from the close. They'll be going to the doctor's, or the hospital perhaps, but Bob is looking after her. We all need someone to care for us. I'm lucky to have Roger.

'We need to meet,' I tell Jason without hesitation. 'Today.'

The sun has gone behind the clouds and an increasingly grey presence looms overhead.

'Okay. Name when and where and I'll be there.'

I jump between my profile and his before I finally remove all traces of myself from the website. I delete my pictures, my profile and sad little biography. How did such an innocent bit of fun go so wrong? Roger would never forgive me if he found out. He must never find out, and I know I need to do whatever I have to in order to make sure.

Jason is standing in a small clearing, waiting for me. Highgate Woods seemed a sensible choice of venue, impersonal and hidden. The trees offer camouflage and protection from prying eyes. We could be any two strangers who are passing the time of day, who have met by chance. We stroll for a few yards before I speak.

'Why, Jason? Was it all about the money? Tell me.'

We find a bench in the heart of the woods and sit, side by side, like any ordinary couple.

'I like you, Susan. You must know that.' He takes my hand and my resolve wavers as I relish his warmth.

'Does Caroline know? Does she know you use online sites to meet people?' I'm unable to stop.

He takes his hand away and sadness fills its place.

'Yes. She's thrown me out.' He looks at the ground, like a naughty schoolboy who's been discovered smoking behind the bike shed.

'How did she find out?'

'I forgot to delete my browsing history and she came across the *Join Me* website. She found my profile on there and put two and two together.' He doesn't hesitate, always so plausible. I sense he's come prepared, ready for the questions.

'What about the money I lent you? I need it back.' I take a deep breath and carry on. 'I can't risk Roger finding out. I'm sorry about Caroline but I want to make my marriage work, for the children.' I don't say for Roger as it still doesn't seem appropriate.

'The problem is that Caroline has banked the money. She deals with the finances; always has. I don't think I can get it back, not at the moment anyway while she's not speaking to me.' He looks contrite with his downcast eyes and something makes me want to believe him. Doing so would make me feel less of a fool.

'Does Caroline know about me?' I'm still confused. Did she know the night of the dinner party? Has she known all along when she has been popping round for coffees? Vince is smartly diverting culpability away from himself. I still think of him as Vince. This is who I am talking to today, not Jason, the husband of my new *so-called* friend.

'She suspects. She saw that I'd been talking to you through the website.'

'Did she know the night you came round for dinner?' I spit. My anger is hot and vicious, ready to explode. Nothing makes sense. I am being played. He takes his hands away rather too sharply as a lady walking her dog strolls past. Perhaps he knows her? Perhaps he has screwed with her head also. His answers are vague.

'I think she might have done but I didn't know we were going to your house, I swear.' I believe him on this one otherwise he would have won an Oscar for his acting skills on the night in question.

'I do like you, Susan, have grown very fond of you but...'

I stand up. He is not going to finish with me first, I won't let that happen. I suddenly realise it has all been an aberration, an illusory moment of madness. He needs to use websites for excitement because he lacks substance and has perfected an outward appearance to fool the most astute of victims.

'I can't see you again, Jason. It's over. I love Roger and hope you can sort it out with Caroline.' Before Vince has time to answer, I tell him I want all my money back. Although I know there's little chance of this happening and that I've most likely seen the last of it, I repeat myself. 'I want every penny, Jason. There were no investments, were there?'

He at least doesn't try to offer more convoluted lies but says, 'It'll take some time but I'll try. I promise.' Something in his manner and in the hang of his head gives me faint comfort that perhaps I wasn't so stupid after all, that perhaps Caroline has been the calculated driver behind the extortion. Perhaps she controls him. Perhaps he had no choice. But I suspect I'm lying to myself.

However, at the moment the money I've lost seems like a small price to have paid for my actions and I now have to walk away, try to forget the whole thing ever happened. As I turn to leave, he utters a single word.

'Sorry.' It tells me all I need to know. He'll not be back.

Roger gets home early, thrilled to see me in the kitchen, fully dressed and made up and as he comes over to kiss me, he sniffs the air inquisitively trying to work out what's in the oven.

'Lamb shanks in red wine with peas and potatoes. Your favourite,' I proudly announce. Tilly and Noah run in from the car, dropping their school bags in the hall, shrieking and arguing and for a brief moment in time, all is right with the world. I am back. My mistakes, like ghosts, have been laid to rest. There is now no reason for Roger to find out. I taste the casserole and add the seasoning and think that perhaps Roger and I should have a weekend away; somewhere without the kids. We deserve time alone and maybe it would give us a chance to ignite our own dormant passions.

As we sit down to a candlelit meal, which Tilly and Noah are mocking with childish derision, Roger says he has heard that the house next door has been taken off the market. An offer has been accepted apparently. I immediately think of the grey-haired man in the Jaguar.

'You'll never guess who the buyer is. None other than your friend Caroline Swinton.' I watch Roger cut the lamb shanks into delicate little mouthfuls and raise his glass to his lips.

'Delicious,' he says, while Tilly and Noah bang their glasses of orange juice rather too heartily together and yell 'Cheers' in unison.

35

ALEXIS

Today I'm meeting up with Jason in my official PI capacity to try to find out for Caroline where he has gone and whom he is seeing. Caroline is increasingly desperate and has sent me numerous texts and emails propelling me towards urgent action. Apparently he has been off her radar for three days and she is becoming increasingly distraught.

I'm waiting for Adam to leave home and go to work before I come downstairs. He's hovering in the hallway, but I can't hear any movement. I know he is there. The front door hasn't been opened yet and I can see his car in the driveway from my vantage point upstairs.

'Alexis!' The sudden yell up the stairs makes me jump. 'I'm off. See you later.' He's acting as if we're a normal loving couple, as if nothing is wrong and he hasn't been screwing another woman and been served divorce papers for his sins. He is waiting for me to drop the proceedings once he has convinced me of his contrition. He won't give up.

'Bye!' I shout down from behind a locked bathroom door which I peel open once I hear him leave the house.

~

An hour later I'm driving to Camden to meet with Eddie 300, whom I now know to be Jason Swinton, Caroline's husband. Gary is at the lock-up ready to follow our mark as soon as I call him. Today our goal is to find out more about Caroline's cheating spouse.

I'm early and as I enter the trendy gastro pub, Freemans, located off Camden High Street, I remind myself that this is not a date but a working assignment. However, as I watch Jason enter the pub I realise how ill-defined such boundaries might become.

'Hi,' he says, kissing me simply on the cheek.

'Hi. Good to see you,' I say, cringing in case he thinks I've been desperate to meet up with him again. He's probably used to this being the case.

We sit down at a brightly lit table like a couple of friends about to share a companionable lunch. Although Jason, in his guise as Eddie 300, acts as if he has all the time in the world, I have work to get done.

'Sorry about the other day,' I begin. I sip my mineral water, determined to keep a clear head while he relaxes back with a bottle of Peroni beer. 'I've got a few problems at home.' I could tell him the truth that I'm married, going through a messy divorce but I don't want to get into personal issues, not mine at any rate and now is definitely not the time.

'Don't worry, no harm done.' His dark eyes crinkle at the corners. His smile is direct and he is definitely being flirtatious.

'Have you met many people on *Join Me*?' I ask, eager to get some answers. 'Where have you been to?'

'Here and there. London Zoo. A few wine bars. Still waiting to take that trip up the Thames though,' he says, his smile set like concrete. 'What about you?'

'To be honest, I only checked out the site when I broke my leg. It gave me something to do and made me realise how much London has to offer. You're the only contact I've made and now I'm back to work, I've not really got much time for sightseeing.'

'What sort of work? Tell me about you.' He tries to divert interest away from himself. This could be a tactic, making his dates feel important by letting them talk about themselves while he feigns interest.

'Nothing much to tell really. I do a bit of consultancy work.' I keep it vague.

'Are you married?' It comes out of the blue.

'Yes, but getting divorced. You?' I turn the question back on him while I spear a small stick into an olive and nibble at the end. The taste is tart.

'Yes, but we've split up too. I'm dipping my toe back in the water and fancy the idea of taking in a few sights around London with new friends. As good a way to start again as any. What happened with your guy?'

'He had an affair. And you?' I have to carry on, get some answers.

'A long story.' He sighs. It's all very theatrical as if he is expecting questions but has primed himself not to open up.

'Do you live around here?' I try a different tack.

'Highgate.' He finishes his beer and quickly offers to get me another drink and something to eat. My phone pings and as I check the screen, I excuse myself and go outside. Gary is exactly on time. We agreed he would text after forty-five minutes and I would call him back.

'How's it going?' The street is busy, chock-a-block with pedestrians pushing up and down the street heading towards the market. I have to talk loudly as the reception is poor and the traffic and bustle make it hard to hear.

'Hi. Thanks for the text. It's like getting blood from a stone.

He's giving nothing away except that he lives in Highgate. Give me half an hour and then wait outside Freemans until we come out. I'm certain he came by tube.'

When I go back into the restaurant, Jason is flirting with a random woman. I'm starting to piece together what my online date does. He sucks ladies in with his easy charm, probably gets them into bed but then what? Perhaps Gary will be able to join up a few of the dots.

~

Gary arrives back at the lock-up around five. After I left Freemans, I decided to while away the time productively and made a start on brightening up our workplace. I've begun to paint the walls, changing the colour from a dirty grey to a bright cream magnolia.

'Love the colour,' Gary says suddenly appearing through the side door.

I plop my paint brushes in the white spirit and use a tattered cloth to wipe away paint streaks from my fingers. I turn the radio down which is blasting out songs from the nineties. 'Did you get anything?' I can't quell my excitement and follow him closely as he deposits his rucksack on the desk. 'Well?'

He extracts a small camera from the bag and attaches the lead from the back of the device into the laptop. It takes about five minutes to download the images.

'He's staying up in Highgate Village. It's a huge house, three storeys with a fountain in the front garden.' Gary is blocking the screen until he's put the pictures in order.

'He doesn't seem to have a front door key and rang the bell for about ten minutes. That's him ringing the bell.' Gary proudly points to the first two pictures. 'Then an old lady came round from the back of the house.' He points to the next two pictures.

The lady may appear old to Gary but to me she looks middle-aged. It's all a matter of perception. I think I must look old to Gary who's hardly out of short trousers.

'Zoom in,' I say as I lean over his shoulder, keen to get a better look. The sixth picture which comes into focus is one of Jason Swinton clasping both hands with the woman and leaning in to kiss her intimately on the lips. I stare at the woman, trying to get a sense of her role in his life. Her hair is tied loosely at the nape of her neck and although it appears light brown, there is a faint but distinct feathering of grey.

'Wait till you see the last picture,' announces my protégé. As Gary flicks through the last half dozen stills, he stops and turns my way, waiting for approval as he presents the final frame.

Jason is standing with his bare chest pushed into this older woman's breasts. They're in a room on the first floor, standing back a short distance from the window. Her breasts are large and their fullness draws the eye. Her younger lover is kissing her passionately and his arms encircle her protectively.

'Well done, Gary, you're a star.' He flushes with pride but as I stare at his work, I wonder how I'm going to tell Caroline Swinton where her husband is staying and with whom.

'Oh by the way, I nearly forgot. I jotted down the woman's name from a small plaque on her front porch. *Francine Dubois B.A., Psychotherapist*. I also took down her phone number, in case we need it.'

36

OLIVE

Bob has turned the heat up high but I'm still shivering. I'm unable to move without the cough starting up again and as I sit by the window I try to stay very still. Alexis has popped in a few times over the last couple of days proffering grapes, magazines and green tea but leaves soon afterwards when she realises I'm not up to talking. It hurts deep down in my chest when I try. None of the other neighbours have called; perhaps it's because they think that Bob will look after me but I think it's more because they can't be bothered. Whichever way they look at it, I'm someone else's problem.

I have my diary open in front of me, trying to work out what is going on. A story is unfolding in front of my very eyes but I'm not sure what it is. Something is afoot in Riverside Close. My mind is fuzzy, cloudy, and I try desperately to wake it up. Bob tells me the antibiotics will take time to kick in, that I must be patient. He knows, after forty years of marriage, that I'm not a patient person.

The mantle clock is ticking with a relentless beat over the background silence and I note it is nearly four o'clock. Bob won't be back until this evening but when I insisted he join his friends at the golf club, he left the phone beside me with promises that I'll call him if I get any worse. I don't think I can get any worse, as the wretched cough is building up again from inside. I need to concentrate. I look at my scribbles.

In my mind I visualise Susan Harper coming and going. She has got thinner, more agitated. She scours the close for people who might be watching as she clambers into her car and drives away, dressed provocatively in short skirts and tight blouses. She's become mutton dressed as lamb. Roger is spending more time with the children, taking them to school and I've even logged a couple of occasions when he's picked them up. I wonder why but perhaps his work is no longer as demanding. Perhaps he will take early retirement like Bob. Susan doesn't know when she is well off, far too much time on her hands. I suspect she's up to no good.

Adam is back with Alexis. I worry for my young friend and have made a careful note of the black-eye incident. You never know, one day, it might provide useful testimony. She has her first real client, a woman who wants her to trail an errant husband. Alexis laughed when she confided that it was a lady she met at Susan Harper's house when a group of ladies were invited over for drinks and canapés.

I blow my nose with a soggy hanky, too exhausted to get up and fetch the tissues. My nose is red raw round the edges and it hurts to wipe. I let the drips drizzle down my nostrils before I blot the ends to stem the flow.

The lady, whose husband she is trailing is, I'm almost certain, called Caroline Swinton. I haven't told Alexis that I am piecing together clues of my own and might soon be able to help her; when I'm better, of course.

I saw a blonde buxom lady, dressed in a bright flashy yellow and navy striped jacket and high heels call at Susan's a while ago. They seemed to be good friends. She stayed for over an hour, probably sharing coffee and gossip. She looks that sort; a bored housewife on a mission. Bob thinks I'm ridiculous in my summations and can't believe that I can make up such nonsense from a five-minute sighting.

I now know her name is Caroline Swinton because Mr Herriott the estate agent let the cat out of the bag after I saw her viewing the empty house at number four. He thinks because I am old and now apparently infirm, that my mind has gone as well. I could have him sued for his lack of confidentiality and report him to his bosses for having let slip the name of inter- ested clients. Caroline Swinton, according to the increasingly desperate estate agent, is a serious potential purchaser. A cash buyer, she told him.

The phone rings and the movement to pick it up stirs the mucus in my chest. I can hear Bob on the other end repeat that he will come home, worried that he shouldn't have left me alone, and I hear him talk agitatedly to a colleague. It's a few seconds before I can catch my breath and speak.

'Don't worry, Bob. I'm fine. Enjoy yourself. I'll call if I need you.' Before he has time to protest, I click the phone off and pull my dressing gown tight. He'll be back by nine o'clock, after the golf club members' dinner. He didn't really want to go but I convinced him to make the effort as I need to be on my own, in the quiet, not having to talk. It's now five thirty and soon I'll have a nap which will help pass the time. The antibiotics make me very drowsy.

I gave Alexis a full description of this Caroline Swinton. When Alexis popped in yesterday I filled her in on people who had been viewing the empty house. She seemed interested but might have been humouring her sick neighbour. She has a kind heart and misses a mother of her own, I think. She was amused when I talked of the brassy blonde friend of Susan Harper's who has been viewing the house for sale. She thinks this might be the lady whose husband she is trailing.

Something has awoken me. I can't breathe. The passageway to my throat won't open, it has stuck. I grasp the edge of my chair and try to stand. Perhaps someone will notice me through the window. I frantically rap on the glass, fearing that I am about to die as I drift in and out of oblivion. Suddenly I gasp for air and the passageway opens up again. The relief floods through me as my eyes try to focus in the dark. I can just make out the time on the clock. It's nearly nine.

I need to turn the lamp on but am very unsteady on my feet. I am wet all over. Water is dripping from my forehead and from the back of my neck. I fumble under my dressing gown and feel my drenched nightdress. Something draws my eye across the road, however, before I reach for the lamp.

I watch Caroline Swinton's husband, the man I assume is her husband as he accompanied her to the Harpers' a few nights ago, approach the front door of the house for sale. Why is he going there at this time of night? There is no sign of Mr Herriott. Perhaps the man wants to look around. But it seems an odd thing to do.

He walks round the darkened building before returning to the front porch and rings the bell. It is a few minutes before the door opens and someone ushers him quickly through and closes the door after him but I can't make out who is in there. I think they are being careful not to be seen.

I have been asleep for the past two hours and things have been happening while I nearly died.

I pull on my little ankle boots and swap the dressing gown for my winter coat. Of course I shouldn't be going out as there is a slight skiff of rain in the air but as I pull down the woollen beret over my ears, I know I have no option. Someone has to find out what is going on and I know no one else will bother. Everyone is too busy behind their closed doors.

A blast of cold air nearly knocks me over as I open the back door from the kitchen leading through to Bob's allotment. There is something in amongst the vegetables, a fox perhaps, rustling through the stalks but it scurries off as I move forward. A full moon illuminates the path to the gate at the bottom of the garden. I stagger slowly along. I clutch my phone in my left hand in case Bob phones. He should have been home by now.

The ragged blades of straggling undergrowth send wet shivers through my body which is shaking involuntarily. I plough on. It seems an eternity till I reach the exit to the outside world, to the little coppice with the river flowing through it. An owl hoots from on high, welcoming me to his night-time world, and the gate creaks open as I grip the fence to circuit the back of the cul-de-sac.

I stop every few seconds to catch my breath and wait for the pain in my chest to die down enough to let me carry on. I switch on the small torch on my phone as Bob taught me a couple of days ago, jesting that it would be useful in a power cut. It lights my way.

It is then I see someone up ahead coming out the back entrance from the empty house. It is too far off for me to make out who it is. I squint in the darkness, frantically trying to switch off the torch as I flail weakly against the wet fence. The cough is rearing up again and for a moment I fear the game might be up as the cough battles to explode. I needn't worry because the person jogs quickly away in the opposite direction, pulling a dark hooded top up round their ears. They hesitate briefly as I stumble to stay upright.

The ground is calling me and I am losing my balance. I manage to shuffle a few yards further. It is enough. I extract the phone which I stuffed in my pocket to conceal the torch and manage to click the camera setting. On the ground there are several footprints which have been left by the disappearing jogger. I manage a couple of close-up snaps before dizziness rocks my vision and balance, and I know I have to get back. The rain is falling more persistently and will soon wipe clean all traces of the recent hooded stranger. I will have the only record of their presence.

I'm scared I won't make it home. Fear grips my heart as the world spins on its axis. I inch along, one tiny step at a time, but quite suddenly I think once more that I'm going to die. I manage to make it through the back gate into our garden and the last thing I remember is Bob running through the vegetable patch towards me, shouting out my name and catching me as I slither to the ground.

37

ALEXIS

The sirens wake me. They are in life-or-death mode. I hear the high-pitched wailing sounds slice through the quiet night air and fade away below my window. The bedside clock is showing ten thirty. I slip out of bed and glance down through the window at the street below. The ambulance is outside Olive's house. A chill premonition of death pervades my tiredness. I pull on my jogging bottoms and sweatshirt, now fully awake.

I rush down the stairs and notice that Adam's door is ajar but there's no movement from within and I remember he told me he was on duty tonight. I unlock the front door and pull on my trainers, watching the small blue light continue its relentless but now silent beat on top of the ambulance.

Across the road, Bob is standing like a robot staring at the stretcher as it is carried out over the threshold. Shock and fear are etched on his face along with something else. Guilt.

'I shouldn't have left her. She told me she was fine,' he mumbles as I draw alongside. He is berating himself for her collapse as if it was his fault.

'What happened?' I gently put an arm around his shoulder.

He doesn't speak but leans over the small bony cadaver

hidden under an oxygen mask and swathes of blankets. I try to comfort him.

'Don't worry. She'll be fine,' I say with as much conviction as I can muster.

He nods and clambers into the vehicle after his wife before the doors close behind them. I walk up to their front door which, in his moment of distress, Bob has left wide open. I slam it shut. It is lucky Olive entrusted me with a spare key.

I try to call Adam as the sirens start up again and the ambulance manoeuvres its way round the close. Lights have been snapped on in some of the other houses as the neighbours spy curiously from behind curtains at the unfolding drama.

His phone goes to voicemail.

'Adam. It's me, Alexis.' I instantly regret the word *me*, it is too familiar, as if I'm still the main person in his life but I need to get his attention.

'It's Olive from across the road. She's on her way to the hospital and I'm coming there now. Please call when you get this.' I'll make him help, make him prove his importance and influence which he so incessantly brags about. Power over life and death is his boast. I've heard it often enough.

I drive too quickly but am desperate to get to the hospital to try to help Olive and Bob. Adam can use his authority to make sure she gets the best care. He owes me that.

When I arrive at the hospital entrance, I soon find myself engulfed by the dimly lit building with its eerie night-time feel. The daytime bustle of concerned visitors with their forced levity is glaringly absent. The smell of disinfectant clings to the sterile corridors and I feel the fear from ghostly patients who wander back and forth. No one talks and I find myself smiling wanly at random people.

Olive is in a small ward on the first floor and I can see, from the corridor, Bob caressing her hand. She is attached to all sorts of wires and tubes but the heart monitor is beating steadily; comfortingly.

'Alexis.' I jump, startled, and turn round to see Adam dressed in his operating attire. Standing alongside, he also peers through the window at the fragile patient.

'She'll be fine. I suspect she's got pneumonia but she's in the right place,' he says in his consoling doctor's voice, as if placating a concerned relative. He places a light hand on top of mine and for a fleeting moment, I'm tempted to forget our differences. Instead I take my hand away and ask, 'Can I talk to her?'

'Just for a few minutes. She's very groggy but aware of where she is.' He pushes open the door and the nurse on duty steps aside reverently as we enter. Bob is still gripping Olive's hand, reluctant to let it go. Adam asks the nurse to get us some coffees and Bob agrees to go with her, relieved for a moment that I am there to hold the fort. I turn to Adam and simply say, 'thanks' as he turns to leave the room.

Olive's eyes are firmly shut and I can hear a faint puff of air escape through her parched lips every couple of seconds. I think she is asleep but suddenly her lids peel back and she stares at me.

'Across the road.' I think this is what she says but I can't be certain.

'Pardon. What do you mean?' I lean down close to her, turning my ear towards her lips. 'Across the road?' I repeat.

'The house for sale,' she croaks before her lids droop together again. Her fingers are agitating, the tips flicking up and down. She's trying to tell me something. I can hear desperation in her tone.

'What about the house?' I probe. There is no movement from the bed and when I think she must have fallen asleep, I hear a mumble. I lean down.

'Something's up. Go there.' I wait while she catches her breath and tries to continue. 'My phone.' She turns her eyes, without moving her head, towards the bedside cabinet. I reach over and look at her phone. The screen is dark and the battery flat. When I turn round, I hear a very faint but light snoring. The medication has sent her into a more peaceful slumber and as I turn towards the door, I see Bob holding two paper cups and smell the welcome aroma of coffee as he approaches the bed.

As I stretch out my hand to take a cup, I notice Adam in the background, watching us all with a faint curl to his lips. I'm not certain if it is because he is pleased with himself for having been on hand to help and curry favour with his reluctant wife, but I feel there is something else. His smile is forced, uneasy rather than victorious. His expression makes me edgy.

Adam won't be home until the morning. I reread his text telling me that Olive is comfortable and he will keep an eye on her. It's well past midnight when I get back and as I park my car in the driveway, I turn towards the house across the road. The rain has died down but puddles dot the pavements. They look like treacherous broken shards of glass under the dull orange street lights. I replay in my mind Olive's whispered words, the urgency of her tone telling me that something's up.

'The house for sale,' she said. I take a few steps towards the little flower bed that sits proudly in the centre of Riverside Close. Before she took sick, Olive planted a few purple and white winter pansies to brighten up the space. It had previously lain barren due to neighbourly apathy and winter frosts.

I skirt cautiously round and across to the other side of the road, shivering as I look towards the empty building which is deathly quiet, like all the other buildings. But the quietness in the empty house has a different timbre. The other houses beat gently with sleeping hearts, but this vacant shell is soulless. I peer through the windows at the front but everything is in darkness and there is a greasy film of dirt smeared across the panes.

I'm about to go round to the rear of the house but hesitate, suddenly overcome by tiredness and something else. I feel brave enough at the front with the smoky street lights for company but something about the blackened silence a few yards further back makes me hold fast. I check my phone screen for messages, unsure what I am expecting to see at this time of night and decide that I'll follow my instincts and call the police first thing in the morning. I'll tell them that Olive was uneasy and suggest they ought to take a look. It might only be the musings of a sick woman.

As I put the key in the lock, I look round for a last glance and notice the front gate at number four is open, swinging loosely on its hinges. It dawns on me that I didn't need to open it to gain access. I'm certain Mr Herriott is religious in closing it after viewings but perhaps my mind is in overdrive. It has been a long night.

I head up to bed, anxious and alert, but am so exhausted I fall into bed desperate for sleep.

38

SUSAN

I can hear a knocking sound somewhere in the distance, somewhere far off but I can't wake up. I am unable to move. I'm paralysed, like a coma victim, desperately willing myself to awaken. The ceiling overhead is listing from side to side, its blue tinted hues rippling like a restless ocean. I feel as if I'm being sucked downwards by an invisible current.

I see a bottle of sleeping pills beside the bed with the lid off and I can make out several small white tablets strewn across the cabinet top. How many did I take? The rapping is getting louder, insistent. Where's Roger? Why can't I move? The room is spinning more violently and a gaping chasm has opened up in the floor, the carpet rent in two. I'm sinking further and further down; plunging to certain death.

The curtain flaps against the window frame. This is the first thing I notice when I jolt back from the drug-induced nightmares. Roger must have left the window open again. He usually closes it when he leaves for work but I can't remember him saying goodbye; I can't remember either him coming to bed or leaving this morning.

I manage to drag myself out of bed and pull on the jeans and sweatshirt from last night which are strewn across the chair before wrenching a brush through my tangled hair.

In the bathroom I splash cold water over my face and neck in a vain attempt to wake up. My eyes are those of a madwoman, unstable and deranged. What's happened to me?

The knocking sound is back, and the gentle rap has increased in intensity and someone is banging heavily on the door.

'Coming,' I yell. 'Coming.' I stumble out of the bedroom and down the stairs. There's no one in the house, school bags have disappeared from the hallway. Natalie was picking the children up this morning. Why wasn't Roger taking them to school? I can't remember. Before I open the front door, I know something isn't right. Through the frosted glass I can see the hazy blue light of a police car. Tilly and Noah. Oh my god. This is my first thought. Something's happened to the children.

A rumpled middle-aged man is standing on the doorstep with his back to me. He turns round when I open the door.

'Mrs Harper?' he asks, holding up some form of identification. Perhaps he's here to read the meters, the gas and electric. 'Detective Inspector Ferran,' he announces.

'Yes. What is it? What's up?' My legs feel weak and my stomach is churning. I put my hand against the wall to steady myself.

'May I come in?' he asks before stepping into the hall without preamble. Over his shoulder I can see activity; police officers, a blue and white tape strapped along the length of the house next door. Why would Tilly and Noah have gone next door? Perhaps Roger was having a look around. I know it is bad news but I can't work out what could possibly be wrong. I suddenly remember Roger's announcement that Caroline Swinton has had an offer accepted on the house next door and a chill foreboding replaces my own personal traumas.

'Is it the children?' I don't let the stranger past until he answers me. He's like Columbo, the dishevelled TV cop, with his gaping raincoat revealing a dark shirt and sensible brown corduroy trousers. His brogues are muddied as if he has been walking in the rain but the sun is out.

'No. Please don't worry. It's not your children. It's something else.' He seems to know that I'm suspecting death, building myself up to hysteria as he closes the door behind us and edges further into the house.

'Is it Roger? My husband?' Where's Roger? Why didn't he say goodbye, why did he leave the window open upstairs. My mind races and I can't assimilate the facts.

'We're not sure at this point, Mrs Harper, but there's been an incident next door,' is all the detective says. I lead him into the kitchen and ask if he would like a cup of tea, coffee. For some reason I feel if I act normally things won't be so bad and it might all turn out to be a big mistake. He might be here to ask casual questions about some matter totally unrelated to my family.

'No thanks. If it's all right I'd like to ask you a few questions. We're knocking on all the doors in the close.'

I put the kettle on anyway, cleaning up spilt milk from cereal bowls which are sitting half empty on the breakfast bar. Natalie wouldn't have put them away but Roger would have. I need to call him, speak to him. He might know what's going on.

The officer asks me to sit down and leads me to the table. Perhaps he wants me to identify my husband's body? Perhaps I'm a suspect in some bizarre crime.

'I'm DI Ferran, Mrs Harper,' he repeats, then pauses as if this is a vital piece of information which I need to grasp. I stare at him, willing him to continue and to confirm that my husband is still alive.

'There has been a death in the house next door and we suspect foul play,' Ferran says. His eyebrows are like thick dark hairy caterpillars crawling slowly across his brow. His weathered skin has a deep red hue, hardened most likely by alcohol, but his eyes are like a hawk's; sharp and focused. He scans the kitchen as if for clues.

'Is it my husband?'

'No. It's not your husband but we can't give out any more information at the moment; but rest assured, it's not your husband.' I slump back in the chair, relieved, and grip the coffee mug in both hands, willing myself to wake up. It's not my husband, not my children but why do I feel so afraid? It's something to do with the house next door, with its connection to Caroline and Vince, Jason, and their offer which was made to ensure it got taken off the market. What's the connection?

'We need to know your movements last night and if you saw anything unusual or suspicious. We'll also need to talk to your husband as soon as possible.' I wonder why they need to talk to Roger.

'I went to bed early,' I say but I've no idea of the time. Liberal use of sleeping pills might cause concern as to my state of mind. 'It was probably around nine or ten o'clock. I'm not sure exactly.'

'What about your husband? Was he at home?' Ferran isn't going to stop until his notebook is full.

'He was later than usual. Again I can't be certain as I think I was in bed when he got home.' This sounds odd as if I'm being evasive but I can't remember. I glance at the kitchen clock, willing it to offer inspiration. It shows midday. 'I don't sleep too well so took a couple of sleeping pills and can't recall much after that.' Perhaps I should have cleared away the pile of white tablets lying on the bedside cabinet in case we're suspects. But suspects in what?

Columbo stands up and hesitates. He's going to ask me one more thing.

'We'll need to talk to your husband as soon as he gets home.'

Ferran hands me his card, circling his mobile number with his pen. 'Please ask him to call me.'

'Of course,' I answer, setting the card down on the kitchen table.

The neighbours are circling like vultures when I finally join them outside on the pavement. The sun is high in the sky but there is an unnatural chill in the air. The milling ensemble hovers patiently, waiting for the first scraps of death meat. I don't recognise some of the faces and am scared to look too closely. Not knowing the onlookers imbues me with hope that I've no part in unfolding events. A young man with a camera clicks his lens. Click, click, click. Another woman is talking gravely into a microphone. I think of a street party with excited but muted chatter which is gaining momentum. Everyone is waiting but no one is sure for what.

'Susan.' It's Alexis from across the road. She steps across and hugs me. I pull my cardigan across my chest and wonder why she's showing me such concern. Perhaps it's a general concern.

'Alexis,' I echo. 'What's going on? What's happened?' She pulls me away, out of earshot from the cameraman, and whispers in my ear.

'Someone's been murdered. I'm not sure who but I telephoned the police this morning. Olive Thompson ended up in hospital last night and I popped in to see her. She's got pneumonia but insisted that she had seen something going on across the road before she collapsed and asked me to take a look.'

'What did she see? Is it anyone we know?' I find it hard to concentrate, take in what Alexis is saying but the fresh air is helping and the activity soothing my personal concerns. It isn't

Roger. It's not the kids. I should be relieved but there's something unsettling about the turn of events.

'I don't know. The cops won't let on.'

We watch as another police car drives up the close, slowly like a brightly coloured hearse. There's someone sitting in the back seat alongside a female officer, and I can make out a bent head which slowly lifts up as the car pulls alongside the gathered group.

The thick bleached-blonde hair is unmistakable and the bright yellow jacket incongruously garish in contrast to the sombre mood. Alexis and I watch Caroline Swinton stagger from the car, staring ahead as she walks slowly towards the blue tape. A young officer efficiently peels back the temporary barrier to let her through and we all watch on in silence, as the little procession moves round to the back of the house.

It is the howl of a wolf, feral and shrill. It won't stop, and the vultures look at the ground, silenced for a moment, their hunger and thirst for blood temporarily quelled. The noise pierces the air and sends shockwaves which vibrate round the houses of Riverside Close. Our middle-class haven of respectability will never be the same again, someone proffers in reverential tones.

The sun dips behind a cloud. Alexis looks at me and I look back at her. She's gone very pale and seems to have shrunk in front of me as I tower over her. She met Caroline at my house. I'm not sure if Alexis knows Caroline's husband but as I turn to seek refuge behind my own four walls, I don't really care. I have to get back inside, away from the baying monster whose desperate screeches from the house next door have become gradually more intermittent. I don't want to hear the silence that will follow shortly. I think of the movie *The Silence of the Lambs* which tells the story of the eerie stillness which follows the separation of the new-born lambs from their mothers. And afterwards, the slaughter.

39

CAROLINE

I can hear a scream. It's deafening but it won't stop. I've collapsed but I'm not allowed to stay where I am. A dishevelled middle-aged man tells me it's a crime scene and coaxes me to get up. I won't go, Jason needs me. He's cold and a policewoman tries to prise my fingers away from his hands but they are locked, tightly closed, and I'm unable to intertwine mine through the hardened bones.

He is sitting on a kitchen chair, slumped leadenly to one side, as if he's asleep but his shape is grotesque. He looks like a macabre Halloween guy botched together for burning. I try to escape the clutches of the woman holding me back, pushing and kicking at her shins. I want her to move aside; she is blocking my view of Jason's head. I need to see his face once more and re-touch his lips, trace the outline of his perfect features and smell his scent. These people are after a positive identification. How can I identify him?

The woman finally moves and I have a clear view. But it's not Jason. Not my Jason. This is the picture of Dorian Gray, ugly and deformed.

'Mrs Swinton.' I hear a voice encourage me up from the

frozen marble tiles which are splattered with dark red pools of blood.

'You need to come with us. We have to ask you a few questions.' Why? What's there to ask? I don't answer, I can't. A doctor, Alexis' husband I think, is offering me some pills. They are small and blue and he says, with quiet assurance, that they'll help calm me down. Why am I not calm and where is the screaming coming from? It's getting louder and everyone is encouraging me to move away. If I leave Jason now, I'll never get back to him. They'll take him away and burn him on the sacrificial pyre. His ashes will mingle with the deadwood and he will be no more.

I'm not sure where I am. I think I'm in Alexis' front room as I see her sitting across from me. Her fine little features and pretty face stare with concern in my direction. I have an overwhelming desire to pick up a heavy object and smash it over her skull. The tablets are making me woozy and I can't think straight but the detective is determined to make me talk, answer his immediate questions. Where was I last night? When did I last see my husband? Had we argued? Alexis is talking to her husband, Adam. I thought they had split up. I had forbidden Jason to meet her because she was newly single, separated. Then I remember that she was following my husband, trailing him to feed me information about his whereabouts. He was having a break away, a short holiday before he came home. I remember now.

Two hours have elapsed and I am alone with Detective Inspector Ferran. Everyone else seems to have gone although I'm still at the Morleys' under house arrest. That's what it feels like and something tells me I need to straighten out my thoughts and my story. The possibility that I might have murdered my husband hangs like an elephant in the room, a bizarre theory that this wizened but hardened cop will be considering. Most murders are connected to someone close to the victim will be his premise.

'Last night. Can you remember where you were?' he begins.

'At home. Who killed him?' I need answers too.

'It's too early to say but we are trying to paint a picture of Mr Swinton's last-known movements.' I don't instantly register who they are referring to. 'When did he leave home?' the detective asks. Jason hadn't been at home. I don't know where he was. Alexis Morley might know but I daren't alert this guy to the fact that I was having my husband followed. Some emotion other than grief is battling to the fore. This guy is going to pry, test the theory that most victims know their killers. Did I have a motive? This is what he wants to find out.

'He had gone away for a couple of days but he was coming back. I don't know where he went.' The truth is easy to tell.

'Had you argued?' He's staring at me, full in the face, probing behind my eyes for answers. What can he see? I'm no longer sure myself what is in there.

'Not really. He needed some space. He was like that.' I'm toying with the truth. Subterfuge will be difficult. I don't really know what sort of man he was, nothing other than I loved him more than life itself. Perhaps I would have killed to keep him. Perhaps I did. Perhaps I was out of my mind but I don't remember. It's the grief and the tablets which are causing the fog.

Through the window I see an ambulance arrive. DI Ferran shifts uncomfortably in his seat and asks if I would like the curtains closed. I shake my head. I watch the cadaver, wrapped in a black body bag, like a huge bin liner, being carried out to the waiting vehicle. That's not Jason. My husband, my lover, is not wrapped up in some rough and ready packaging being carted away to an incinerator; he's waiting for me at home.

'No. Leave them open. I'll be going home soon anyway,' I say, looking blankly at the cop. I will him to believe in my innocence.

~

I have managed to escape back home and have an over-whelming urge to down the whole bottle of pills Adam Morley has given me and go to sleep. Instead I pull the blinds across and boot up the laptop. I need to wake up, for a short time anyway, and get my affairs in order. I haven't decided yet whether I will join Jason or not.

I fill a pint glass of water and pour it down my throat. It's cool and cleansing but violently hits my empty stomach and bile spurts back over the kitchen surfaces. I scrub the mess clean with a cloth and only stop when I hear a noise.

The phone rings. I have already turned off my mobile and proceed to pull the landline out of its socket before I sit down and log in to *Join Me*. I need to be alone with my thoughts and to talk with you in private. I wonder if any of our clients might have considered who would delete their profiles in the event of sudden death. As the screen flickers to life in front of me and faces fuse in and out of view, I consider that perhaps Jason might not be the only deceased member. I stare at my husband's pictures, clicking through the individual images of his perfect face and body, touching the outline of his cheekbones delicately with my finger. The bottle of little blue tablets sit on the desk beside me and, like *Alice in Wonderland*, I'm tempted by their magical lure. Perhaps they would make me small and I could disappear across to the other side before anyone realised I'd gone.

The room is cold, silent like a morgue. I see you hover in the corner of the room, urging me on.

I methodically delete my dead husband's profile, all his

pictures, his browsing history and all email communications since the site was launched. I don't reread the dangled verbal carrots that we concocted to entice unwitting users, but cut every piece of evidence that earmarked Jason as a member of our cleverly masterminded machine.

You are smiling at me and have raised a transparent, ghostly arm in the air. I know what you're saying and I smile back. We're still working as a team but as I get up and move towards the filing cabinet, your spectral image fades.

I lift out the banking files and start, one by one, to feed every single statement and cheque book stub through the shredder. I only destroy the evidence of my husband's bank accounts; the secret accounts which house the large payments extorted for the bogus investment schemes. These amounts have nothing to do with me and I will feign ignorance. When the money might eventually come my way, I will act unsurprised by the large amounts confirming what my husband used to say, that he would always look after me and make sure I wanted for nothing. No one will ever know that I knew of his dalliances and the monetary scams. What wife would allow that, everyone will ask? It will be our little secret, something that worked for us. No one else would understand.

The balance on the private Jason Swinton bank account has reached a six-figure sum but I need to deny all knowledge of this. 'You don't want me to take the rap for the extortion, do you?' I search for you in the room, letting my eyes flit from corner to corner, but you have disappeared from view. 'I know you won't mind. All the cheques were made out in your name for a reason. If I don't join you straightaway, I'll need to go some-where, escape and perhaps the money, if no wrongdoing can be proven, will one day soothe the pain.' I talk out loud. I know you're listening.

There'll be no paper trail to the money; nothing illegal will be pinned on my dead husband to tarnish his good name. No one will come forward, I'm certain, to own up to their stupidity in handing over such ludicrous sums.

Susan Harper was to be our blackmail victim but she's had a lucky escape. You don't answer me but a window in the bathroom must be open because something falls off a shelf. It's not windy outside so it must be you telling me that my plan has your approval. I always was the brains behind the scheme and you happily let me take the lead.

I bag up the shredded documents, lock up the house and load it into the car. I start the engine and turn the music up loud so that it blasts around my ears, rendering further thought impossible, and drive. I'll go to Brighton and we can walk hand in hand along the beach, sharing ice creams on the promenade and perhaps we'll browse the lanes for souvenirs like we did when we got engaged.

First though I need to dump the paperwork. The police have told me that I mustn't go anywhere but they'll not miss me for a day or two if I decide to take a dip in the sea and follow the waves all the way to France. Whatever I decide, my work here is done and as I drive away, out of North London, I don't look back.

40

SUSAN

I don't recognise the number flashing up on my phone. I'm in the kitchen, drinking camomile tea to soothe my nerves when I hear the beep of the message. It will probably be Roger.

Slut, whore. Do you think it ends here?

I stare at the message and immediately think it's a wrong number. Someone has sent the message to me by mistake. As I reread the words, the phone rings and the incoming call screen hides the message. This time it is Roger.

'Hi,' I say.

'You called.' He's busy on yet another very important high-powered legal case and has no time for small talk. He doesn't yet know what has happened.

'You need to come home. The police want to talk to you,' I say.

'What do you mean?' I have his attention but instead of telling him in concise logical sentences of what's going on, I cry; large blubbering sobs. My thoughts are in a jumble, all over the place, and the threatening text message has added to the confusion.

'Susan? Are you okay? Is it the children? What's happened?' I hear him excuse himself from some hovering colleague, most likely his secretary, and head outside.

'Can you come home? It's not the children. It's the house next door. Someone's been murdered.'

'I'm on my way.' The phone goes dead.

After I jot down the number of the caller who left the message and delete the text, I wander round the house like a caged animal. I don't know how much to tell Roger, whether now is the time to come clean. What can I tell him? That I joined some online sightseeing website and the man I've been to London Zoo with is none other than the dead body next door. That he was also the man who came to dinner at our house recently, the husband of my new friend, Caroline Swinton.

A constant hum of activity bubbles through from next door and I watch from the window as people move backwards and forwards round the building. I have to get out of the house for a bit, before Roger comes home, act normal as if nothing unto-ward has happened. No one needs to suspect me. What is there to suspect? Having a bit of fun is not a criminal offence, although, where I'm concerned, I know Roger would put it down as such. He would have me hung, drawn and quartered. He has always told me that the one thing he would never tolerate in marriage is deceit.

Relationships are built on trust and without trust he sees no point. In his wildest dreams, I would be the last person he would suspect of having an affair as he has told me often enough that he only sympathises with abused or battered wives who seek escape routes. He deals with enough divorce cases to have little time with bored, spoilt or philandering spouses who think they're clever enough to get away with cheating.

I go upstairs and wash my face, scrubbing it hard until the red flaky patches appear again on my cheeks. I apply a thin layer of foundation and lightly rouge my cheeks in an attempt to hide the damage. I dampen my hands and run them through the ends of my hair, trying to flatten it out but this only makes it more unkempt. I look deranged.

I must calm down and not draw attention to myself. I'm an ordinary middle-class housewife who is as shocked as everyone else by the turn of events. I'm not a criminal. Yet the picture in the mirror tells another story.

I text Roger to tell him I'm popping to the shops as I need to get some fresh air. I shouldn't be too long and will see him soon. I thank him for coming home. A message pings straight back. As I look down to note the reply, his default and concise *Ok*, I drop the phone. There's another threatening text on the screen from the same random number as before.

Dirty little bitch. I'm watching you. Do you think you can fuck other people's husbands and get away with it?

41

ALEXIS

I'm at the lock-up with Gary who's got in early at my request. The thick cloying stench of grease is slowly fading and our new offices, with the strong smell of lavender air freshener, have started to have the feel of a professional outfit.

It doesn't end here, you little slut. Watch your back because I'm watching you.

I turn the message on my phone round to Gary for him to read and for a moment he doesn't seem to register what I'm showing him.

'I've no idea who it's from but this is the second text in the last couple of days; since the murder.' I save the message and the number as I think they might be of future importance, evidence of what though I'm not sure. I know they'll be untraceable and most likely from the murderer; probably sent from a cheap burner phone. There's no reply when I dial back and it automatically goes to a generic voicemail. Yet for some reason it seems vital to log the details.

'Who's it from? I'm missing something here,' Gary asks as he unloads his backpack onto the desk. His black T-shirt has *The Grateful Dead* emblazoned across the front in fluorescent orange and I grimace at the words.

'Great T-shirt,' I say. 'Very fitting.' He looks embarrassed and pulls a chair over beside me, settling in to hear the whole story.

I begin by showing him the home page of the *Join Me* website, with its teasing façade, which offers innocent sight-seeing opportunities around London for its residents. Although I told him, albeit in a casual throwaway manner when Caroline engaged our PI services, that I had also been enticed to join the surfers on the site, I now feel foolish and naïve. I was easily sucked in by the offers of meeting like-minded people to enjoy London's gems, especially when I was bored and alone after Adam had gone. The £50 enrolment fee seemed value for money.

'There's a connection between the website and the murder, I'm certain. It's all too coincidental otherwise. This guy Jason has been posing on the website under some phoney aliases and if he's sucked in Susan Harper and me, then God knows how many other idiots he's been seeing. I wonder what sort of places he's been offering to take them.' If Gary senses my humiliation and stupidity, he doesn't show it. I like him for his sense of respect but perhaps it's his gratitude at the chance I've given him that stops him making sarcastic or belittling comments. I feel ridiculous enough as it is.

'What do you think?' I wait as Gary slowly reads through the blurb on the screen. It's not the first time he has looked at the site, but this time he concentrates hard, poking at the detail.

'I hear what you say but I can't find this Jason Swinton anywhere. His profile seems to have disappeared. Even if he's using an alias, or a bunch of aliases, I can't find a photo of anyone remotely resembling him. Someone must have deleted it, possibly after he was murdered. Any ideas?' Gary turns the question in my direction. 'I doubt it would have been his wife, as I can't imagine he would have shared intimate details of his online dates with her.' Gary continues to click over the keys, scrolling through the pages.

'Try Susan Harper. She was on there. I'm sure that's how she met Jason in the first place.' I watch, willing her face to appear.

'No. Nothing. Have you deleted your own profile?'

'Yes. The first thing I did.' I speak with a light-heartedness I'm not feeling. 'The police will soon make their own assumptions and start piecing together the facts.'

I want to get things straight in my head and try to work out what's going on. Somehow I'm involved but I'm not yet ready to tell the police about the threatening texts or my inroads into the online network, despite its apparent harmlessness. My father taught me that the police suspect everyone and they dig especially deeply in murder cases by delving into the seediest corners.

My dad never gave up on a case until he got answers, trawling through evidence into the small hours, pinning up faces and names along every inch of wall, slowly and methodically joining the dots. When he was working on really high-profile cases, Mum and I never saw him. He darted in and out of our lives, mumbling vague words of greeting or farewell as he carried on with his mission. 'We need a whiteboard, Gary,' I announce. 'We need to find out what's going on before the police jump to any wrong conclusions. Can you get one and make a start on the evidence? I know how the police operate and we need to keep one step ahead of them. I can't take any chances of being put in the frame for homicide, however unlikely it might sound.'

'Aye aye, boss.' He salutes with his right hand in my direction. 'I'm onto it.'

As I hand him some cash, I pick up my keys and tell him I've someone I need to talk to while he sorts out the shopping list.

'Susan Harper is involved. Caroline knew she had been seeing Jason. I think I'll pay her a visit and try to find out some more. I suspect she needs someone to talk to.'

Adam is mooching around the house when I get back from the lock-up. He seems to be using the events to his advantage although perhaps this is unfair. The house is spic and span and the smell of fresh polish hits my nostrils as soon as I open the front door. I turn and glance across the road at the crime scene where a huddle of police officers and reporters still mooch around. The blue tape has been extended round the perimeter of the house and the circle of the cul-de-sac has been closed off except to residents. I feel an icy coldness in my bones.

'Hi. I'm off to work,' he says when he sees me, lifting his briefcase and throwing a coat over his arm. I detect a distinct whiff of aftershave biting through the polish and wonder if the former is also for my benefit as I know the latter certainly is.

He doesn't ask where I've been. He sees that I'm in jogging clothes so will assume I've been round the woods early, to clear my head. This was my intention. He doesn't know about the lock-up and I won't be telling him. It's my haven until the divorce comes through.

Adam thinks I've been overly shocked by the murder and also by Olive's condition and seems intent on making the most of my trauma to feather his own nest. Little things have ostentatiously been added to his daily routine, small stuff to showcase his attempts to make amends and to get things back to where they were several months ago; before he started the affair with Debbie and before he knocked the shit out of me. He's started making me tea in the morning, adding toast and marmalade with freshly cut grapefruit and also empties the bins knowing that this has been a bone of contention since we got together. It all makes me uneasy as I need to move on and get the divorce sewn up.

'Thanks for tidying the house,' I say. 'I'm grateful.'

He bends over and kisses me on the cheek, ignoring the bracing of my body in response.

'A pleasure.' He turns to leave. 'By the way, that policeman was poking around this morning, DI Ferran. He's checking out alibis of everyone living in the close the night of the murder. I've no idea who the poor dead guy was but you might know him. He was Caroline Swinton's husband. I think you mentioned you'd met her at the Harpers'?'

Adam closes the door gently behind him, the stench of aftershave trailing in his wake. I reach for the chain and pull it across, securing the bolts top and bottom.

Fifteen minutes later a text pings through on my phone.

Tart, whore. How many times did you fuck him? One too many, I think.

42

SUSAN

Roger sits alongside the detective. His long legs are crossed and he looks composed, relaxed. I'm on the other side of the room, a non-participating spectator. This is Roger's moment. I need to listen, to hear what's being said. There's been no mention of *Join Me* and details haven't yet been made public with regard to the victim's name or background.

'We need to ascertain where all the residents were on the night in question,' the foggy throated detective begins. I feel like I'm watching some TV drama; this sort of thing doesn't happen in real life. Roger doesn't look to me for help in confirming his responses. He's not looking for an alibi. This is as well as I have no idea what time he got home. I sit and stare self-consciously at the floor. I feel bizarrely responsible for putting my husband in this position although I don't really know why other than I have the weirdest feeling that something about my trysts with Jason are going to come back to haunt me, sooner rather than later. Our marriage might be hanging by a thread if the truth comes out.

'I got home around eleven. I was working late. Susan was in bed when I got in.' He glances over. I don't remember. The sleeping pills had done their trick and I don't even remember him leaving in the morning.

'Is there anyone who can confirm your movements?' The detective carries on taking notes and I wonder if he's compiling a shopping list. He can't suspect Roger and would have nothing to write of any importance where he's concerned. Cereal, bread, bacon and eggs will be his staple essentials; probably a bottle or two of malt whiskey as well.

'Yes, my secretary and I were working together and we shared a nightcap before I left.' This catches my attention. He hadn't said but then perhaps I hadn't asked. 'We often have to stay late. Legal cases involve mountains of paperwork.' This time Roger looks at me more directly. I straighten up in my seat and try to concentrate on the conversation.

'We'll need her details please: name and contact number. It's a formality.' Ferran bends over to make more notes; bananas, apples and milk are being added to the list. Roger won't provide him with many clues. I watch my husband bend down and scratch his calf muscle, a strange place for a sudden itch. He looks uneasy but then he doesn't like to be the centre of attention. He'll be finding this whole exercise very unsettling.

'Yes of course.'

The detective stands up and rubs his back, grimacing as he straightens. He snaps closed his notebook, slips it into his pocket, and glances at me with a definite hint of sympathy. I move across to join Roger and wonder what Ferran has gleaned from the interview that I haven't. Does he feel sorry for me or does he suspect Roger?

I need some air. My mind is in overdrive. As we reach the front door, the bell goes. I can see the outline of Alexis Morley from across the road through the side glass panel. Before I have time to disappear upstairs with one of my threatening migraines, Roger opens the door and invites our neighbour across the threshold. He's relieved by the intrusion as I sense one of his shutdown moods when further conversation will be impossible. He has an uncanny ability to brush problems aside until a later date when he might have a better ability to deal with them.

'Hi. Come in,' I say but Alexis stays on the doorstep.

'Do you fancy a coffee? Thought you might like to get out of the house. Adam's gone back to work and I could do with the company.' Before I reply, Roger announces that he's off to his mother's to check on the children. He tells me he won't go back to work today but wants to take over some toys and games as he thinks it best they stay where they are for the time being.

'Yes. Why not,' I say to Alexis. 'Give me ten minutes.'

Strange, but I've never been in the Morleys' house before. It is the mirror image of our own in construction but it lacks character, personality. The décor is bland, unfinished, and it has an unlived in feel.

'Sorry,' my hostess apologises. 'It's a bit of a mess.' She doesn't say why and I don't like to ask. The walls are bare, no paintings or photographs break up the insipid magnolia. There's a glaring absence of something; permanency I suspect.

'At least you don't have Lego strewn across the floor and broken toys under your feet,' I quip, but instantly regret my tactlessness. The absence of kids might not be by choice. She leads me into a similarly unfinished kitchen and I notice a couple of unpacked boxes by the utility door.

'Still settling in,' she says. I suspect the rumours of a split in marital harmony might not be far off the mark. I sit down at the small breakfast bar and mentally compare its unaltered dimensions to our large granite work surface.

I wait for her to start up the conversation. She's not easy company but perhaps it's because we don't have much in common. When she throws down her opening gambit, I sense a hidden agenda.

'Did you know the victim?' she asks. Alexis is dressed casually in bright jogging clothes, and as she leans back against the cupboards and cradles her mug with both hands, I realise I'm about to be interrogated.

'Who?' I play for time.

'It was Caroline Swinton's husband. Jason. I can't believe it.' Alexis grimaces with a look of disbelief and waits for my response.

'Yes, I heard.' I sip my coffee and swill the bitter taste slowly round my mouth, scared to swallow in case it won't settle. She tries to put me at ease by offering some plain biscuits which she lifts out of a tin and sets on a plate. Perhaps she senses my struggle with the coffee.

'Did you ever meet him?' She's watching me. Does she suspect? I need to get out of here. I don't need this.

'Yes, they came to dinner once. He seemed nice. Did you?' It's something to ask in return, a way to engage in conversation until I can finish my drink and go home. Her reply is the last thing I expect.

'Yes.' Alexis sets down her mug and takes a stool alongside me. 'I need to tell someone and I know this will sound ridiculous, but I met him through an online website.'

I'm not quite sure what she means. Who is she talking about?

'Really?' I sound surprised and open my eyes wide. 'Shit. Sorry, I'm a bit clumsy. It's my nerves.' I apologise as coffee dribbles from my mug. 'It's all been very unsettling.' I hear my voice rise a few decibels and I begin to shake.

Alexis must notice but she carries on, perhaps too polite to comment.

'*Join Me*. Did you see the flyers? It's an online website where people link up with other members to sightsee around London. It isn't a dating site, or it's not meant to be.' She hesitates and then continues. 'I fell for it. It offers a chance to meet people with similar interests. Jason Swinton was on there, posing as someone called Eddie and I met up with him a couple of times for a drink.' She takes a sip of coffee. 'Adam and I weren't getting along and it was something to do after I broke my leg. I was going crazy in the house on my own.'

She waits for me to respond. She knows something. I don't feel too well. The panic attack is building and my breathing is becoming increasingly laboured. I'm sweating but perhaps it's the heat in the kitchen.

'Yes. I saw the flyers and had a quick look but that was all,' I manage. Something tells me not to deny all knowledge.

'I don't know whether to tell the police. I'm scared they might jump to conclusions and as his name as the murdered victim hasn't become public knowledge yet, I don't want to be too hasty. What do you think?'

She's toying with me. She knows about Jason and me. I look at her athletic little body, toned and slender with her crisp neat hair and faintly tanned complexion. Her bright snugly fitting peach top outlines the girlish curves and the little scar over her left eye has started to twitch. I hate her. She's made things worse. Vince would never have wanted anything from her. I was his secret woman, his longed-for passion outside a loveless marriage. I'm certain. I stand up.

'Sorry, Alexis, but I don't feel too well. Do you mind if I go home? It's all too upsetting.' I set the mug down and drag my stool back. 'I wouldn't bother saying anything if I were you. I doubt if the website has anything to do with his murder. For all we know, Caroline might have killed him.' My laugh is high-pitched, hysterical, but Alexis doesn't react. She's controlled and I don't trust her. She's goading, teasing me, and I'm desperate to get away.

As I step out into the close, I turn and ask a question that has been niggling away. It's been lurking somewhere in the recesses of my mind for some time.

'Who runs the website? Do you know?'

43

CAROLINE

B RUTAL MURDER IN NORTH LONDON LINKED TO
AN ONLINE SOCIAL NETWORK
Scott Wilson of the London Echo
Jason Swinton, a local man from Highgate, aged 32, was found brutally murdered in an empty house on Riverside Close NW6. He was savagely attacked and it is understood that broken glass shards were used to disfigure his face and features.

His wife, Caroline Swinton, is the owner and founder of the London-based website called **Join Me.** *The website offers its users a chance to link up with like-minded professional people to share tasteful exciting experiences around the capital. The site, with over 1000 members, is currently shut down pending police investigations. Detectives are looking into possible links between the murder and the website.*

The skies are azure blue and the seagulls cruise overhead, limousines of the skies. I watch them swoop and soar through the air. Children are playing on the beach, their squeals and shouts batting back and forth over the distant steady rumble of the sea. I can feel your hand, warm and wet in mine, the sand grains rubbing gently between our fingers.

We walk slowly, a young couple in love, hand in hand, along the seashore with our trouser legs turned up in age-old beach-fashioned style. We dip our toes in and out of the water and shriek as the icy coldness invades our warm bodies, before I streak away, careering towards the headland willing you to follow, catch me and never let me go.

I crumple the newspaper up and throw it in one of the litter bins that line my route. I have quite some way to walk to reach my destination and to escape from prying eyes. I have one last thing to do before my final journey so tiptoe with caution over the increasingly rocky landscape to an isolated boulder which juts out from the surrounding platform. The flat top is warm to the touch and I take off my cardigan, spread it across the surface before sitting down and beginning to write.

Dear Alexis

I'm enclosing a cheque for one last job I would like you to do for me. I no longer need your help in locating my husband as I've found him. We'll be together shortly. You'll see I've included a more than generous amount in good faith because I want you to make sure that his murderer is brought to justice.

The police will try to put me in the frame and will pick through our lives like vultures over a carcass. They won't believe that I could never have murdered Jason. They will suspect me of being a jealous wife and lover and won't understand that I could never have hurt him. He was my love, my life, my reason for being. I won't stay around to watch them destroy what we had.

Join Me was our invention, mine and Jason's. It was never about the money. It was about allowing Jason the freedom to feed his addictions yet provide me with a way to stay in control and keep him close. I'm glad it's over. It was all an illusion. I've learnt that love has no controls but is free flowing and sexual fantasies are momentary aber-

rations of the mind; nothing more. I will sleep peacefully at last as nightmares can no longer torture my soul. My love is calling me.

Please find his murderer and make sure they take the blame for my demise as well as his.

Yours,

Caroline Swinton

~

I find a tiny postbox slotted into the seawall at the far end of the beach. I say a silent prayer before I pop the envelope inside, and will my final act to bring justice. I then turn and head back towards the rocks and step out over the craggy outcrops which have become green and slimy from the salt water as it encroaches across their surface.

I count to ten, slither down over the edge and gently release myself into the swirling ocean. I swim, violently at first, and then more calmly out towards France. We can start our new life in Dieppe and from there make our way to Paris and onwards to the Riviera.

Cannes is lovely this time of year, off-season, and perhaps we can dander along the coast before taking in the film festival. The red carpet will welcome you, with your film-star looks. I will be your plus one and we will stroll into the bright lights together, hand in hand, having conquered the world.

I'm coming, I'm on my way.

44

ALEXIS

Gary has made a start at staging the lock-up as an incident room. The whiteboard is smeared with all manner of scribbled words and symbols, arrows darting back and forth, and he's cut out head and shoulder lookalikes from magazines which are labelled underneath with the real names of the players and stuck them alongside.

'George Clooney?' I laugh with a raised eyebrow. 'More Ted Bundy.' I finger the various pictures and stop when I come to the one meant to represent Jason. Even Gary has picked up on the victim's film-star looks. Gary looks embarrassed by his amateurish attempts at mocking up a suspect collage but I high five him, impressed by his improvisations.

'Marilyn Monroe isn't a bad choice for Caroline,' I add, amused by the snap showing off her cleavage. He has been astute by homing in on her sexuality. 'But Susan Harper is nothing like Julianne Moore. The hair maybe, but Susan is much more insipid and insignificant.' I'm slightly shocked to see Adam's name labelled under a picture of Matt Damon although I can't deny his vague likeness to the actor.

'Adam? You don't see him as a suspect, surely?' I don't sound convinced. Gary looks awkward at perhaps having overstepped the mark. A rush of red floods his cheeks.

'Sorry, boss. I'm trying to be as thorough as possible.' He tries to justify what he thinks I've taken as a slight but underneath my rhetorical question, I have my own misgivings. Look at the unsuspecting, go at it from all angles and rule no one out. I can hear my father as if it were yesterday. I now wonder where Adam was on the night in question.

'Roger Harper looks nothing like Bill Nighy! How did you come up with that one?' I laugh, amused by his summations and relieved to have moved on from my own husband's possible involvement.

There's a picture of an aging Bette Davis pinned at the bottom of the board.

'Who the heck is that meant to be?' I peer at the grainy black and white cut-out and try to decipher the name attached to it.

'Fannie? Francis? I can't read your writing,' I tut in mock irritation at the illegibility.

'Francine, Francine Dubois,' he says. 'Sorry. I'm more used to a keyboard than a pen. I thought she might come into the equation somewhere. Remember she was the last woman we saw Jason with; in Highgate. I took some pictures.' Gary pokes around through a pile of images strewn across his desk and hands me the stills of Jason with his muscled torso pressed into her bare breasts.

'You've done well,' I say, amused but impressed by his efforts. 'What's the large random group of people alongside Bette Davis?'

'They represent all the users of *Join Me*. It could be any one of them, don't you think? Anyone playing away could have a partner at home, jealous enough to kill or perhaps one of the users might be a psychopath. Jealousy seems a likely motive though.' Gary sits on the edge of his seat and swirls the end of a felt-tipped pen in his mouth. Faint blue streaks of ink have smudged across his chin and I take out a tissue, wet the end and proceed to rub the offending marks.

'Jeez. I feel like your mother.' I laugh as he blushes again, his acne becoming angry from the attention.

'Thanks,' he mumbles.

'That last picture, off to the side. Let me guess.' I look nothing like Meg Ryan but must say am pathetically flattered that Gary has chosen her image as my representation. 'Thanks for the choice of picture but you can't seriously think I'm in the frame?'

'No, of course not but the police might. You said to think outside the box,' he adds in justification for my addition.

'Here, let's sit down. I've something to show you which looks as if it might eliminate one of our suspects.' I pull my chair alongside and we sit, side by side, like teacher and pupil. The new strip lighting overhead flickers on and off as if it's about to fuse and the overcast gloom from outside seeps through the narrow window slits of the room. I extract the plain white envelope from my bag.

'This arrived this morning. First class from Brighton. It's from Caroline Swinton,' I say. 'There was a hefty cheque inside which will more than cover our little investigation. I'll be able to give you your first proper pay packet.' I wait patiently while he reads through the contents. It takes him a few minutes to digest what has been written before he comments.

'It doesn't mean she didn't do it, does it? She wants us to prove otherwise but perhaps she wants to get herself off the hook?' He hesitates and then asks the obvious. 'Do you think she's dead? Committed suicide?'

The light overhead suddenly implodes and sends lethal shards of glass all around the room. *She's been listening*, I think. Perhaps she's only pretending to have killed herself and has maybe fled the country instead. Despite the quandary, I know, deep down, that Caroline Swinton is dead. Gut instinct. Ninety-nine times out of a hundred it's correct. Dad is also listening.

'Christ,' Gary yells as he automatically shields his head with his hands from the downpour of shattered glass. The room is plunged into darkness and I switch on my phone's torch.

'Are you okay?'

'Yes, just missed me though.' Gary shakes his head from the fallout of glass dust.

'Listen, I'll go and locate the fuse box if you get the ladders so we can change the bulb. There are a couple of spares over there. What a bloody nightmare.'

'You can say that again.'

Gary has gone home. After we got the lighting back on, we spent several hours trawling through the evidence, meticulous in our efforts, and before he left, I insisted that he treat himself to a takeaway and a few beers. He sheepishly accepted some cash and asked if I'd like to join him. I'm not sure if he was being respectfully polite to his boss or whether he has no one else in his life to share the simple pleasures with. When it's all over I'll treat him to a real night out, spoil him and perhaps find him a girlfriend. That will be my next project.

I toy with the crime scene possibilities, trying to order my thoughts which are throwing up more questions than answers. Everything is masked in confusion.

Is Caroline Swinton really dead or did she fake her own suicide to get the police off her trail? Where is she? Perhaps she murdered Jason, as she certainly had the most reason of anyone to be jealous, and has fled the country, perhaps to Brazil or some other far-flung destination to escape justice. I put a line through this theory. She's dead, I'd bet my life on it.

Susan Harper is next on my list. I smile at the picture of Julianne Moore thinking that Susan completely lacks the actress' substance and rather comes across as a neurotic, bored and spoiled housewife. Roger has given her everything: money, kids and a gilded lifestyle. Perhaps she was scared that her relationship with Jason was going to come out? Perhaps Roger was somehow about to learn the truth and she was driven, through sheer desperation, to silence her lover. She hasn't got the nerve. Selfish, spoilt and self-seeking maybe but the label of murderess doesn't ring true.

Susan has definitely played away from home though, I'm certain. Her reaction to my mention of *Join Me* was too knee-jerk, too definite. By trying to deflect the conversation away from the website so quickly, it alerted me to the fact that she knew more than she was letting on and has most probably been using the site. Caroline must have known and that's why she asked me to follow her. Why did Caroline want her followed? And by me. My mind is going round in circles and the possibilities as to what might have happened are endless.

The thought of blackmail suddenly pops into my mind and I wonder if the police have got access to Jason Swinton's bank accounts. Why was he so readily seeking out anonymous women for innocent fun when he could have had his pick of beautiful women? Of course. He must have been in it for the money. Perhaps he was blackmailing Susan Harper and goodness knows how many other women. This seems like a distinct possibility. If this was the case then Susan Harper might have had more reason to kill him than simple fear at being found out. However, I draw a line through her name. I can't see it. I visualise her pristine kitchen, dust-free surfaces and unblemished paintwork, and the mess of blood and gore doesn't fit with her obsessively spotless and organised lifestyle.

Roger Harper is bothering me. As I try to order my thoughts, two messages bleep through on my phone. I swallow hard, bracing myself before I check the screen. I toy with leaving it till I get home, dreading what I might see, but go ahead and pick up anyway.

Join Me is dead. Who'll be next?

The first message is followed by one from Adam.

Hope you're ok. Going to pick up fish and chips on the way home. I'll buy enough for two. All the more for me if you don't fancy it. A x

Whereas the first message is menacing, the second one almost makes me more uneasy. How dare he think I'll fall back into our old ways, sharing late-night takeaways while he drones on, with boring self-obsession, about his operating prowess? The *x* at the end of the text is an arrogant assumption that I've forgiven him and am prepared to carry on as if nothing has happened. I delete both messages and get back to my task. Another thirty minutes and I'll shut up shop.

Did Roger know that Susan was having an affair or that she was using the website for amusement? If so, perhaps he trawled the profiles himself. I suddenly feel uneasy as I imagine him sending me the threatening texts. Perhaps he saw my face on there, along with Susan's, and is hiding his anger under a very cool composed façade. Lawyers toy with words, know how to be manipulative without giving the game away. But I don't know much about the guy other than brief sightings across the close.

Perhaps I'll pop across again one evening when he gets back from work.

~

It's seven o'clock when I finally decide to shut up shop. I wander round and close the small windows, using a set of tiny steps to reach up and secure the bolts. I tidy the desks, straighten out the papers and wonder what I'm missing. The picture of Matt Damon warns me that Adam, like Roger, might have been aware of the website but I'm certain he wouldn't have known I was using it to look at profiles. There's nothing I can think of that would lead him to suspect I had any involvement with the victim. As I turn out the lights and prepare to lock up, I realise the only way that he would have been able to track my browsing history was if he had got access to my laptop.

Outside it is cold and dark. I set off to walk the few blocks to pick up my car. The steady buzz which fills Camden in daylight hours has calmed down and the bars and cafés are slowly filling up with after-work trade. I pause when I reach a small greasy kebab shop where a flashing red neon sign lights up *Kamden Kebabs* and I glance through the steamed-up window.

In the corner I spot a lone figure, hunched over a plate and tucking into a large meat platter. The shop is otherwise empty. I watch Gary, unselfconsciously, enjoy his meal for one. I'll make it up to him. I promise myself, as I wander on, that I'll join him next time he asks. I owe him.

45

SUSAN

*J*OIN ME, THE ONLINE WEBSITE, BECOMES FOCUS OF MURDER ENQUIRY.
Scott Wilson of the London Echo

Police investigations into the murder of a North London man are now being concentrated on the **Join Me** *website which attracts Londoners to enrol and enjoy the sights of the capital with other users. Members can invite people with similar interests to join them for days out.*

The dead man, Jason Swinton, had added his own profile to the site and met up with different female users. This has proved a valuable line of enquiry.

Jocelyn Oakley, a subscriber to **Join Me**, *whose online alias was* **Jos 040**, *has come forward and is now helping police with their investigation. Mrs Oakley, recently separated from her husband, claims that she met Mr Swinton on half a dozen occasions at various venues in Central London. It transpires that she lent him two thousand pounds to help towards a business venture that he was investing in. Asked about the nature of her relationship with the deceased, Mrs Oakley declined to comment. Their individual profiles showed a shared interest in fine wines and gourmet dining.*

*Police believe that Mr Swinton may have met up with several ladies through the website and would ask anyone who met him in this way to come forward in an attempt to eliminate them from their enquiries. The police are stressing that all **Join Me** users will be interviewed in due course and anonymity can no longer be guaranteed for the site's users. Website members are urged to contact their local police station or to call the confidential hotline number below.*

Meanwhile Caroline Swinton, the deceased's wife, has disappeared and police would appeal for information concerning her whereabouts. It is believed that she was the mastermind behind the website and it is unclear at this time whether she knew that her husband had been using it for his own pleasure.

Roger has lifted the paper out of the bin and asked why I threw it out. I'm trying to act as normal as possible but Roger's attitude makes me increasingly uncomfortable. He's taking longer than usual leaving the house and from my vantage point at the kitchen sink, I'm aware of him behind me silently reading the article which is plastered across the front page of the local newspaper.

'It's a joke that police expect people to come forward and own up to cheating.' There's sarcastic amusement in his tone. He doesn't look up but carries on scrutinising the printed detail. 'Who's going to own up to playing away from home?' His laugh is loud, over the top.

I watch him sip his coffee and butter his toast with measured tardiness.

'Don't you agree?' Why is he asking my opinion?

'It's not a dating website,' I say, scrubbing hard at the sink. 'It's a way for people to make new friends and go sightseeing.'

He snorts, making a phoney theatrical splutter with his coffee.

'Don't be so naïve.' He stands up, wipes his mouth with a serviette and pushes the stool neatly back under the breakfast bar. 'The website's wording is clever, I'll give you that. It's managed to suck in plenty of bored idiots and offered them a ready-made cheating platform.' He pulls his suit jacket on, straightens his sleeves, gently tugging them down at the cuffs, and comes across to kiss me goodbye. It's an automatic gesture but today it feels particularly false, manufactured for effect. He takes his time, waits for my response, willing a reaction. I don't know why. I carry on scrubbing.

'I can't think of anyone I know who would be stupid enough to pay money to make friends.' He's a lawyer, clever with words, discerning and professional. I think he knows. If not, why do I feel so cheap and pathetic?

I fell for the clever wording. I pretended that it was all a bit of innocent fun. I was conned into handing over obscene amounts of money for the pleasure of seeing one particular member again and again. Roger could have told me in advance, if I had asked, that meeting people online, no matter for what seemingly innocent reason, would almost certainly go horribly wrong. I smell his cologne, faint and subtle, as he brushes his lips against my skin. I have the most horrendous urge to own up, tell him everything and beg his forgiveness. I want to tell him I'm sorry, that it was all a big mistake. However, his next words jolt me back to reality.

'I'm not sure what I'd do if you did anything so ridiculous. I wouldn't know where to lay the blame if you'd met up with this guy Swinton.' Roger makes a wringing movement with his hands, a silent strangling action and his eyes are wide open. 'Would I kill him or would I kill you? That's a difficult one.' He's amused by the question.

His behaviour is slightly manic, off-kilter, for someone so calm and measured.

I watch as he picks up his briefcase and leaves the house.

The sun is bright overhead and a pleasant heat hits me as I step outside. There is still a steady buzz of muted activity coming from the vacant house. A police officer shoos away a stray dog persistent in its efforts to gain access. The officer turns when I appear.

'Morning, ma'am,' he says. I nod brief acknowledgement and scurry on. I cross the close and walk away from the cul-de-sac on the opposite side of the street. There's no one else about and as I pass the incident board with its boldly printed notice, black on yellow, I shiver. The board signifies a death. Stuck to the board is a notice requesting people who may have any relevant information to come forward.

When I reach Church Street, I pass a young mother with a pram. She smiles at me with the tired weary eyes of a first-time mother. I used to walk Tilly round and round the park and wish for sleep to come so that I could escape the heights of awakened anxiety and join her in much-needed slumber. It seems a lifetime ago.

The steady buzz of traffic away from Riverside Close sucks me back into the real world. The turn of events in the cul-de-sac now seems surreal; other worldly. My legs feel leaden and I try to speed them up, spur them into action. All around, people carry on as normal. Don't they know there has been a murder around the corner? I seem to bear the weight of the incident alone on my shoulders.

I check my mobile every couple of minutes, like a programmed automaton following instructions. It no longer matters what messages might say. There'll be none from Vince, as I still think of Jason, to quicken my pulse and send adrenaline surging through my body. There are none from the school, so the children are safe. The head teacher would only leave a message though if I didn't pick up. In an emergency they would call Roger and he would be there to share a crisis. I walk on, head down, looking at the threatening words which light up the screen.

Bitch, whore. I'm still watching you. Lying little tart.

The words no longer frighten me. I've had enough. I'm going to give myself up. I feel like a criminal on the run and even though I've done nothing legally wrong, it feels like it. Cheating on Roger won't warrant a prison sentence. I want someone to help me, listen to my story and tell me that I have nothing to worry about. The meetings, the dinners out, the champagne were all innocent diversions. No one need ever find out about the wild rampant sex on silken sheets. My insatiable lust for Vince's perfect body will forever be my guilty secret and I'll learn to live with it and keep it deeply buried. I'll deny any suggestions of wrongdoing and my tears of foolishness when I get home will melt Roger's forgiving heart. He'll tell me I've been very stupid.

I walk on with a more determined set to my stride and smile at the possibility that Roger might even try to take some blame for my ridiculous behaviour. Perhaps he'll spoil me and offer to book us a weekend break to Bruges, or Rome, and apologise for his neglect by working such long hours. This is the time of year to visit Venice, or Barcelona perhaps. Destinations pop into my mind, one after the other. The bright midday sun helps to fuel my romantic imaginings.

As I turn the corner of Station Road, my stomach does a nervous flip and for a moment I waver. For a second I consider turning back but know I can't. The police need my help. They'll understand if I explain myself properly and they'll be able to get the vicious texts to stop.

Up ahead I see another woman walking into the station and I notice she is putting her mobile phone back into her pocket. Like me, she'll have turned it to silent mode in deference to authority. It's only when I reach the entrance, framed by heavy metal doors, that I recognise her.

'Hi Susan.' Alexis Morley holds the door open for me. I know why she's here and I suspect she knows why I'm here too. It will all soon be over.

'Hi,' I reply as we cross the threshold together.

46

ALEXIS

I sit in the dimly lit interrogation room, a volunteer here of my own accord to offer up information to help police with their enquiries. Yet for some reason I feel anxious as I wait, alone, for the interview to begin. I'm nervous and don't know why. I got a call from the station earlier in the day, asking me to pop by. It all sounded innocent enough but I feel uneasy. I am going to own up that I was a member of *Join Me*. Something tells me of the need for honesty.

The room is a square box with a long table in the centre, four red plastic chairs neatly pushed underneath and a notepad with half a dozen pens placed on top. There are no windows in the room which is stuffy and increasingly claustrophobic as the minutes tick by.

The door opens after what seems like an eternity and DI Ferran comes in, carrying a paper coffee cup; the strong rich aroma fills the room. Although he is no longer wearing a rain-coat, he still looks dishevelled in a manufactured sort of way. His hair is unkempt, uncombed, and his brown jacket doesn't match his black slacks. I wonder if he deliberately dresses down to put suspects at their ease or if his personality is such that he isn't one for timewasting on what he perceives as irrelevant personal grooming.

'Would you like a coffee, Mrs Morley?' He sits without waiting for an answer, which he assumes will be negative. He's guessed right and that I'll be anxious to get on with matters.

I have the fleeting notion that I might intentionally have been left alone in the room for so long. It's a well-known tactic to make suspects feel uneasy, give them time to sweat. I breathe deeply and try to relax, and remind myself that I've done nothing wrong and have nothing to hide.

'I hope you don't mind if our conversation is taped. It makes life much easier for the investigating team if interviews are recorded.' Ferran looks at me, awaiting affirmation, while his right hand hovers over the machine, preparing to click it on. It doesn't feel like a casual chat. He seems to know that I might have relevant information that will be important in the case. I wonder how much he already knows. The door swings open and a young female, whom Ferran introduces as WPC Taylor, joins us and sits down opposite me and alongside the SIO, the senior investigating officer.

'Can you begin by telling us how you knew the deceased, Mr Jason Swinton, please, Mrs Morley?' The recording machine has been kick-started into life and I tell them what I know. I don't tell the whole story though as I'm leaving out the fact that Gary and I are carrying out our own investigation into what happened. It's likely that we would be warned away from this course of action. Private investigators are not the police force's favourite people. I fidget, twisting my finger through the ends of my hair as the questions come thick and fast.

'You say you met Mr Swinton, who was using the alias of Eddie, through *Join Me*. Let me get this straight...' Ferran pauses as if considering the possible implications. 'You only met up with him after his wife had engaged you to follow him as she suspected him of cheating. Didn't you think this was a bit coincidental? You say you only met him twice, is that correct?'

'Yes. It was only after the first meeting that I realised it was the same guy Caroline wanted me to follow. She seemed to know he was cheating. I'm certain she knew about his affairs and she probably also knew I'd been in contact with her husband before she engaged my services.'

'Did your own husband, Mr Morley, know you were using online websites?'

I stare at the cop, provoked by the sudden deviation from his interest in the Swintons.

'No, of course not. We're going through a divorce and I only checked out *Join Me* after problems we'd been having reached a head.' It's none of his business whether Adam knew or not. I can't see the relevance.

There's a small fan overhead which clicks every time it does a revolution. It creates an ominous presence in the silence. Ferran waits for me to continue. I don't.

'So Mr Morley still has no idea you met the deceased online?'

It's all a bit confusing. I don't want Adam to know about any links I had to Jason, through Caroline or the website. It's none of his business. If it comes out later, it will probably be easier when he has already moved out and accepted that our marriage is over. I know at the moment he wouldn't take finding out what I'd been up to particularly well. He might be trying to lure me back with over exaggerated displays of remorse, but it's not easy to forget how quickly his moods can swing towards violence.

I extract Caroline's letter as my coup d'état and hand it across. Ferran pauses the tape.

'What's this?' I have his attention. Adam is relegated to the background.

'A letter from Caroline Swinton. It was sent from Brighton. I think it might help you to trace her whereabouts,' I say, proud to be one step ahead of the game. The fan clicks again. A small bluebottle is buzzing in competition and the female police officer tries to swot it away with a folder. I realise I'm too closely linked to the deceased and his wife to be given an easy ride. The cogs in Ferran's brain are working overtime as he scrutinises the letter's contents, turning it over and over and back again. He checks out the postmark on the envelope and hands the evidence to his colleague.

'Thank you. We'll hold on to this for now, if that's okay. One last thing. Can you let me have your mobile phone number please?' It's a simple request. I assume it's so that he can try to trace the source of the sinister messages. I've saved all the threat messages which he has already logged, dates and times carefully noted.

'Am I the only one getting threats?' It's an innocent question. I assume the murderer has targeted other users, having somehow obtained their private numbers. Perhaps it's a hacker, a hate nerd who has managed to break into members' details.

'I doubt you will be.' Ferran is evasive. Perhaps no one else has come forward yet. However, something makes me sit up when the cop throws out a curveball. I freeze. The fly is on its back, WPC Taylor staring smugly at her handiwork.

'For God's sake, get rid of that bloody thing,' Ferran snaps while the officer proceeds to wrap the dead insect in a tissue and throw it in the bin. For a second, her composure fails as she reddens, embarrassed by the remonstration.

I am uneasy at what is about to come. It's going to be something I don't like but I can't put my finger on it. I write down my mobile phone number on a proffered piece of paper and watch while the DI compares it with another number extracted from his file.

'Mrs Morley. This number you have given us is the same

number that was used to send a text message to the deceased on the day of his murder. He received a text asking him to meet up in Riverside Close, in the vacant house where his body was found. It was sent from this number. We got the information from his mobile phone found at the scene.' The fan clicks through several revolutions while I try to digest the facts. What does he mean? What message?

'In a text sent to Mr Swinton, the words *Join Me* were used as an enticement and the sender signed off with a capital A. I wonder if the A was for Alexis?'

47

ALEXIS

My thoughts swirl round in my head as I run back to the house. I can't make sense of what's happening. I skirt the refuse bins set out on the pavement for collection. There is a stench of rotting rubbish in the air. I turn first into Church Street and then on up to Riverside Close. I check my watch. Two o'clock. I pause at the front gate, frantically trying to get my phone out of my back pocket, my fingers damp with sweat and catch it just in time before it slithers to the ground.

I leave a voicemail when Gary doesn't pick up.

Gary, it's me, Alexis. I have to see you urgently. Can you make the lock-up about seven? I need your help. Please.

Once inside, I dash upstairs, rip off my damp clothes and jump into the shower. I stand under the boiling water and let it stream over my tense body. Who had access to my phone? It must have been someone who knew about my interest in *Join Me*. Adam possibly, but he didn't know about *Join Me*, or did he? How would he have found out? I try to remember when he might have had a chance to pick up my phone, or browse my laptop when I wasn't around.

As I reach for the towel, my stomach knots. It looks increasingly probable that I'm being put in the frame for something I didn't do. I sit on the bed and tug a brush through my wet hair, and suddenly wonder if Caroline might not be dead after all. Perhaps she managed to lure Jason to the house herself and in a jealous rage finished him off and is trying to put one of his lady companions in the frame. It's all too ridiculous. I've definitely watched too many cop movies. How would she have got hold of my phone or used my number to lure him to the house? I can't think of any other options. I pull a T-shirt over my head. I need to calm down; my mind's all over the place. A text beeps through on my phone. It's from Adam.

> Hi. Olive is much better today and is asking to see you. Perhaps you can pop in. Am in theatre till about five. X

My pulse races as I hurry downstairs. At first I can't find my car keys as they're not in the bowl by the front door. I'm not sure what time Adam left this morning and why would he have taken my keys? I poke around blindly in my clutch bag and find them at the bottom. I need to calm down.

I realise as I walk through the front doors into the main reception area of the hospital that I haven't eaten since eight o'clock this morning and my head is spinning through worry and lack of sustenance. There's a small café on the ground floor and I decide to have a quick coffee and biscuit before I go and find Olive who's recuperating on the third floor. I need to stay alert.

I notice the woman before she notices me. She's sitting in the corner with a newspaper spread out on the table. At first I can't work out who she is, although her face is familiar. Her hair is scraped back severely into a knot at the nape of her neck and under the light blue uniform it's difficult not to be drawn to the large bust which appears to be sitting on the table. Then it clicks. Debbie. Adam's dirty secret. As I pay for my coffee, she gets up. Perhaps she's seen me and wants to get away, save us both the embarrassment. Instead she walks towards me, momentarily blocking my way.

'Alexis? I thought it was you. I'm Debbie. I work with Adam. Do you have a minute?'

Why does she want to talk to me? To pour her heart out, cry over spilt milk, apologise. At the moment she's the last person I want to see. She doesn't seem particularly at ease and I suspect an insincere apology might be on the cards.

I follow, somewhat reluctantly, back to the corner but I am interested to hear what she might say; how she'll explain things. She folds the newspaper and sets it on a vacant chair.

'I've wanted to talk to you. I'm sorry about what happened with me and Adam. It wasn't serious,' she begins. I conjure up Gary's black and white photos of this woman and my husband at the upstairs window, bodies entwined, wet lips stuck together. I let her carry on. 'Adam can be very persuasive,' she says, looking down at the table as she speaks and adds more quietly, 'threatening actually. Doctors seem pretty powerful and sometimes the nurses get sucked into things that in other circumstances they wouldn't ever consider.' She's going to try to pass the buck, blame it all on Adam. I sip my coffee through the small hole in the plastic cap, watching Debbie carefully, my lips drawn tight.

'Promotions were on the cards for junior nurses when Adam first approached me and I fell for his offers of help in fast tracking a pay rise. I was pretty naïve.' I suspect she is telling the truth here as I've no doubt Adam flaunts his position of authority among the more junior sycophants. It sounds like him.

However, I'm not convinced of her naivety until she continues. 'When I told him I was married and that I regretted what I'd done with him after the Christmas party, he became threatening. I told him I was happily married and it had been a big mistake.' At this point she pulls up a long blue sleeve and shows me dark angry welts across her forearm. I can make out a small but livid scar near the wrist. 'He warned me by saying if I showed anyone, he'd tell them that I'd been self-harming because he wasn't interested in my advances.' Under the dim wall lighting, I notice a tear filter from her eye. Self-consciously she rubs it away, as if ashamed of the weakness.

'Listen, Debbie. Don't cry on my account. It's water under the bridge,' I say with a barely concealed sigh, resisting the urge to pat her comfortingly on the arm. There's only so far I'm prepared to go.

'I try to avoid him at all costs and have requested a transfer out of London.'

I stand up, drain the contents of the paper cup, scrunch it up and throw it in the bin.

'Good luck with that,' I say and move smartly away.

For now I've much more pressing concerns. I need to see Olive and then get hold of Gary to help me work out what's going on. Together we need to come up with the best way to deal with the complex turn of events. I have to clear my name.

I mount the stairs, two at a time, checking the ward names on the walls as I go up. The bizarre notion that Adam might be capable of murder is starting to freak me out. If Debbie spurned his advances and at the same time he found out I might have been cheating on him, he may well have been capable of anything; pushed to unknown limits. But murder seems far-fetched. He's arrogant and controlling but surely not homicidal.

I reach Oasis Ward and peer through the window at the small row of beds, whose occupants are hidden under a camouflage of blue and white bedding. Bleeping monitors are hooked up to a couple of the patients and bright overhead fluorescent tubes flood the room with a bland impersonal light. As I push open the door, I notice there is no one other than the patients inside the ward. A couple of nurses hover outside by the desk, busy with the drugs trolley.

'Olive?' I'm not sure if it is Olive. I walk over towards the last bed nearest to the window and I have to get up close before I'm certain. She's so small and frail-looking but sharp beady little eyes alight on me immediately.

'Alexis. You've come. Thank goodness,' she croaks, as she struggles to get upright. I bend over, kiss her gently on the forehead, and pack the pillows tightly behind her for support. 'I need to talk to you. Are you okay? You don't look so good. What's up?' She doesn't wait for an answer as she's desperate to tell me something.

'It seems ages since I came in here and I must talk to you, show you something.' She wheezes with the effort of speaking and her eyes dart from side to side.

As I pull a chair up close, I see Adam hovering in the doorway, stethoscope dangling from around his neck, his hand raised in acknowledgement. Olive spots him and quietly sets her fingers reassuringly on top of mine. I exhale slowly, realising I've been holding my breath for a long time.

'Don't worry,' she whispers, barely audible. 'We'll get the bastard.' It's Adam. That's what she's telling me. I can't move, as if I'm manacled to the chair and begin to make what is intended to sound like vacuous small talk. My voice is shaky and shrill. Adam strolls across, throws professional caution to the wind, and leans down and tries to kiss me on the cheek. Olive closes her eyes for a second; she doesn't want to watch.

'How are we today?' He's going to use his stethoscope, perhaps to strangle her I think, bizarre thoughts invading my common sense. The patient keeps her eyes closed. It's deliberate. Olive is pretending to be asleep but suddenly she opens them wide and stares accusingly at him.

'My phone. Where is it? Someone's stolen it,' she snaps in his face. Adam smiles in a calm self-assured professional way while he straightens her top sheet.

'Don't worry, Olive. One of the nurses has it at her desk for charging. You remember you were worried it had run out of battery?' He's plausible; very plausible. It's his forte. Perhaps I'm too tired, my mind overactive. The bitter taste of coffee has furred up the inside of my mouth and I can feel a persistent throbbing in my left temple.

'I'll go and get it for you now. You should be ready to go home in a couple of days.' He smiles, wide and gleaming. I'm meant to be proud of him, in awe of his bedside manner and dedication. Perspiration is dripping from my forehead and Adam leans across me to reach the window clasp.

'Would you like me to crack the window, Olive, let some air through? It's very hot in here. The nurses can shut it if it gets too cold.' Olive doesn't answer, but ignores his gestures of concern.

'I need my phone now. Bob is expecting me to call him. I didn't ask you to take it away.'

Once Adam has left us alone to get the phone, Olive says she's something to show me. She tried apparently to send them through to me seconds before her battery died. Photographs she took. She asks if I got them. I'm not sure what she's talking about. We watch Adam return with the phone. He hands it directly to the patient.

'There we are then. Fully charged.' He sounds as if he's talking to a small child, after having successfully located an errant football from behind the bushes. He is seriously underestimating my elderly friend.

Adam disappears again, stethoscope swinging and his green

gown gaping loosely open which means his work day is nearly over. It'll take him about an hour to change his clothes, scrub down and make his way home. I have an hour left with Olive and I need to hear what she has to say and see what is on her phone.

48

ALEXIS

The traffic is unending as it blocks the roads home from the hospital. The seven o'clock news announces the latest terrorist attack with gruesome descriptions of bloodshed and gore broadcast over the airwaves. I turn off the radio and concentrate on getting home. I need to reach the house before Adam.

The rain batters the windscreen and the inside of the car has steamed up. I slowly wend my way up through Hampstead and when I stop at the next set of traffic lights, I phone Gary and curse the poor signal at the lock-up, being forced to leave yet another voicemail. I tell him to wait for me that I might be a bit late but that I will definitely be there. I check the time again and realise it will probably be nearer nine before I get to him but I need to go home first.

I crawl up Riverside Close, prepared to turn round if Adam's car is in the driveway but the house is in darkness with no obvious signs of life. I scan the neighbours' homes for bright lights to help quell my fears and calm my pounding heart. I fumble with my keys and drop them on the ground as I anxiously keep checking for the appearance of vehicles.

I don't turn on the hall light as I enter as I don't want to illuminate my shadow. I begin my search. Time is of the essence.

The door keys which are used to gain access to the patio and back garden have been moved. They're not in the usual drawer. I wrench open all the drawers in the kitchen, then move into the hall to check in the sideboard but can't find them. I decide to go out the front again and skirt round the other properties and gain access into the rear garden, through the gate by the river.

There's still no sign of Adam. I scurry across the road, down the small side alleyway, and follow the path through the woods behind the houses.

It seems to take forever to reach the gate and for a moment I'm confused in the dark as to which one belongs to our property. My phone lights the way and I finally click open the gate leading back into our garden. There's a small shed tucked neatly in the corner which houses Adam's lawnmower and garden tools. I enter in the combination, fumbling with the rusting lock as I swivel it round to the four digits that make up the day and month of our wedding anniversary. It's a date I plan to forget.

Once inside, I switch on the light. The bulb is weak, making only faint inroads into the gloom. There's a neatly arranged row of gardening equipment leant up against one wall; a rake, hoe, broom and a large pair of secateurs. 'Shit.' I bang my head on the rafters when a tiny grey field mouse scuttles across my path and I have to put a hand over my mouth to stifle an automatic yelp.

My husband is methodical, organised, and I imagine his operating instruments displayed with similar precision to the gardening equipment. His outdoor footwear is lined up to the left of the door. There are walking boots, gardening shoes and an old pair of tennis shoes. His trainers are nowhere to be seen. He always leaves them here after a jog in the woods as the mud and wet debris get caked in the ridges of the soles. I wrack my brain trying to remember when I last saw him wearing them. I pull the tarpaulin off the top of the lawnmower, checking if they might have fallen down the back. I then lift out a pair of small step ladders and clamber up so that I can run my fingers along the top shelves of the metal rack. I'm sweating, my breath rasping. My ears are alert for a car which might pull in at the front of the house.

I stumble off the ladder when I hear a door slam and quickly flick off the light switch and stand very still. Through the small window I see the lights come on in the house and I can make out Adam's silhouette in the kitchen. He's looking out into the garden. I watch his back retreating into the hall and I quickly open the shed door, fumbling to reclose the lock and in a blind panic hurry towards the back gate.

I jog, follow the path of the river, glad that I had the foresight to wear my own trainers and build up pace, faster and faster away from our house. About half a mile further down, near where the river meets the motorway, I'll turn right and wend my way back up to Riverside Close from the opposite direction. I need Adam to believe that I've been out jogging, trying to clear my head.

I pound on and will the exertion to calm me down. Up ahead I see a figure coming towards me. I emerge out on to the road and realise it's another jogger. Only when they draw close do I realise it's Adam.

We meet under a small street light and the first thing I notice are his trainers. They're brand new, bright blue and orange, with the distinctive Nike logo emblazoned along the side. He will have carefully destroyed and thrown away his handmade Italian running shoes, the ones with the thick round black expensive maker's mark embossed deeply into the underside of the sole. The imprint which Olive told me she had photographed. I know now that my husband is the killer.

49

SUSAN

'What do you mean you were a member of this website?' Roger is spitting, furious spurts of disbelief. '*Join Me* or whatever it's called. Did you meet up with men? Is that what you're telling me?' For an awful moment I think my husband might be having a heart attack. His face has turned red, mottled and his cheeks have taken on a distinct ashen hue. He's gripping the back of one of dining room chairs to steady himself. I move towards him. I need to get closer and make him understand, let him look in my eyes and see that I've done nothing wrong. He needs to believe me; let me explain. No one will ever know otherwise.

'Don't come near me. While I'm out busting a gut to pay the mortgage, fund your gym fees and pay for unnecessary child-care, you're out dating perverts you've met online.' He's not going to hear me out. Frightened, I step backwards. I've never heard Roger shout before because he is the one who listens. He's the calm steady influence in our family and always quietly placates when I fly off the handle. He pacifies Noah when Tilly has sneakily nipped her brother when no one is looking. He soothes Tilly's tears when she can't do her homework. I'm scared. Roger is my rock, whatever was I thinking? I'm torn between guilt and a desperate need to get my story across, telling the half-truths necessary to keep my marriage intact. I can't lose Roger.

'Can we sit down? Please,' I plead. Roger stares at me as if he's seeing me for the first time.

'Did you know this Jason before he came to our house? Christ. He's been in our house and you already knew him, didn't you?' I watch in horror as he puts a hand over his chest and seems to struggle for air. I go to pull a chair out for him, and insist he sits down. He ignores me but carries on with the venom. 'Tell me the truth. When did you meet him? Did you have an affair with him?'

'No, it was nothing like that!' I exclaim, rather too loudly. Will he know I have the answers all prepared? 'Lots of the ladies at the gym were having fun on the site, taking trips around London with new friends and I didn't see the harm.' I daren't move.

'You were sleeping with him, weren't you?'

I've been practising. This is the part I need to get right.

'No. It was only a bit of fun. I met him once. We went to London Zoo. I had no idea he was Caroline's husband until he came to dinner. I was as shocked as anyone.' That at least is the truth. Images flash past of the naked afternoon trysts in seedy hotel rooms and I can no longer make sense of what happened. Was I that bored or was it something else? As I look at Roger, bowed by the revelations, shoulders slumped in despair, I feel an emotion like I've been given a terminal diagnosis; or at least what I imagine it must feel like. I can't lose this man. He's my rock, my life, my love. I can see the end in sight but I need to fight.

'Why did he turn up near my offices?'

Roger paces round the dining room, picks up picture frames,

stares at the happy family images, and sets them down again. 'Seems too much of a coincidence to me.' He's the prosecuting lawyer in full flight. 'Why would he want to come and see me? Surely not to check out the competition.' He laughs and waves away the preposterous notion with a swish of his hand. 'I'm sorry, Susan, but I don't think he was fighting for your heart. He didn't strike me as the needy type. Now why would he turn up at my offices?' Roger won't stop. He's like a dog with a bone, on a mission, as he prowls round the room. The jury is out. 'Do you know what I think?'

I don't want to hear. 'Please calm down.' I start to cry; it's my only weapon against the ensuing verbal assault. I sit down and put my head in my hands and let the emotions pour out. He doesn't come near me but carries on.

'I think he might have been considering blackmail,' he hisses, pulling my head up gently by my hair. 'Look at me,' he demands. White spittle has congealed in the corners of his lips. He looks as if he's having some sort of fit and for a moment I don't recognise his features, they've become so distorted by anger. I carry on crying, bawling like a spoilt child who has been discovered stealing forbidden sweets.

'What do you think, Susan?' He waits, and waits. 'Tell me!' he yells.

I blubber, desperate to make him understand, choking on the words as I speak. 'I met him once. We went to the zoo, shared a coffee and went our separate ways. That was all. Then he came for dinner with Caroline and I realised what a dreadful mistake I'd made. There was no harm done.'

'There's talk that he extorted money from other ladies he appears to have met on the website. You need to tell me now if you ever gave him money.' He emphasises the word 'now' in all its importance. I can't own up to this. It would be tantamount to admitting we had slept together. I sniffle. Theatrical little noises emanate from my nose and I use my sleeve to wipe away the wet drips which have collected at the end of my nostrils.

'Don't be ridiculous. I'm not a prostitute, sleeping with men for money,' I shout, not daring to look at him. I hear the words and suddenly the truth hits me in the face. That's exactly what I am. Boredom, sex, lust, deceit, money, security; they all belong in the same melting pot, the melting pot of my life. The laughable thing is that I paid for the pleasure rather than the other way round. I daren't imagine what Roger will do if he finds out about the missing cash. I've no idea how to replace it.

He goes silent, hovers for a brief second. He then heads for the front door and storms out of the house.

I hear the door slam. I don't know what I'll do. My first thoughts are for the children. I can't lose them. I need to think. But as I get up and wander blindly into the kitchen, I realise that my future is no longer in my hands. Only Roger can save me; that and whether I might yet be able to convince him of my innocence.

50

ALEXIS

As Adam and I reach our driveway, side by side, I see Roger Harper leave his house and slam the door on his way out. His face has the thunderous set of a black cloud.

'He doesn't look too happy,' Adam quips as he takes my arm and leads me up the path. I wave at Susan who is looking out from the downstairs window but she doesn't wave back. At least she's seen me which suddenly seems to matter.

It's eight thirty and I need to get to the lock-up, away from the house. Something makes me hesitate from telling Adam that I have an appointment; an evening client to meet. He won't believe me. He's pushing me forward, prodding insistently in the small of my back, daring me to try to escape. He stops on the doorstep and unties the laces of his new trainers, unmuddied by sticking to the roads, and sets them in the porch. He'll put them in the shed later.

'Don't worry. I'll not bring them inside. I wouldn't dare dirty the hallway.' He thinks he's funny but he's toying with me, testing the waters and pressing some buttons to see how I'll react.

'Was Olive okay when you left?' I change tack, unlace my own trainers which I place alongside his. The close is deserted. I anxiously scout round for signs of life. Susan has moved away from the window, Roger has gone and darkness cloaks the other houses. The blue tape still marks out the grisly crime scene. Only a dim light glows in the Thompsons'. Bob will be home by himself, waiting patiently for Olive to phone and come back to him.

'Yes, fine. Only she thinks someone deleted all the photos on her phone on purpose. I think she's hallucinating. It was touch and go for a while you know.' His eyes also skirt round the road and the action makes me uneasy. I don't want him to register the black empty homes which would let him relax in the knowledge that we're alone.

'Bob's home again,' I point out, doubtful that the dim light behind the net curtains will cause Adam much concern. Bob is too old for him to worry about. Adam relocks the front door after us and pulls the chain across. He secures the extra bolts, top and bottom, the ones I installed after the night of his birthday.

'You'll not be going out again?' It's a rhetorical question. He knows I won't and he's making it quite clear it's not on the agenda.

'No. I need an early night. I'm exhausted. See you in the morning.' I head towards the stairs, desperate to get away when I feel him tug me back by the arm.

'Not so quick. I think we need to have a few words, don't you?' His eyes, which bore through me, are like hard lethal bullets; ready to fire if provoked.

'What about? I'm tired. Can't it wait?' I try to act normally, carry on as if I've no suspicions so that in the morning I can escape from the house and get to Gary. He'll be able to help. I won't sleep but Adam mustn't know I'm worried.

'No, not really. This *Join Me* thing. When were you going to tell me?'

My legs threaten to give way as I try to push his hand off my sleeve and carry on up the stairs.

'Can we talk when I've had a shower? I'm filthy. I'll only be ten minutes.' I play for time, it's my only option.

'Okay but don't keep me waiting.' He smirks. 'I'll open a bottle of wine. What do you fancy? Rioja? Merlot? Your choice tonight.' He lets go of my wrist and heads for the kitchen. I manage to reach the top of the stairs, my legs like jelly, my head reeling. I need to collect my thoughts and decide what to do.

Outside, there is an enormous peel of thunder and lightning cracks through the skylight, sharp and piercing. Rain pelts against the glass and I manage to get into the bathroom and lock the door before my phone beeps. I cough to cover the sound and quickly turn the volume to mute, leaning my back against the wood. A sudden knock at the door makes me freeze.

'You don't need to lock the door. I wouldn't dare come in.' Adam has followed me up the stairs. Perhaps he's checking I haven't tried to climb out the window. My heart pounds. I glance down at my phone. There's a message from Gary with four pictures attached.

Hope you're ok. Assume you can't make it to lock-up so going home. Catch up tomorrow. Got these pictures from Olive, by the way. Any idea what they are? See you later. Gary

Three of the photos show footprints left by the handmade Italian trainers. Adam had treated himself when he decided to do the London Marathon last year. The distinctive embossed logo, Giro, the maker's individual calling card, is clear and defined. I've got him. I keep all receipts and have their images backed up on the Cloud.

When we first married I used to try to buy clothes for Adam until I realised that he would return them or exchange them for something of his own choice. I now realise it was a less than subtle attempt to belittle my choices rather than a dislike of the items themselves. It was another way to undermine my confidence. As a consequence I started to photograph all receipts with my phone and back them up along with other important data. He's put the nail in his own coffin, ungrateful bastard. I remember photographing the receipt for the handmade trainers, staggered by the obscene amount of the purchase. They'll be his downfall.

'I'll only be five minutes. Promise,' I answer, trying to quell the shake in my voice. I forward the message and attachments back to Olive and tell her not to let the phone out of her sight this time and then reply to Gary telling him to back up the photos urgently and that I'll see him tomorrow.

Olive will confirm that she saw the wearer of the trainers leave the murder scene on the night in question. She will tell the police that she photographed their footprints as they sped away. I also have the proof that the shoes belonged to Adam. I finally delete all the messages from my phone, including the photographs, before turning it off.

51

ALEXIS

I sit tied to a chair in the kitchen. Adam has secured my feet to the metal frame, warning me that any sudden movement might topple the chair and lead to a potentially fatal bang to my head, perhaps against the corner of the working surface or alternatively on the cold marbled floor tiles. He has lit a small candle which is placed on the table beside me and turned off all the other lighting in the house. He doesn't want anyone to know we're at home.

'Cheers,' he says, offering me a glass of wine to join him in a toast. The thunder and lightning continues its background cacophony of noise and deafens my response. Adam extracts some keys from his pocket. They are those for the patio doors which lead out into the back garden.

'Have you been looking for these? In case you had plans to change the locks again, I didn't want to take any chances.' He proceeds to unlock the doors 'to let some air through. A bit too hot in here, don't you think?' I watch as he cracks open the back door. Another violent streak of lightning flashes overhead.

'You're not scared, are you?' he taunts. 'You don't like thunderstorms I seem to remember.' He glances over his shoulder before turning back to face me.

He forces a filled glass into my hands and curls my fingers roughly round the goblet. 'Drink,' he snarls as he pulls my head back and proceeds to pour the Merlot down my throat. 'Is this what you drank with that bastard? Wine, or did he prefer champagne?' I can't breathe and am soon spurting the red liquid in a projectile trajectory across the floor. It looks like darkened blood, as it spurts back up over my clothes.

'Come on; tell me what was so special about him?' Adam is up close staring at me, holding the bottle of wine high in the air, checking how much is left in his glass before he pours himself out another full measure.

'Who?' I dare to ask, knowing he means Jason.

'Don't play with me. Tell me. That fucking dead bastard, Jason Swinton,' Adam hisses.

'Nothing. I didn't know him.' I try to stay calm, dissipate his anger. I must sound convincing, it's my only chance. 'I promise. Nothing happened. I met him for a drink only once, after you were seeing Debbie.' I manage to resist the urge to scream at him about what a bastard he had been and keep my temper in check, reminding myself that the unknown stranger in front of me murdered Jason, and I'm probably next on the list.

'I finished with Debbie. I told you, bitch.' He pushes his face tight up against mine and breathes rancid fumes over me. He prods my chest with his finger. 'Go on. What's your excuse?' I know I should try to logic with him but it seems too late to believe that he's going to walk away before he's finished what he's started. I explode in fury.

'I met Debbie today at the hospital. She finished with you and showed me her scars. No one wants you, you sick fucker.' I scream the words. I've gone too far. Adam prowls round the kitchen, lifting bottles of wine out of the fridge and putting them back. I conjure up the ghoulish images, reported in the paper, of Jason with his skull smashed in with disfiguring scars across his cheekbones and blood oozing from a severed carotid artery. The injuries had been done by glass from a wine bottle. I cough and vomit more globules of red mess across the floor.

Suddenly a loud noise shatters the night silence. The door-bell rings and someone is stabbing persistently at the button. Adam is by my side in an instant and thrusts his hand over my mouth.

'Don't make a sound. I'm warning you or it's all over.' I know he means it. As I try to bite through his hand, his grip tightens. 'Shut up.'

We wait for what seems like an eternity. The bell rings once more before we hear a retreating tread wend its way back down the path. I look at the clock. It's eleven. Who would have been calling at this hour? Adam is spurred on by the caller, a new urgency about his actions.

'Did you sleep with him? Was he good in the sack?'

'How did you find out? Were you following me?' I play for time. I coax him to listen, to believe me. It's my only chance.

'After you changed the locks, I guessed there was someone else. Why would you have been so keen to get rid of me other-wise and not give me a second chance? Most wives forgive their husband the odd one-night stand.' He has forgotten the bruises and the black eye which he inflicted after my discovery of his affair. 'I checked your browsing history. I'm not a moron. *Join Me* seems to have sucked in a sad bunch of losers, you amongst them. It was easy after that. I used your phone when you were in the shower and texted Jason asking him to meet at the empty house for sale in Riverside Close. The prick turned up on cue. You must have been good.' Adam snarls like a rabid wolf, teeth bared, and paces back and forth.

We are like a lone pair of actors on a stage. I think of *Waiting for Godot* and know that no one will ever come. The lightning is crackling through the windows but the peels of thunder have moved on, leaving the ragged streaks as an accompaniment to our final act. He is going to kill me. I've done nothing wrong except choose the wrong man. My whole life flashes before me in a second.

'You're in the frame for murder, Alexis. There's nothing to link me to the act, so this will be a provoked crime of passion. I'll tell police that you owned up to murdering your lover when you discovered that he was going out with Susan Harper. You're a jealous woman, deranged, unhinged. Anyone using that website must have been mad.'

He is completely insane yet he believes what he's saying. No one would believe I had a motive for murder. If I had invited Jason to meet me in Riverside Close, what possible reason did I have for killing him? We never slept together. I only met him twice. No one can prove otherwise. Adam is going to kill me because he has lost control. He believes what he's saying and convinced of his own infallibility. He thinks he will be able to con the police.

'Did you send those stupid texts threatening me? Did they make you feel better calling me names?' I squirm in my seat. If he is intending to kill me, I must try to reason with him. It's my only chance. I quieten my voice.

'Adam.' I use his name; a long-acknowledged way to entice a suicidal victim back in from the ledge. 'Adam,' I repeat, waiting until he turns back towards me. I'm facing the patio doors, looking out into the garden and my assailant has his back to the glass, standing directly in front of me.

All at once, by moving my head ever so slightly to the right, I make out the faintest movement outside. The gate at the end of our garden has been opened and closed and a shadowy figure is creeping across the grass. I have to keep Adam engaged. My life depends on it. He's gripping the wine bottle and I can see his bony knuckles are white from the effort.

'You don't need to kill me. The police will never suspect you because I didn't really know Jason and you would have had no reason to be jealous. I only met him because Caroline asked me to trail him. She was suspicious of him having affairs.' I don't need to tell Adam that my first meeting was out of curiosity and boredom. I'll make him think I only browsed the website in a professional capacity, to help with my work for Caroline. A momentary doubt flickers across his face as he considers that I might be telling the truth. He's wondering if I am and trying to work out in his manic state what he should do. He will have had no idea about my working for Caroline. Perhaps, he's now considering that I didn't have a passionate interest in her husband.

'I don't believe you. Why would you browse the website if Caroline asked you to trail him? How did you know he was on the site anyway?' The thoughts swirl round in his brain. 'You're lying. Like you always do. Shut up, you little whore. Shut the fuck up.' As Adam moves up close and starts to raise the bottle high in the air, he yanks my hair back and finally moves round to stand behind me and face the patio doors.

At first I think the thunder is back. A loud crack blasts through the air like cannon fire. Only in the silent aftermath do I realise that it was no act of God but rather the sound of a bullet. Blood spurts have appeared out of nowhere, coating the tiles with slimy red rivulets. In the background I'm aware of the keening wail of a wild animal in pain. I want it to stop but it goes on and on. I put my hands over my ears.

'It's okay, dear. Let me help you.' Bob Thompson has

appeared out of the shadows and bends down to untie my
ankles from the metal chair frame before he helps me up. 'The
police are on their way.' Bob leads me to another chair and only
when I am sitting down again do I dare to look round.

'Is he dead?' I ask.

'Of course not. What fun would there be in that?' Bob's eyes
have a wicked twinkle. He's done this before. 'I've kneecapped
him. It'll shut him up for a while. An old tactic we used in
Belfast when we needed information. Bloody painful though.'
He picks his way carefully over Adam who is squirming in
agony, although more silently now, and pours me a glass of
water.

'Here. Take this, love, and drink it all up. I can hear the cops
outside. It's over; you're safe.' He pats me on the shoulder, reassuringly, before he adds, 'I wouldn't make a habit of leaving the
back door open though.' He smiles. 'Might tempt the wrong sort
of person through.'

It's midnight. Blue lights again flash on and off in the close.
Several police cars and an ambulance have arrived. I am led out
by the same policewoman who questioned me earlier in the day,
WPC Taylor. My eyes wander round the houses and scan the
circular enclave. Bedroom lights click on and curtains are
twitched back. No one will understand what's happened. No one
will yet connect tonight's unfolding events with the murder a
few days ago. I realise no one really knows their neighbours
properly as everyone is too busy with their own self-serving
lives.

In this one moment I offer up a prayer of gratitude for the
elderly; for the old and infirm who have all the time in the
world. Olive and Bob have saved my life and Olive, with all her

silent vigils, will help me put my husband away for life. As soon as I left the hospital this evening, she phoned Bob and sent him round. She guessed what was going to happen.

I stand and watch the ambulance drive away, Adam having been stretchered aboard clutching his kneecap and screaming in pain. Two uniformed officers have accompanied him. He'll not be left alone again. Bob is also being taken away in a police car for questioning and to give his version of events. He gives me a little wave and thumbs up as he is driven off. He wants me to know that I don't need to worry about him. He's a soldier after all, an old hand in battle. But I'll not forget he saved my life. I promise myself that I'll make it up to the Thompsons. When tomorrow comes, I'll be there for them.

I finally head back to my own house accompanied by WPC Taylor who needs to take down my version of events while they're fresh in my mind. She'll stay with me all night and in the morning she'll accompany me to the police station to begin formal proceedings.

52

SUSAN

THREE MONTHS LATER

Alexis has turned out to be a good friend. I hand her a mug of hot coffee and suggest we sit in the garden. The sun is out and summer is finally trying to break through. I pull over a couple of chairs and a small mosaic-topped table to set our drinks on. I sit down and turn my face up towards the sun, letting it soak through my bones.

'No, I won't be going tomorrow. Are you definitely going?' The geraniums, reds and pinks, sprout vigorously from the pots which I planted no more than a week ago and the lavender which edges the lawn wafts out a calming scent of summer.

'Yes, I've decided to go. Gary's coming with me and Olive fancies getting out of the house for a couple of hours. We'll make a merry little band of mourners.' Alexis sips her coffee, delicate mouthfuls and wipes the top of her lips with slim shapely fingers. I sit on my white veined hands, embarrassed by the ugliness of the tiny brown sunspots that age my skin. It is the curse of my pale Irish colouring, according to Roger.

I miss him and the children so much, a dull ache having lodged itself round my heart. A robin perches on the top of the barbecue which sits, rusted and forlorn, up against the fence. I daren't look at it or I'll hear Roger moan about the damp fire-lighters and the children's voices impatiently asking every two minutes when the sausages will be done.

'I'm working hard at winning Roger's trust back, and getting the children to come home. Going to Jason's funeral wouldn't be a wise move,' I say. 'I see the *For Sale* sign is up again on the house next door.' I change the subject. I don't want sympathy. I know I've messed up but don't want to dwell on it. It'll take time but I'm determined to get my family back.

'So I see. Not sure who'll want it though. The price has plummeted and Mr Herriott's no longer so gushing.' We laugh together, as friends, and lift our mugs in unison. White fluffy clouds glide softly past and for a moment I think it might all turn out okay.

'How's Adam getting on?' I don't like to pry but it would seem strange if I didn't ask. The murder has brought Alexis and me together and our inroads into *Join Me* have cemented our friendship through an unspoken bond of momentary madness.

I like to think that my new friend was as foolish as me but I haven't dared ask if she slept with Jason. It wouldn't seem right and anyway I don't want to hear the answer. I'll never forget Vince, who for a short period was mine. I'm not prepared to accept that his feelings weren't real. It was all too real for me.

The sun pops behind a cloud and I shiver as I remember the unbridled lust we shared. I close my eyes and recall the churning stomach, my animal desperation for consummation and the wild abandon that he stirred in me. He may have been playing a game but I don't want to believe this. It was never meant to last, that was its nature; torrid yet transient.

Roger and the children, Tilly and Noah, are the future. They will last forever. Perhaps it was the forbidden nature of the fruit that made it taste so sweet. I can't make sense of it all. It'll be hard to forget but I need to try.

'I've no idea except I know he has been refused bail and I never want to see him again.' Alexis isn't going to open up and as I offer her another biscuit, a leftover custard cream from Tilly's stock of sugary treats, Alexis tells me about her job.

'Being a private detective sounds great fun.' I laugh. 'I need to get a job, show Roger I can change, and perhaps make at least a small contribution to the family purse.' I don't tell her, however, that I've also promised to repay the money I lent to Jason. Roger didn't want to talk about it, as the money was the final nail in my coffin when he heard the amounts involved.

We haven't yet sat down so that I can explain properly. I want the chance to make him understand that the money was a loan to a friend, someone whose company I enjoyed. I'll never own up to the abandoned sex when handing over money seemed the only way to ensure its continuance. Roger must never see me in the guise of wanton mistress. I'll play the naïve gullible card but not the passionate dormant sex devil who remembers, only too vividly, the animal release that Vince gave me. I've a lot of work to do but a job might be the best way to start. I'll check out local sites online, perhaps, later this afternoon. I have enough time now, that's for certain.

'You'll need to employ Olive Thompson. I think she could be Miss Marple in the making,' I suggest, amused by my moment of levity. It must be the sunshine and the positive ideas that are trickling through.

'Yes, Olive's going to help me. I'll make sure she's kept up to speed on any new clients. She's happy working from her front window but has promised she'll stop logging our comings and goings in the close. I don't think the neighbours like being watched so intently.'

Perhaps I'll ask the neighbours round for drinks, start being more sociable and get to know them all a bit better. Roger likes married couple get-togethers, good food washed down by smooth wines augmented by stimulating conversation. It's so simple really. That's all Roger has ever really wanted.

I'm scared I might start to cry so I stand up, lift the mugs and wipe the few stray biscuit crumbs onto the ground. The robin hops closer, concentrates on the crumbly offerings, and waits patiently until we've gone inside and closed the door. Life carries on as the river of life wends its way inexorably to the sea. I'm through the rapids and must now steer a careful course to get back on track. I'll prove myself to Roger and hope that he'll wait and watch for my redemption. He has the patience of a saint.

'Fancy a walk out the back? Why don't we stroll along by the river and perhaps put on our trainers and jog part of the way?' I lock the door and watch through the glass as the robin swoops in for the leftovers, his vigil finally over. His little head moves nervously from side to side as he checks for predators, before he pecks savagely at the crumbs. He then soars away, high up over the fence and disappears heavenwards, safe and free once more.

For a moment, I think of Vince and close my eyes and hope that he is also safe and free. It's time for us all to move on.

53

ALEXIS

I support Olive as we stroll through Highgate Cemetery. The wind gusts around our ears and my frail friend is very shaky on her feet. But she was determined to come, without Bob. She needed to get away from the house and be with her two new best friends. Gary wanders along behind us and every so often stops to read the inscriptions on the gravestones, taking snaps of the more elaborate tombs and ghoulish deathbeds. I throw him a few dirty looks to try to quash his overzealous photographic activities.

Bonnie is off the lead, scurrying along the ground; her little stomach hangs so low that small dried sticks and leaves attach to her fur. Every few seconds she stops, smells the grass and runs on again. But not before her wary little eyes check I'm still here.

'Why don't you get a proper dog?' Gary makes a derisive snorting sound.

'Bonnie is a proper dog, thank you all the same.' I give him a stern look. 'Just because she's small doesn't mean she's not a proper dog.' Bonnie comes bounding back and I scoop her up and feel her pimply wet little tongue lash my face. 'If I had a so-called proper dog, I wouldn't have this pleasure.' Olive watches us as she rests for a moment on a wooden bench.

'Yuk. That's disgusting. Anyway, I thought she belonged to someone else.'

'She's mine now. Her owner's gone to live in France and I offered to keep her.' I don't tell Gary that I always wanted a dog but Adam forbade it. 'It's either me or a dog,' he'd said on more than one occasion. Perhaps I should have stood firm and chosen a dog.

As we move on, Gary stops again and takes a photograph of Bonnie with her little leg aloft against a headstone. He thinks it's hilarious. We all laugh, amused by the irreverence.

'Show some respect,' I call over my shoulder. He smiles, determined to ignore his boss on this rare occasion. He's been talking of a scrapbook to record all the details of our first real case. The fact that Olive solved it isn't relevant and he's milking his involvement with childish enthusiasm.

We finally reach the graveside and mingle with the motley gathering of mourners who keep silent vigil by the gaping hole in the ground. I wind Bonnie's lead in and she lies down quietly, puffing out a steady stream of hot air, tongue hanging loosely to one side.

'Must have cost a bomb to get a plot here,' Gary whispers in my left ear.

Olive, clinging once more to my arm for dear life in case she topples over, answers for me. 'At least twelve thousand pounds. I've been googling,' she announces.

'Since when did you google?' I can't help a wry smile as she bobs her tiny head towards me and winks.

There are no more than twenty mourners, who wait patiently for the vicar to begin his eulogy. The sight of three random women, standing separately, all dressed in dark reverential colours, makes me wince. I surmise that they might all have known the deceased from their inroads into online activities. One of the ladies blows into a tissue, finding it difficult to keep the noise down.

'Ashes to ashes,' begins the minister. I let my eyes wander further afield. There's a large oak tree off to the right of the mourners and I can see an older woman whose head is covered by a dark netted veil. She looks familiar. I nudge Gary and nod in her direction. He stares at her and I have to dig him somewhere below the ribs to get him to avert his eyes. He knows who she is and smugly waits until the service concludes.

'Go on then, Sherlock. Who is she?' I ask.

'Don't you remember the pictures I showed you? That's the last woman Jason was seen with. It's Francine Dubois. The psychotherapist from Highgate.' Of course. She lifts her veil and starts to move away.

'Here, Olive. Hold on to Gary. I'll not be long. Gary, you hold on to Bonnie.' I pass him the lead before he has time to object. Bonnie's eyes follow me closely.

Olive knows where I'm going. We work well as a team. I move a little faster across the rough ground and join the small path which leads back to the car park. I don't want to alert Francine that I'm following her. She seems intent on getting away, unnoticed.

'Hi,' I say as I finally catch up and fall into step alongside her. 'At least the rain's held off. It's still threatening though.' I glance heavenwards. She doesn't look at me. I notice dark bags under her eyes and the pale bloodless complexion. I carry on.

'Did you know the deceased?' I'm intrigued by this woman as I think she might hold some more clues as to Jason's life. Who is she?

We walk in silence and I'm about to give up when she stops, unpins the veil from her hair where it's been clipped neatly into place. I watch her fold the lace and put it carefully into her black handbag. Her eyes are a deep mahogany brown and her high cheekbones augment what would once have been a breathtaking beauty. I think of Sophia Loren, the aging but timeless Italian sex siren. A squirrel runs past, bobbing and weaving between the trees before it pauses.

'Perhaps that's Jason,' Francine muses, watching the tiny animal stand up on its hind legs and survey the landscape. The furry creature has something small clasped between its tiny front feet, a nut perhaps or an acorn. 'I don't think he'll leave me altogether. He always comes back and I let him go when he asks.' She drops a glove and bends to pick it up. Her thick brown hair is highlighted through with subtle blonde streaks but stubborn grey strands are discernible in the sunlight. It falls free of the clipped restraints as she bends and her thick tresses rest softly on her shoulders. I'm mesmerised by her beauty. I realise why Jason would have been drawn to this enigmatic woman.

'Yes, I knew him. We go back a long way, to the beginning of time really,' she says facing me, a smile on her lips. As she speaks, her full mouth opens to display perfect white teeth. She falters and puts a hand against a random gravestone to steady herself. She reads the inscription out loud. It helps steady her voice and calm the emotion.

George Mortimer, aged 25 years. Beloved husband of Greta and son of Paul and Rachel. Taken too soon. 1956–1981

She runs her finger along the wording lost in thought.

'Yes I knew Jason. Since he was born actually.' She turns round. 'He was such a beautiful baby and an even more handsome child.'

We are alone among the gravestones, the other mourners linger some distance behind. I hold my breath, and suddenly realise what her next words are going to be.

'He was my son. My only son. My perfect child.'

I've left Bonnie in the car, exhausted from all the activity, but she'll not lie down until I get back. I'll make it up to her later. Tonight we'll snuggle up on the sofa, wine for me and doggy treats for her, and while I watch a movie, she'll fall asleep, safe and secure at last.

Meanwhile Gary, Olive and I have ended up in tearooms in Highgate Village, having decided against tea and sandwiches in the old rectory with the vicar and the motley crew of mourners.

'Not sure I could cope with any more gruesome revelations,' Gary chirps as he shakily deposits two full cups of tea in front of Olive and me as we settle down by the window. When he goes back to pick up the scones and jam, Olive turns to me.

'Looks can be so deceiving. I've watched families come and go for years and often wonder what really goes on behind closed doors. I try to guess from the smallest details but I don't think even I could have worked out what was going on in the Swinton household. Just imagine. Sleeping with your own mother.' Olive's teacup wobbles in her hand which she tries to control with her gnarled fingers. I lean across to wipe at the dribbling hot liquid with a serviette but she shoos me away.

'Don't worry, love. There'll be a few more drops before I've finished.'

Gary returns and the three of us sit at a small square table. The red and white linen tablecloths give the room a homely feel and freshly cut flower posies emit a delicately scented aroma. I lift my cup and reach it into the centre of the table towards my new friends.

'She must have reverted to her maiden name of Dubois or else conjured it up as a more exotic surname for working purposes,' Gary suggests. 'Anyway, it would have taken the sharpest detective in the world to have worked that one out.'

'Cheers. Glad you could *Join Me*,' I say and we all laugh, cautiously touching our cups together.

'And here's to many more successful cases,' Gary says. He seems to have grown in stature since we first met and as I glance round the small tea shop, I surmise that people will think we are three generations of the same family; grandmother, mother and son. Although I must admit that Olive and Gary do feel like a real family to me. I sip the warm sweet tea and realise I'm excited about working together and getting to know them better. As I call the waitress over to ask for the bill, Gary produces a small notebook from his suit pocket.

'By the way,' he says, pointing to some scribbled writing inside. 'We've got a new client. Mrs Pennington from Bishops Avenue.'

'Another errant husband?' Olive asks.

'No. She wants us to find her cat. It's gone missing apparently.'

Olive and I burst out laughing as Gary reads out a full description of the missing pet.

ACKNOWLEDGEMENTS

Writing is frequently a solitary lonely task but it is the people along the way who keep you going with their unwavering encouragement and belief.

I would like to thank all my friends and family who offered support and survival tips. Firstly, thanks to my sister Linda Pigott who has always believed in me and pushed me to persevere when things got tough. Thanks to Susan McCarthy, Lindsay McQuillan and Gloria Green for their enthusiastic feedback on all my work, and to Jane Badrock who encouraged me to contact Bloodhound Books, which turned out to be the best home for this novel. To Margaret Fitzpatrick who took the time to read early drafts and to the many other people who ask me every day how things are progressing.

I am so grateful to all at Bloodhound Books, especially to Betsy Reavley who believed in the manuscript on first reading, and to her wonderful staff who have worked tirelessly to get it ready for publication. Morgen Bailey has been the most amazing editor with her sharp and focused attention to detail. Thanks also to Tara Lyons, whose prompt response to so many questions marks her out as a true professional.

Finally biggest thanks of all to Neil and James, the two men in my life. Neil for giving me the time and support to get on with the job, and James for promising that one day he might get around to reading my books.

ABOUT THE AUTHOR

Diana Wilkinson graduated from Durham University with a degree in geography then after a short spell in teaching, spent most of her working life in the business of tennis development. A former Irish international player, Diana finally stepped off the tennis court to become a full-time writer.

The inspiration for much of her work has come from the ladies she coached over the years and from confidences shared over coffee. *4 Riverside Close* is Diana's first crime novel.

Born and bred in Belfast, Northern Ireland, during the height of the civil unrest, she now lives in Hertfordshire, England, with her husband Neil and son James.

Printed in Great Britain
by Amazon

66629790R00184